KU-271-378

The Weeping Women Hotel

Alexei Sayle

The Weeping Women Hotel

SCEPTRE

Copyright © 2006 by Alexei Sayle

First published in Great Britain in 2006 by Sceptre
A division of Hodder Headline

The right of Alexei Sayle to be identified as the Author
of the Work has been asserted by him in accordance with the
Copyright, Designs and Patents Act 1988

A Sceptre paperback

1

All rights reserved. No part of this publication may be
reproduced, stored in a retrieval system, or transmitted, in any form
or by any means, without the prior written permission of the publisher,
nor be otherwise circulated in any form of binding or cover other
than that in which it is published and without a similar condition
being imposed on the subsequent purchaser.

All characters in this publication are fictitious and any resemblance to
real persons, living or dead, is purely coincidental.

A CIP catalogue record for this title is
available from the British Library

ISBN 978 0 340 83122 9

Typeset in Sabon MT by
Palimpsest Book Production Limited, Grangemouth, Stirlingshire

Printed and bound by Clays Ltd, St Ives plc

Hodder Headline's policy is to use papers that are natural, renewable
and recyclable products and made from wood grown in sustainable forests.
The logging and manufacturing processes are expected to conform to the
environmental regulations of the country of origin.

Hodder & Stoughton Ltd
A division of Hodder Headline
338 Euston Road
London NW1 3BH

ACKNOWLEDGEMENTS

Firstly I must express my deepest thanks to Sifu John Kelly: without his extensive and occasionally disturbing knowledge of Oriental martial arts I would not have been able to write this book.

Secondly I have to thank Siobhan Redmond whose neighbourhood, flat and occasional items of furniture form the basis of the place where Harriet lives.

And, as ever, Linda.

Contents

POINTLESS PARK.

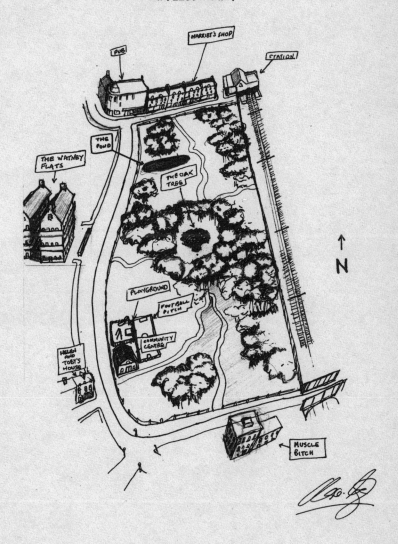

Oh! Mister Porter, what shall I do?
I want to go to Birmingham
And they're taking me on to Crewe,
Send me back to London as quickly as you can,
Oh! Mister Porter, what a silly girl I am!

I

I stared at the poster stuck inside the darkened window of the nightclub and wondered why the President of the Ukraine had chosen to have his picture taken wearing a blond nylon wig, pink tie and a bright yellow jacket. Underneath the President there was printed in big red letters the claim: 'Yussuf Younos – undeniably Cheshire's Premier Rod Stewart Tribute Act'. At the bottom of the poster was a white space – an oblong inside which there was scrawled in black marker pen, 'Tuesday, August 29th 2007's the Night.'

Even in the darkness I could see that the window was crammed full of posters, pale rectangles clinging to the inside like moths. Trailing my finger along the warm glass I tried to read them all; the most frequently repeated seemed to feature a group of allied airmen from the first Gulf War recently released from torture. Above the prisoners of war it read: 'Pret a Manger definitively the UK's Number One Depeche Mode Impersonators. Pret a Manger will be appearing at . . .' and written in another white oblong: 'Guantanamo Bay September 4th 2007'. Guantanamo Bay was the name of the nightclub spelt out above my head in dead neon lights. The club formed almost one half of the ground floor of a huge red Gothic revival hotel that teetered on the edge of the narrow pavement like an uncertain fat man on the rim of a swimming pool.

A distant clanking and the squeal of metal grinding on metal caught my ears: it was the sound of my night train leaving.

Pushing at the carved wooden door of the hotel, above which

a single light burnt, half expecting it to be locked or to resist my touch in some way, it swung open easily enough so, with no reason not to, I slipped through and entered. Finding myself in a small reception area, I saw that ahead was a locked single half-glazed door, to my right a reception desk and beyond it a view into the silent pub that took up the opposite corner of the hotel to Guantanamo Bay; on my left there were double doors through which could be seen some sort of dining room, again deserted since it was the middle of the night, but already laid for breakfast.

In the cluttered space behind the reception a young woman was seated at a battered wooden desk, clacking away at the keys of a computer. As I approached the counter the receptionist looked up, smiled and said, 'Hi, can I help you?' in a voice extremely bright for this time of morning. I had been worried that the people at the hotel might send me away or ask in a sympathetic voice if I was in trouble and call in the police or social services since it was 3 a.m., I was a woman whose only luggage was in a carrier bag, whose face was patched and roughly bandaged and whose hair still had traces of blood streaked through it; but though the girl seemed to take all this in quickly it didn't affect in any way the warmth of her smile or the neutrality of her welcome.

'Yes, if you don't mind I'd like a room . . . for a few days,' I said.

'Of course,' the girl replied, reaching behind her and taking a blue fob with two keys on it from the board. Then she rose and came to the counter, held one key up to me and explained, 'This one lets you in the front door and through this door here' – she indicated the half-glazed door – 'and the other's for your room: number three on the first floor.' She also handed over a small piece of paper slightly larger than a postage stamp with printing on it. I read: 'Station Hotel. Restaurant Pass. Breakfast Only. Room Number . . .'

'Oh, I'm not sure I'll want breakfast,' I said to the receptionist.

'Oh, you'll want the breakfast,' the girl replied confidently and turned back to her computer.

Letting myself through the door and mounting a hefty, dull brown varnished, carved wooden arts and crafts staircase, I ascended to my room. It was much larger than I had imagined, furnished with two narrow, single beds on each of which had been placed a folded towel, a square of soap wrapped like a biscuit and sachets of shampoo and shower gel; there was a small TV on a wooden chest of drawers. I had planned to have a wash but instead lay down on one of the beds and was almost instantly asleep. Drifting away I heard the high-pitched insect sound of a two-stroke motorbike far into the countryside; it came fast down the arrow-straight road, rattled past my window before fading off again into the night.

My only plan was that I would sleep till at least the middle of the morning but instead I was woken at around 8 a.m. by a voice that intruded into my dreams chanting echoey things about Glasgow, Preston and Carlisle. I groggily deduced that the voice was coming from Crewe Station in its trench across the road.

Now irredeemably awake, I thought I might as well try the famous breakfast. Having stayed in quite a few provincial hotels over the years, descending the stairs I glumly thought I would be able to paint the ingredients from memory in all their fried colours.

I entered the fragrant interior of the dining room. Some time during the night, along the back wall of the restaurant a long buffet table had been laid out; walking its entire length twice, my sense of amazement grew as I studied the food set upon it. First there was a row of brown ceramic jugs, elegantly handwritten labels before them on the stiff white-linened table describing the contents of each: there was orange, mango, melon, peach and pear juice, and all of them seemed on inspection to be freshly squeezed. Then there were platters of cheeses, sliced ham, fresh figs. Further along were lidded dishes with a little paraffin flame burning beneath each: these were labelled 'bacon', 'sausages', 'scrambled eggs', 'wild field mushrooms', and 'today's special – huevos rancheros con chorizo'. There were piles of toast wrapped in thin creamy linen and freshly baked baguettes, pots of thick home-made jams, slabs of farmhouse butter.

I took some bread, jam, Spanish manchego cheese and figs then seated myself at the only available place, a small table with a single wooden chair in the far corner of the room. A pretty young waitress soon came from the kitchens carrying a coffee pot in each hand. 'Can I get you coffee?' she asked. 'Our special this month is Kenyan Blue Mountain.'

'Er . . . sure,' I replied, more used to being served watery brown outflow to drink with my British hotel breakfasts.

While the waitress was pouring the coffee I slipped out into the foyer and looked at the room tariff displayed in a glass frame by the desk: a single room apparently cost thirty-five pounds a night; this seemed incredibly cheap for such luxury – most hotels in Britain could only manage shabby, dirty indifference at that price.

As I ate my breakfast I looked around the dining room: coming up to eight thirty most of the guests were already finishing their meals and preparing to leave – they were all men, sitting either singly or in groups; some wore papery thin office-worker suits, others were more casually dressed in golfers' shirts, neat jeans and very clean trainers. The men in the most exuberant groups wore synthetic overalls in blue, green or orange emblazoned on the back with company logos: 'GEC, Alstrom', 'Amec' or 'Bentley'.

At exactly ten minutes to nine all the men got up and left the dining room. I realised then that I'd been wrong, there had been women there all along, at the edges of the room like corner flags, four solitary women. One was in her mid-fifties, tears ran down her cheeks and with pale fingers she nervously shredded a freshly baked peach muffin; another was no more than a teenager, she had her head in her hands and her whole body was racked with silent sobs; the third was middle-aged and expensively dressed in a Nicole Farhi matching pale jumper and trousers, gold necklace round the neck and gold bangles at her wrists, she was eating bacon and sausages rapidly. I noted that both hands which gripped the knife and fork were wrapped in bloodstained bandages and tears dripped on to the bacon. The fourth was me.

In the following week my only meal was breakfast, I found I was able to pack enough away at the buffet table to last me until the next morning, occasionally supplemented by my sneaking a few pieces of fresh fruit or a sausage up to my room for later.

After the mental confusion of arriving at the hotel, my mind subsequently settled into a reasonably pleasant state of numbness. I knew there were things I would have to think about but the time didn't have to be right now. During the day as my wounds slowly healed I took long walks into the rich Cheshire countryside along disused railway tracks overhung with copper beech and Scotch pine, or I wandered through the flat, amorphous town marvelling at the number of confident, beefy girls in their skimpy tops striding along the greasy pavement clutching carrier bags full of outsize clothing.

Often older women, catching sight of the cuts and bruises on my face, the black eye and the stitches, would give me a sad, knowing, sympathetic look. 'No,' I wanted say to them, 'it's not that.' Sometimes I would go down to the station; it gave me particular pleasure to watch the new modern expresses slide like fat silver eels under its dirty, glass canopy. Maliciously on occasion I would occupy the same end of the platform as the train-spotters, their flapping anoraks giving them the appearance of cormorants perched on the edge of a pier; this strange intense female standing in their midst made the men extremely threatened and twitchy; they shielded their male children from me with their plastic coats.

In the evenings the women who guarded the door of Guantanamo Bay were happy to let me slip inside without paying. I would sit in a corner sipping at a glass of tap water and watch the entertainers onstage. The main business of the club was tribute acts who performed four or five nights a week. I soon noticed that, strangely, the popularity of these acts was linked more to the fame of the people they were imitating rather than to the quality of their imitation. The Abba tribute band Bjorn Cjrazy got a full house though they couldn't match any of the Swedish group's complex harmonies and despite the fact that the singer who I initially thought was supposed to be Benny was in fact attempting to do Agnetha. On the other hand the Scottish Peter Gabriel impersonator Jock the Monkey, who was an almost exact copy, both vocally and visually, of the real former lead singer of Genesis, drew only a handful of discontented locals who threw empty beer cans at him during his almost entirely authentic rendition of the video for 'Big Mouth'. I was also nearly certain that the Gene Pitney impersonator who appeared there one Saturday night was actually the real Gene Pitney.

Of the three weeping women who had been in the breakfast room on my first day, one was not there the next, one stayed a week then was gone and the third, the woman dressed in the accessorised Nicole Farhi, I saw one morning in the corridor on the first floor, pushing a cleaning cart, going from room to room singing a tuneless song to herself, wearing a blue nylon overall, her face free from make-up and her arms unadorned by bracelets.

After breakfast on my eighth day at the hotel I went to the reception desk and spoke to the young girl working at the computer.

'Hi,' I said.

'Hi there,' the girl replied.

'Look, I think there might be a bit of a . . . erm, problem with my bill. I can pay up to today but after that my funds are going to get a little low. I need, I guess, to speak to the manager, maybe about some sort of a job?'

Rather than treating this as a problem the girl smiled sweetly, then with a couple of sweeps of her slender fingers put her computer to sleep and said, 'OK, we need to find solace.'

'Yes, I suppose we all do,' I said. 'That'd be nice.'

The girl lifted the flap of the counter and beckoned me through, led me across the little reception and through another door at the rear, down a narrow wood-panelled corridor past the hotel's clattering kitchens to another small office with a battered cream-painted door.

She knocked and a woman's voice called for us to enter.

We both squeezed into a tiny space lined with shelves on which box files, stacks of papers and accountancy books were precariously balanced. On the wall was a year planner covered in stickers and a calendar from an organic farm.

Seated at a cheap office desk was a black woman in her mid-forties; her skin was that black that is almost blue, her head and body might have been taken from a Benin sculpture, while her clothes had come from B&Q. The woman was dressed in a grimy overall dress of murky shades of orange as worn by employees of the DIY store and in a space above her left breast was written in Biro the name 'Solace'.

'Solace . . .' the young girl said to the African woman, indicating me with a wave of her hand, '. . . Room 3.'

'Room 3,' said Solace, looking up at me, 'sit down, dear.'

Once I was seated on a wobbly, cracked plastic stacking chair the older woman leant forward and asked, 'Did you hear the voices, dear? Did they tell you to come here, the voices?'

'Eh?' I asked, primed as I was for some kind of quizzing about my financial resources.

The young girl said, 'Some hear voices, some see pictures in their minds like a film.'

Getting no response from me, Solace added, 'Or drawings; other women get letters through the post addressed to them in their own handwriting and inside are maps on how to get here and a bus timetable. One said a statue of Florence Nightingale told her to cycle all the way to Crewe from Lincoln but she was a bit . . .'

Finally I said, 'I took a train, I took a night train and I don't know why but it seemed like a good idea if I got off here.'

They moved me out of my room in the kindliest way as if it was my idea; instead I was given a bed in a cramped, wooden-walled little cubicle slotted into the hot roof space of the hotel. In addition to the narrow metal-framed bed, the cubicle contained a small hardboard wardrobe, a desk and a bedside table; it felt like that was enough.

To pay my way they assigned me a job in Guantanamo Bay serving behind the bar, something I found I was unexpectedly bad at. Yet Solace never even hinted that they would move me, and because the drink was cheap and the atmosphere unthreatening none of the customers seemed to mind the occasional wrong order, incorrect change or cranberry juice knocked down the front of their white T-shirt. For my part the brainless work was a balm for my overheated nerves and I felt safe and looked after. The big beefy women who manned the door of the club looked like they would be a match for most men in a fight, though somehow it rarely came down to violence, they always seemed to be able to defuse a situation before it climbed out of control and became irreversible; unlike a lot of male security staff they never acted like they had anything to prove.

In the early hours of the morning once all the customers had reeled off into the night, those who had worked late would sometimes sit around in the staff canteen: a large, bare, functional room at the rear of the building, white-painted, lined with simple wooden tables and benches, where they would recount how they had come to the Station Hotel Crewe. I sat and listened but never joined in, to tell the truth I'd hardly had time to digest it myself. Important, crucial bits I'd forgotten would suddenly slip back into my mind, often with a jolt of shame, fear or sadness.

When you came down to it many of the women's tales amounted to extended nervous breakdowns, all sort of the same in the end though the details could be unbelievably shocking. A lot had had terrible things done to them, a few had done terrible things to others; some were clear on their motives, others told their tale still wrapped around with self-justification and evasion that only they couldn't see. I found all the stories I listened to during these early morning sessions absolutely riveting, apart from one. There was a woman there named Mrs Costello whose duties around the hotel seemed to consist of occasionally putting a spoon out at breakfast and whose crisis seemed to consist solely of her husband once slightly burning a corner of their living room curtains. This paucity of incident did not prevent her relating this yarn over and over again on nights such as this.

We'd had a particularly busy evening with a spirited performance by The Jim, a Paul Weller tribute act fronted by a lead singer whose real name was Jim, so it wasn't until after 2 a.m. that the empties had been cleared away and the mistakes I'd made in giving change had been accounted for so the cash could be counted and locked in the safe. It was a warm night and the windows were propped open; nobody from the club staff wished to go to bed yet and before anyone could stop her Mrs Costello was off again. Drifting away, I wondered to myself whether I would ever tell my own story like this, during one of these early mornings. I was certain if I ever did, even though I say so myself, the story would have a lot more to it than somebody setting fire to the curtains.

2

Toby stood in the doorway of Harriet's shop, letting the September wind rush in to riffle the clothes hanging on racks behind the counter; he was straining to see the police helicopter that was slowly and noisily circling the neighbourhood. The machine itself was so low in the sky that it was hidden by the tall trees in the park opposite but its searchlight backlit them in black, angular silhouette, giving the appearance of a sinister wood in a Balinese shadow play.

'The Pointless Park airshow beginneth early tonight,' Toby said, coming back into the warmth and closing the door so that the clothes abruptly stopped their frantic dance.

Harriet looked down and smiled to herself – her brother-in-law was the only person in the world who called the neighbourhood that they lived in 'Pointless Park'. Even she didn't, though from time to time she tried really, really hard to do it, to say the words 'Pointless Park'. Mentally Harriet would rehearse little scenarios in which she used the name in a conversation with Toby, saying in her mind, 'The Japanese Strangleweed is flower-ing this week in Pointless Park,' or 'I hear they found another dead body in Pointless Park today,' knowing how happy it would make him if she did. She'd set out to say it and he would stare optimistically at her, like a little kitten crouched waiting for a ball of silver paper to be thrown to it but then some other words would emerge from his sister-in-law's mouth and Toby would deflate like a punctured weather balloon. One of the hazards of having a conversation with Toby was that he gave his own names to lots of people and lots of things but would never explain what they were or admit there was anything odd about what he was saying: for instance he called the Prime Minister 'Mrs Mitchum' and the European Community was 'The Banana Club'. It could be quite difficult for people who didn't know him or weren't familiar with his personal glossary to understand what he was talking about a lot of the time when he said things like, 'I see Mrs Mitchum gave a big speech to the Banana Club last night.' He would also always sing a few bars of the *Marseillaise* whenever he saw a black person reading the news.

It was just a guess of Harriet's that he'd like her to use the same phrases as him, she didn't know for certain, nothing had ever been said out loud. Maybe, she thought, he was happy being misunderstood, yet she did remember how briefly delirious Toby had seemed to be when he discovered that he'd persuaded a married couple to use the phrase 'soup, swoop, loop de loop' every time that they drank soup. The couple were called Tori and Paul and they had been friends at college with Harriet's younger sister Helen. Toby too had been at this college but at that time not part of the same circle. He'd belonged to a crowd of rugby-playing business studies students who Helen and her friends only encountered puking drunkenly into wastepaper bins on the campus as they left a play or a madrigal concert.

In the early years after Helen and Toby married they gave many dinner parties for Helen's old college friends, while not returning the phone calls of Toby's mates. He would cook the first course which was always soup and when serving it he would invariably say, 'There we are, soup, swoop, loop de loop,' then he'd smile at everyone as if he'd just done a magic trick.

What Toby wasn't aware of was the process by which the married couple Tori and Paul had come to use the phrase 'soup, swoop, loop de loop'. After the dinner party they would start drunkenly talking about what an arse Toby was as soon as they were in the minicab going home; they would say to each other in a high-pitched, mocking imitation of Toby's voice, 'Soup, swoop, loop de loop,' and 'Please do have some more of this delicious soup, swoop, loop de loop,' then they would collapse against each other laughing, convincing the Algerian or Bengali taxi driver once again of the impenetrability and corruption of Western society. Tori and Paul would also repeat after Toby, 'Soup, swoop, loop de loop,' when he served the soup and give each other secret looks. Pretty soon when they had soup at home Tori and Paul would say to each other, 'Soup, swoop, loop de loop,' at first still ridiculing Toby but eventually they forgot why they were saying it and it became part of the private language every couple develops, employed long after they'd gratefully ceased having soupy dinners with Toby and Helen.

When Tori and Paul had children one of their au pairs was a Maori girl from the Southern Pacific Cook Islands who, when she returned home after a couple of years, took the phrase 'soup, swoop, loop de loop' with her and spread it amongst her extended family until finally the phrase appeared in an anthropological dissertation: '"Soup, swoop, loop de loop": Shamanistic Incantations in Raratongan Food Preparation Rituals', University of Topeka, 1998.

Toby was a great many things to Harriet: he was her brother-in-law, he was married to her little sister, he was father of her beloved nephew and he was her best male friend, but sometimes she still wished that he didn't have quite so much free time to hang around her shop. Harriet thought to herself that it wasn't as if he didn't have a job, a good job and a job he was good at. When she sporadically visited her brother-in-law at his work it always amazed her to see how all his quirks and idiosyncrasies disappeared and that around the office he was focused and businesslike like a normal person; those who only knew Toby from the office were astonished to witness his eccentric behaviour in social situations and those who only met him socially were startled to learn that he held down any kind of job at all and didn't live in some sort of sheltered accommodation.

But Harriet knew it was part of his cleverness that he'd always looked for employment in administrative posts that didn't stretch him. Until quite recently Toby had been deputy chairman of the Penrith Fairground Disaster Fund, a charity whose main purpose as far as she could tell was to avoid giving any money to anybody involved in any way in the great Penrith Fairground Disaster – either those actually on the Ferris wheel or the ones crushed by it as it travelled down the A66.

A few months ago he'd left that position and now administered the estate of a famous playwright who'd died in the late 1980s. From what Harriet knew the playwright had been an easy-going, genial sort but his estate was now controlled by several distant relatives whom he'd never met. Toby's job was to stop anybody ever putting on any of the work of the playwright ever again unless they agreed not to change a single syllable of the sacred text. As far as possible, following orders from the estate, Toby did his best to prevent students from studying the sacred text and to forbid the transmission of any clips of the plays on radio or television unless a gigantic fee was paid to the distant relatives.

Harriet's younger sister Helen – Toby's wife – also worked full time for a charity, this one going by the name of Warbird. Warbird wasn't always called Warbird: when it was founded by a group of philanthropically inclined citizens in the early Victorian era to look out for the interests of canaries being sent down coal mines it was known as the Society for the Protection of Our Feathered Chums. In the modern age Helen's charity primarily concerned itself with the treatment and welfare of parrots, macaws and budgerigars that were trapped or needed to be rescued from dangerous war zones. A few years before, the family including Harriet had been on holiday in Cornwall when Helen had got a call saying there was a famous parakeet trapped in the middle of the tribal massacres in Rwanda; the parakeet belonged to a British millionaire who had a wildlife sanctuary in the rainforest, all the human staff had fled or been hacked to bits and the word was that the bloodcrazed Hutus would soon start on the wildlife. Helen right away drove back to London and organised a private plane to fly into the middle of the fighting. Harriet tried to be proud when she saw her sister being interviewed on Sky News with Montmorency sitting on her shoulder. Though really, she'd thought to herself, you'd think the bird could have flown out of there by itself if they'd simply told it where to go.

Then immediately Harriet felt guilty about having mutinous, unsupportive ideas such as these. They came often to her and her response always was instantly to try and squash them flat and replace them with nicer, more kindly thoughts. Unfortunately, however quickly Harriet caught and squashed them, she was still left with feelings of shame over being the sort of person who had such malevolent ideas in the first place, so she would then have to perform some penance to make amends, maybe buy a little present for the person she'd had the bad thought about, resolve to be super-nice to them forever in thought and deed, praise their shoes extravagantly when she next saw them or do tedious little jobs for them even though she really had better things to be getting on with.

'There you go, Toby,' Harriet said, 'your jacket's done.'

'Ta, thanks a lot,' her brother-in-law replied, taking it and staring at where the acid burn hole had been – there was now no trace at all.

'Golly, Hat Hat,' Toby said, 'you're a magician.' Then he stood in the centre of the shop clearly wondering what to do next. Though he didn't necessarily do that much work Toby was scrupulous about not going home until the end of the working day. Harriet imagined that he knew if he started staying at home during the week he might eventually never leave the house. Toby looked at his watch, then he did a bit of tuneless singing to himself. 'Yeehoo, yahh, yeegata yam yam,' he sang. Then finally he said, 'I think I'll go and visit that exhibition of new ceramics in that gallery at the furthest end of the parade.'

He really could be so sweet, Harriet thought as Toby left the shop, forgetting to close the door behind him. She could hear him singing 'Yach a yang a yach a yoo . . .' the sound trailing off down the pavement. Now she felt a bit despicable about wishing he would leave, picturing with a stab of guilt how whenever they were out and they met any of his mates that she didn't know, like the gang he played football with on a Thursday, he would always put his arm around her and say right away, 'Guys, this is my sister-in-law Harriet,' like he was claiming her, pointing out to them that she was somebody special in his life.

Toby thought the woman behind the counter in the gallery was having some kind of fit hissing and tutting and sighing like that; it was only when she strode out from her desk and slammed the door that he realised he hadn't shut it behind him. Staring at the tortured lumps of glazed clay, he'd become engrossed in thinking of his sister-in-law. Toby's personal theory, for what it was worth, was that Harriet had been attracted to invisible mending because she herself was so visible. Harriet reminded him of one of the misshapen, hand-thrown milk jugs he was standing in front of: huge, pot-bellied and lumpy. Whenever he was out with her and they bumped into somebody he knew who wasn't from their social circle, some of the fellows from the footy club for example, he would point out immediately that this big fat thing he was with was his sister-in-law just in case they thought she was some girl he was having sex with. Toby felt guilty about doing that because Hat was his best friend, but still and all a fellow had his reputation to think of.

To this day he still found it hard to believe it that the slim, vivacious, petite Helen, the woman he was married to, was the sister of such a hippo.

Even after eight years of marriage, every day Toby still considered it his greatest achievement in life to have managed to snag a woman as beautiful as Helen. That and of course his 'soup, swoop, loop de loop' triumph with Tori and Paul, but the soup thing was years ago now.

Toby also wasn't sure whether he should really be proud of the 'soup, swoop, loop de loop' thing. He seemed to remember that before he'd made the decision to stop drinking (well, Helen suggested it pretty forcefully and the stipendiary magistrate had implied it might make sense too) he hadn't said or done all these weird things. Still, most of the time he didn't regret his choice – there had been a demented, sprayhose quality to his drinking that had frightened him in the few brief hours when he'd been sober. If it took a tremendous effort of will to steer clear of alcohol and if he still thought about having a drink an awful lot of the time and if as it turned out the poison in the liquor had somehow been deadening or killing off the runaway thoughts that now carommed day and night around his head and he monthly seemed to acquire some new strange idiosyncrasy, quirk or tic, well, that was all a price worth paying.

Stubbornness was something Toby noticed and admired in Harriet; you had to give her credit for the dogged way she kept trying to lose weight despite a total lack of success and so many obstacles being put in her way. He'd asked her earlier in the shop, 'Can you babysit Timon tonight? Me and Helen are going to a charity dinner attended by Bono out of U2.'

'Yeah of course,' she'd replied. 'Helen's already asked me. But you'll have to wait till after seven, when I get back from the gym.'

Toby was surprised to hear her say this. 'I didn't know you

were going to the gym again, Harriet, after . . . you know that thing that happened, the incident . . .'

'Yes, well . . .' Harriet said, poking her jaw out so she looked like a fighting dog, 'the boss of the gym agreed that that woman had no right to say those things to me. Apparently she was suffering from postnatal depression over not getting her figure back two weeks after giving birth; but still, shouting all that stuff about how I looked and the smell of my sweat . . . They've told her she has to attend another branch and they've offered me six months free membership extension to sort of say sorry. So I have to go back really.'

Stubborn, see?

As Harriet huffed along the pavement she once more castigated herself for not being able to say out loud Toby's name for the patch of land she was skirting; she really should have been able to use it, especially since it did so perfectly capture the flavour of the place: it truly was a pointless park. The fitness centre Harriet was heading for was on the boundary road at its southern tip, but though tarmac paths snaked through the black trees and one streetlight in five was working she would not, certainly after nightfall, enter its pitch-dark interior. Harriet recalled when she'd been a child in the early 1970s in Southport that a park had been a very different thing. There were big wrought-iron gates guarding the entrance that were firmly locked at sunset every night, there were substantial black-painted spiked railings all around the perimeter, inside there was a band-stand and a boating lake, clipped grass as neat as a Guardsman's haircut, a crystal palm house, flowers and stout native trees and a head gardener who lived in a little house by the gates and kept an eye out. Not in this part of north London where she lived now; those into whose charge fell the open spaces during the 1960s were having none of that old malarky – they couldn't quite explain to you how a bandstand could be oppressive of racial minorities while simultaneously putting down women, they just knew it somehow did.

The authorities at that time had high hopes of building a grand eight-lane highway linking Walthamstow in the east with Fulham in the west, demolishing large parts of antediluvian London on the way and vaulting St Paul's Cathedral on a long-legged concrete flyover. Any building on the route might be pulled down at any moment, so while they waited for it all to happen they thought they might as well stick modern non-hierarchical urban utility spaces along its entire length.

Composed of interlinked Second World War bomb sites, an abandoned asbestos factory and the grounds of a long-vanished stately home, Pointless Park was laid out by graduates of the new town planning courses from the best polytechnics in Britain, disregarding all the laws of both Eastern and Western aesthetics. The disruptive, unbalanced random distribution of weedy, ill-looking trees, ugly, common plants, concrete, tarmac, dead-end paths leading to blank walls, sinister hollows, unsightly brown hummocks, stretches of grey metal fencing only suitable for a poison gas research facility and scrubby dead grass emitted such a strong sense of malevolence that anybody entering the park immediately suffered acute feelings of anxiety, fear and depression. The only ones able to endure its aura of malignancy were those whose brains had been numbed by drinking cider or floor polish, or those who were taking powerful anti-epilepsy medication.

Only in the very middle of the park in a shallow bowl perhaps two hundred yards across was there a sort of calm. Over the years pollution had killed off all the native woodland trees that had surrounded the bygone stately home, apart from a single ancient oak right in the centre of the grassy depression. Four hundred years old with many long-dead branches not cleared by any tree surgeon and stumpier than a healthy oak should be, growing only about fifty feet high, it had a cave-like hollow in its trunk where somebody in the late eighteenth century had lit a fire at its base and the tree had grown around the damage.

Fringing the edge of the bowl a tangle of living and dead trees – beech, horse chestnut, hawthorn and sycamore, curled about with damp undergrowth, thorny berberis, rhododendron and strange creepers of unknown origin – was neglected by the contractors who visited the rest of the park a few times a year to flail the grass, pick up a few of the discarded syringes and trample the flowers round the edge but who never penetrated further to its heart of darkness.

In Harriet's mind the park was roughly the shape of an upside-down pork chop, fatter at its base, a quarter of a mile wide and approximately a third of a mile along both sides, the eastern margin formed by a high brick wall beyond which ran a railway line buried in a deep cutting. The steep sides of the cutting were almost an extension of the park, untrodden by humans from one year to the next; rare species of rodents and reptiles flourished beneath its long grass and often above the track birds of prey – kestrels and hawks – hovered and swooped.

Her invisible mending business was in a small terrace of shops on the road at the northern end of the park. In some ways Harriet didn't need a shop as most of her trade came from repair contracts with many theatres in the West End, but as she lived alone and worked alone, the few walk-in customers she got during the day at least meant that she talked to some human beings just to reassure herself that she was real. Harriet's brain, free to fret itself into increasingly baroque circles, worried that all those people you read about who went missing every year had simply faded away, their molecules giving up the effort of holding together simply because nobody had taken any notice of them for so long.

The work was never-ending – performers were always tearing

their clothes, either in accidents or fits of actorish passion – and secure, since once managements found somebody they got on with to do their repairs they tended to stick with them. And despite the big sign above her window stating 'Harriet Tingle, Invisible Mending Services' she was constantly turning away people who entered the shop clutching bundles of dirty clothing who wished to have their dry-cleaning done. 'I don't do cleaning,' she would tell them in a clear, slow voice, 'I do invisible mending; it's a highly specialised craft, I don't stick on patches to repair a hole like they do in the dry-cleaners.' If they hadn't already turned round and walked out without a 'thank you' or a 'sorry' she would continue to explain to them: 'I take a tiny strand of fabric from some place on the garment that you can't see and I weave it around the damage so that once it's done you'd never know where the repair was. I charge forty pounds a hole.'

'About the same as a high-class prostitute,' Harriet had once remarked to her friend Rose.

'Darling, how naïve you are,' Rose had replied. 'You've no idea how much some men would pay for the right hole. Especially if it's telling them things they want to hear.'

Looking over her shoulder she smiled at her building and thought, I own that. Harriet's shop was in the middle of the parade and sat alongside a number of ethnic businesses such as Halal Meat And Videos and a Turkish social club, some businesses that catered to the newer, more wealthy inhabitants of the area like a fromagerie and a gift shop and gallery called Galerie Giscard d'Estaing of which she was the best customer. There was an old-style hardware store that was very useful and a Valueslasher Mini Market for the white working classes. On the corner there was a pub and over the road in the other direction a sweet little railway station with cream-painted filigree fretwork edging the platform canopy and a slate roof, from which trains ran into the Lagos-like madness of Finsbury Park and past whose silent platform late at night slid sinister grey trains carrying nuclear waste from the power plants on the Suffolk coast to the north near Penrith, where the people didn't matter as much, where it was stored in leaky concrete holes in the ground.

It was a guilty pleasure for Harriet that she held the freehold of the whole building; she thought she shouldn't be the sort of person who took pleasure in property, that she should be wild and free and ready to move to New Zealand at a moment's notice, nevertheless it was the thing Harriet secretly felt proudest of that she'd had the sense to buy, even though some months the mortgage repayments could still be a problem, before prices in the area went completely mad.

The road curved east, giving her the first view of the gym towards which she was heading. Housed in a former five-storey garment factory, a stocky cube of a building faced with yellow brick, the ground floor was now occupied by her gym which was called Muscle Bitch – it was one branch of a middle-market chain with an all-female clientele. Harriet had joined three months ago on her thirty-eighth birthday. The three-month introductory membership had been an unsubtle birthday present from her sister Helen. Harriet liked to think there was nobody better at buying presents than her: she possessed a comprehensive collection of jewellery brochures, a definitive list of florists, extensive contacts amongst muffin basket vendors and each gift she gave to someone was crafted for their particular personality and was a joy to own. Whereas the presents her sister gave, at least to Harriet, were invariably an imposition: they always required her to go somewhere and do something, a voucher for beginners' violin lessons, a three-week walking tour in the Alpujarras or a course of introductory Arabic in a six CD boxed set.

When Harriet had reluctantly gone to join the gym the man in the suit who filled in the membership forms and took her voucher as if it was contaminated went off to find a teacher to devise her exercise programme and was gone for a very long time. Occasionally people who looked like instructors would stick their heads round the door then withdraw them quickly when they saw her.

Nearly half an hour passed before the manager came back trailed by a tall, slim but muscular, pale-skinned young man with close-cropped blond hair, who had the name Patrick stitched on the breast of his light green instructor's polo shirt.

'This is Patrick,' the manager said redundantly, 'he's said he'll show you what to do.'

'Great, thanks, great,' Harriet babbled, grateful that at last somebody was prepared to take her on. Without a word the young man turned into the body of the gym with its sweet smell of air freshener mingling with the clang of weights rising and falling. As she dragged around behind him Patrick would brusquely order Harriet to climb into a machine, he would strap her in, belt her up and then tilt her heavy body backwards so that her legs were spread wide apart and all her fat tipped towards the floor; after that he would lean across her prone body to minutely adjust something, with her thinking that this was much closer than she would ever normally get to a stranger. Harriet held herself stiff as her nose brushed his sinewy white skin and her breath riffled his translucent, pale eyelashes.

After a few strained pushes on each machine at weights with the combined heaviness of a couple of mice, Patrick marked out on a pale yellow card what she should do during subsequent visits then abruptly left her, still pinioned inside a machine, without a word.

Harriet had not wanted to get changed at the gym, exposing her hectares of dimpled flabby skin to the other women, so she walked home in the clothes she'd worked out in, the icy wind drying her sweat in salty rings on the towelling fabric of her tracksuit.

*　　*　　*

After the trauma of the induction she almost didn't return to Muscle Bitch but in the end found herself unwilling to add the gym to the long list of things she had given up on after one visit or lesson, things such as archery, dry-stone wall building or introductory Arabic. Harriet was determined that 'going to the gym' would at least be on the slightly shorter list of things she'd abandoned after a few months, along with learning to play the violin and Marxism.

So over the next couple of months once or twice a week, experiencing an inner sense of dread as if going in for painful and embarrassing minor surgery, she would drag herself there along the pavement.

It was only the thought of Patrick being there to help her through it that persuaded her to make the trip. He always seemed to be the one nearby when she needed somebody to hit the emergency stop button on the treadmill, to lift some weights off her or to whisper that she was trying to do leg presses on an arm curl machine and when, as often happened, she became confused at the settings on the machines, unsure whether '15' was the weight or the seat height it was always him she would seek out for advice.

Harriet would rather have gone to the gym during the day when the place was presumably emptier but a sense of guilt kept her constantly in the shop from nine to five so she was forced to attend in the evenings when the place was always packed with demented women, running on the treadmills, crazed expressions on their faces, dancing madly as if auditioning for *A Chorus Line* or pedalling static bikes as though pursued by hordes of mounted cossacks with rapine on their minds. Yet amongst the frantic female crowd Patrick seemed to glide with solemn composure. Finding herself oddly comfortable with his looming, sallow presence, Harriet assumed, although he gave no sign of it, that he felt some sort of fondness for her. All the same, she realised, the main reason their relationship grew was because he was the only instructor that she ever saw twice. The entire staff of the gym, including the receptionists, the office staff and the cleaners – all the small Mediterranean muscled men and the slender blonde South African girls – seemed to change entirely between each of her visits.

At first Patrick struggled conscientiously to perform his job with Harriet, to encourage her to push herself, to strain after progress, to work her body. 'Cccc'mon!' he would growl, or 'Yes, yes, that's good!' but throughout all the damp hours she spent at Muscle Bitch none of her weights or reps went up at all. Harriet could just about chest press five kilos – the lowest weight – on her first visit and she was still just about chest pressing five kilos now, three months later. After a while Patrick had given up trying to be a motivator and simply sat down next to her staring into space or chatting in a disjointed fashion.

He seemed to be able to talk at length without Harriet actually getting much information about his life. He possessed a strange elliptical way of speaking about himself, mentioning the names of people without any context so that she thought she'd found out things about him but was never entirely sure. There seemed to be a child and possibly a mother, though whether they lived with him or not remained obscure, and there definitely seemed to be a best friend called Martin who had a great deal of sage advice though Martin might have been a cat, and there'd possibly been an important trip to Belgium but perhaps not. It was hard to know even what age he was; given the number of things he'd done he had to be at least in his late twenties though sometimes to her he seemed little older than a child.

Indeed Patrick never seemed younger to Harriet than when one day, more direct than usual, he told her that he would really like to be a stunt man in the movies. She grabbed on to this solid piece of biography and pressed him to expand. 'You have to be at Olympic level in two sports, though, and you have to, like, know people in the business,' he told her. She shyly said that she often repaired costumes for theatre and film productions and knew a few people in the business but he didn't seem interested in any practical help she could offer. Patrick's speech, usually flat, became more animated as he went on. 'They have this annual stuntman's ball every year, right? And when the bloke announces who you are at the entrance to the ball-room, you have to come in and throw yourself down the stairs, to get to like where the tables are and the dance floor and that . . .' He paused, then said, 'I don't know whether the wives and girlfriends have to throw themselves down the stairs too. I suppose if they were stuntwomen themselves they could but walking down the stairs would be optional . . .' Harriet got the feeling from his tone that he thought the wives and girlfriends really should throw themselves down the stairs too, even if they weren't stuntwomen, out of loyalty.

When she checked in to the gym with her personalised swipe card, the entrance way, as it often was, was filled almost entirely with red and purple balloons, making her feel as if she'd walked into a giant berry pie.

'Hi, er . . .' said the female receptionist brightly, reading her name off the computer screen, '. . . Harriet, you coming to the party then?'

There was frequently a party at the gym that went with the balloons though sometimes there were just balloons for their own sake. 'No, I don't think so. What's this one in aid of?'

'It's going to be great,' the receptionist explained breathlessly. 'Relay run on the treadmills from London to Penrith for the Fairground Disaster Fund – one of the girl's brothers ran a hoopla stall in the path of the Ferris wheel – and, well, you know . . . the party's compulsory for the staff so I won't get home until after midnight but hey! That's great too.'

Feeling as if she was already carrying heavy weights, Harriet passed into the interior of Muscle Bitch and moved amongst its crowd of grunting women. Her exercise programme was the usual mixture of light weight-lifting and aerobic exercises. After some half-hearted stretching that usually gave her backache, she climbed into a sort of bathtub-cum-recumbent bicycle with a TV screen clamped on the front of it. She was supposed to pedal the bathtub for twenty minutes round a badly computer-rendered tropical island shown on the TV screen. After only a quarter of her allotted time she would usually steer the bathtub over the edge of Pirates Cliff or pedal out to sea from Mermaid Beach, hoping to drown or be smashed to bits on the rocks of Coconut Inlet, but the implacable computer inside the machine simply steered her back to dry land, generally after a stern fish told her not to be so silly.

Sweatily pedalling around the imaginary island, Harriet's thoughts were on a journey of their own to an equally uncomfortable destination. She realised that she had for some time been approaching the point invariably reached in her efforts at self-improvement – Giving Up Cove.

A few years before, she had been introduced to an Iraqi man at a party by her friend Lulu. Lulu said this man was a healer who had completely cured her mother's arthritis and she was sure he could do the same for Harriet's obesity. Filled with optimism at a cure for fatness that required her to do nothing, she visited him at his shabby rented rooms in Harley Street and for ninety pounds a session he wrapped her in hot towels and prodded and pinched her body seemingly at random. At the end of six hours' 'treatment' she had gained nearly half a stone, so Harriet told him she was emigrating to Argentina and stopped the visits. A few weeks later she bumped into Lulu's mum who told Harriet that her arthritis was worse than ever and she wished she was dead.

One thing, however, that had stayed with her from her six sessions with the grave Iraqi, apart from the half a stone, was a phrase he'd used. In attempting to describe the complexity of her mind, he had endeavoured to liken the inside of Harriet's head to the Boeing Corporation. The healer had wanted to conjure up a vision of rows and rows of desks, mile upon mile of tiny office workers dedicated to the elaborate business of managing Harriet's thought processes and actions. Except he ruined the profundity of it by pronouncing the Boeing Corporation as 'the Booing Corporation'. To her this seemed a much more apt metaphor for her thinking – not a huge, efficient global planemaker but instead the Booing Corporation: a gigantic organisation installed inside her head dedicated to the business of booing, heckling and general discouragement of any kind of positive behaviour. The only time the Booing Corporation ever became encouraging was when they were suggesting it might be a really good idea to eat a whole frozen tuna pie at six thirty in the morning. Except, as her wobbling legs strained against the pedals and perspiration rolled down her face, she resolved that this time things were going to be different, this time she had a foolproof plan to get fit and lose weight.

Two weeks before, sitting in the place where she went to be ritually abused about the state of her hair, she'd read an article in an old copy of *Marie Claire* concerning an incredibly fat woman, much fatter than her, who'd got fit and slim simply by hiring a personal trainer. There were snaps of the woman when she'd been fat, at family parties and at long tables in restaurants, smiling dazedly into the lens like a barnyard animal that somebody had put a wig and big glasses on. Funnily enough Harriet thought to herself all these 'before' photos were fuzzy as if the camera itself was angry at the woman for being such a gigantic pig. Then there were pin-sharp, acid-bright pictures of the way the woman was now, youthful, thin and confident, her face full of happy intelligence. That was what Harriet was going to do, that was her plan: she was going to ask Patrick if he'd be her personal trainer.

Harriet was pedalling the bathtub through what was either a tropical forest or some animal heads stuck on spikes when Patrick came over.

'Hiya,' he said, picking up her chart. 'How's it going?'

'It's going at exactly the same speed as it was three months ago.'

'Yeah . . .' he replied, studying the exercise machine's digital readout, 'your laptime's identical to the second; it's a remarkable achievement in its way.'

'What way's that exactly?'

Patrick shrugged. 'Well, you know it isn't really any sort of achievement but they like us to be positive.'

'I'm getting sick of this place,' she said

'Well, you need to stick with it, not get discouraged . . .' He struggled to find something more inspirational to say, 'or . . . something.'

'No, no,' she persisted. 'Patrick, I do sincerely want to get fitter but this gym isn't working. So I was thinking . . . do you do personal training?'

'Personal training?' he asked.

'Yeah, yeah.' Harriet realised she was talking fast now but couldn't stop. 'I've got this big empty room above my shop, nice springy wood floor, and I was talking to a couple of girlfriends Lulu and Rose and we . . . they thought we could sort of hire you to come round and give us a workout, a personalised programme, personal training. What do you think, what do you think?'

He paused for several seconds then said, looking around, 'We're not supposed to make side deals with the clients.'

'Oh come on,' she wheedled, 'please . . . I'm never going to get into shape here. We both know that. I assume you've done personal training before, most of the instructors here have, it must have been part of your own training.'

'Yeah, sure, obviously . . .' He was silent for a further moment then asked, 'You'd pay me?'

'Yes of course, whatever the going rate is . . . I dunno, forty pounds an hour?'

He considered a little longer then said, 'Well, I suppose the gym don't need to know about it. I guess I could come round one afternoon next week to meet your friends and work out . . . you know, a personalised programme and that.'

One of the muscular dykey weight-lifting women had asked Patrick to 'spot' for her, that is to stand above her while she bench-pressed the weight of a small car, to make sure that she wouldn't be crushed by the chromed bar if her strength suddenly went. In fact he wasn't giving her any attention at all but was thinking about what it might be like to be a personal trainer. It was kind of stupid that Harriet thought anybody at Muscle Bitch, least of all him, held any qualifications, unless you thought looking nice in a tight polo shirt counted as a qualification.

Not that it was a particular shock for him to be asked to do something he didn't know anything about. He didn't have any memory of it happening when he was a kid but sometime around the time he became a teenager Patrick began to notice people would always be asking his opinion on stuff when he only had the vaguest idea what they were talking about. At school the teachers would often turn to him to answer questions on all kinds of subjects and even when his replies were stumbling or just plain wrong many times they acted as if he'd said something dead intelligent and when they marked his essays he got grades that were much better than he reckoned his confused ramblings on ox-bow lakes or the rise of the Nazi Party in pre-war Germany really deserved. For the longest time Patrick couldn't explain it, beginning to think that perhaps he was brighter than he thought he was: until he failed every single one of his GCSEs.

Very confused, he took ages to figure it out. Slowly the fact dawned that those people who marked the exam papers from the exams *didn't know him*. Or rather they couldn't see him. Staring at his face in the mirror and trying to imagine how he appeared to others he saw that the stillness, the blankness with which he held his features, added to the way the planes of his face fell, the bright clear blue of his eyes, the sharp, straight line of his nose, the firm cut of his mouth, made him look really, really, really intelligent. Patrick thought, turning his head from side to side in the pitiless light of the shaving mirror, that if he didn't know the true ordinariness of his own mind he'd ask himself for advice on all sorts of difficult and baffling matters.

Beneath Patrick's spread legs, on her eighteenth lift the woman's strength did suddenly leave her and she found herself unable to straighten her arms, and the silvery bar barely held by shaking limbs began slowly to descend on to her windpipe. While the customer gurgled and gagged, her legs waving in the air, Patrick mulled over what might happen if he became a successful personal trainer. He assumed that if he did a good job for Harriet she might recommend him to her friends, then to her whole social circle and if he did a good job for them too then they might want him to be their friend. He knew this because sometimes he liked to eavesdrop on the customers at the gym and from time to time he'd hear the women discuss the valued people who came to their houses. 'You really must use our painter and decorator Vaclav, he's more of a friend than anything else,' he'd heard them say more than once, or 'We're spending our summer holidays with the nanny's family on their farm just outside Kraków,' or 'We're taking our Colombian cleaner to a comedy club on Saturday night, she doesn't speak any English so we're not sure how much she'll take in, but still . . .'

Only if they were good though, they didn't seem to recommend those who were bad; he imagined people didn't say to their friends, 'I've found this really unreliable, incompetent and expensive plumber, you really must use him as soon as he's finished wrecking my central heating.' Mind you, from what he heard at the gym most plumbers still seemed to be unreliable, incompetent and expensive anyway so how did that happen? It was another mystery.

Not for the first time he wished Martin was there so he could discuss these things as they had done so many times in the past. He'd tried again to e-mail Martin last night but the satellite uplink wasn't working, just as it hadn't been for the last month and a half.

From beneath him Patrick heard a strange gurgling sound, a final death rattle from the female weight-lifter; he looked down and easily lifted the chromed bar from the woman's throat just as she was heading towards the white light and the welcoming outstretched arms of her mother.

3

Three years before, on her second day of property ownership, still settling into the shop and the flat above it, slowly sorting through boxes of books and wondering where to hang pictures and just about deciding to set fire to the whole lot and start again, Harriet had noticed through the big shop window a smartly dressed man of about thirty-five standing at the bus stop a little way along the parade talking animatedly into a mobile phone. As she got to work on her very first job, repairing several knife slashes in the ballgown of a transsexual, she saw a number of the little red buses that served the stop race up and rock to a halt, she saw their doors hiss open and the man shake his head, refusing to board; the driver would shout some insult or exhortation then, getting no response, would drive off in a fury, the bus often becoming airborne as it crested a nearby speed hump. Throughout all this the man continued to talk rapidly into his phone.

At lunchtime, guiltily skipping next door to console herself with a large shawarma and chips at what had then been a place called Shashlik Happens and was now Mon Fromagerie, Harriet passed near to the man and heard him describing somebody to whoever it was he was speaking to on the other end of the phone. 'Yeah, he looks like one of those big Irish farmers,' the man said, 'that never marries then fails to commit suicide with a shotgun in the mouth, huge hands, probably a repressed homosexual . . .' Following the man's electric gaze up the road she saw that the big repressed homosexual, failed suicide Irish farmer person he was referring to was Toby lolloping towards her along the pavement, making the first of his many visits to the shop and now beginning to wave a cheery hello at her with his huge hands. In turn the businessman shifted his gaze to see who Toby was greeting, moving his head in a stiff arc like one of those silver-painted street performers she'd seen that terrible time she went to Barcelona for the weekend on her own, who made money by impersonating robots. The man with the phone stared directly, disturbingly, into her eyes. Unable to take the intensity of his gaze, she looked away slightly and saw that what she had taken to be the smart metal-effect mobile phone which he had been holding to the side of his face was in fact an unopened tin of sardines.

'Gotta go . . .' the man said, before slipping his tin can phone into an inside pocket of his jacket, then, crossing the road with stiff movements, walked straight into the park where he was soon swallowed up by the moist grey-green vegetation.

Now three years later the Tin Can Man was still at the bus stop most days or walking up and down the parade or striding along the perimeter roads of the park; though his smart business suit was now filthy and torn, he still clutched his sardine can to his mouth and would still generally be describing those around him. 'Big, enormous, porky girl, can hardly breathe she's so fat, greasy black hair, gigantic gig lamps, obviously not been fucked for years . . .' was what Harriet heard him say about her one afternoon, forcing her to laugh out loud when he said it, since there was really nothing she could find to argue about in this portrait.

Though she was inclined on occasion to get extremely upset with those she thought had insulted her, much to her own surprise Harriet never felt any fury towards the Tin Can Man. When thinking of him she recalled the look briefly observed in his eyes on that first day when she had seen his 'phone'. A look of sadness and panic as if the words were saying him rather than the other way around.

Also sometimes, usually if returning to her flat late at night, when she heard him talking he appeared to be involved in a different kind of conversation over his imaginary phone, where he listened more to the other person and his tone was unlike the bombastic, crazed voice of daylight hours.

The Tin Can Man was caught up in one of these calls as she shut the side door of the building on her way out to meet her two best friends Lulu and Rose at the pub on the corner.

'No, Lynn . . .' the Tin Can Man was saying, '. . . yes, I understand that, darling, it's just that I've got to do the . . . yes, Lynn . . . yes, Lynn . . . please I wish you wouldn't . . . yes, Lynn . . . but please, darling, if you'd just listen for a second I can . . .'

His pleading tone carried with Harriet up the road for once almost unheard and unnoticed; instead there was a rushing sound of fury in her ears. About ten months after she'd moved into her shop the building next door had been acquired by a housing association dedicated to the interests of elderly Namibian women. At first things had gone terribly well, the elderly ladies were an interesting mixture, the majority African of varying shades of blackness but a few of Indian or Pakistani extraction and one or two stiff old white women in cardigans and pearls. In their brightly coloured robes, their saris and salwar kameez, they had regularly visited her in the shop, bringing baked yams, onion pakora and sponge cake with them. They would often tidy up the chaotic workroom while Harriet devoured the food they'd made and sometimes the women might do little pieces of intricate embroidery for her to cover a particularly difficult hole.

However within half a year the young grandsons and the great-nephews of the Namibian ladies found out that Granma was living in a spacious, freshly decorated, rent-subsidised, architect-designed flat and moved in whether they wanted them to or not. Rapidly the old ladies died from the upset or moved back to Whitechapel or Totteridge or Africa so that soon the entire building became occupied by rough young men who played loud music and held mysterious parties late into the night and didn't appear to have regular jobs. Despite the absence of the grannies the meals on wheels still came every day delivering stacks of dinners in foil containers and the pavement outside was blocked by BMW 3 series coupés and Subaru Impreza Turbos allowed to park freely on the yellow lines because of the disabled parking badges the young men had coerced out of their grandmothers' doctors, insisting that they regularly took Granny down the hospital, though if they went anywhere the cars seemed most regularly to be parked outside nightclubs in Wood Green and Crouch End.

All of this made Harriet furious, she hated the injustice and the cruelty of it and she missed the little old ladies. Most of all though, she objected to the way the boys who lived rent-free in the adjoining house constantly piled rubbish bags and mounds of rotting food against her front step. As she stepped over the garbage she'd felt herself seethe with rage, a rage that was swiftly followed by a crushing sense of powerlessness. Harriet fantasised often about confronting these rough-looking boys with one of those electric gatling guns you saw in Hollywood movies, laughing insanely as the bullets ripped into them and feathers flew from their big puffed-up jackets. Outside her head she scuttled out of their way and said nothing and kept her head down, since they seemed to be so many and she was frightened of enraging them. Harriet suspected some of the boys had pushed their own grandmothers down the stairs, so there was no knowing what they'd do to her.

A few months before, she had been burgled and the police said that it was most likely the Namibian boys who'd done it, since there were CCTV cameras that covered most of the pavement, though not the adjacent front doors, and nobody suspicious had been spotted approaching her place. She felt another huge rush of hate for the young men as she thought about the brooch, her only memento of her mother, which they had stolen. Harriet's fury wasn't cut off until she stepped through the doors of the pub on the corner.

Until the year 2000 the pub had been a typical north London boozer called the Admiral Codrington, then it was gutted like an organic salmon and began serving a different kind of food and drink to the new people moving into the area. A few old-time drinkers hung on still, never moving out of an area of stripped wooden floor that had once been the public bar, though now they had to nurse pints of Czech Staropramen Pilsner or a stout from the Aleutian Islands called Gleck in place of their fizzy keg London bitter.

'Hello, Jago . . . Hello, Alaric,' Harriet said to the barmen, 'pint of Gleck please.'

Her two friends were already there, seated at a pine table, a half-drunk bottle of white wine between them. She picked up the beer – it was cloudy and the greasy glass was only three-quarters full but she still paid the price of a budget flight to Corsica for it – and went to sit down. Rose had been on the same fashion course as Harriet at the college in Middlesex that they had all attended. Now she was a successful costume designer working on TV programmes and films. Though she lived alone, while she was away on location she often had affairs with married men on the crew, usually a senior electrician or the cameraman. Once Harriet had asked her, 'Don't you feel guilty about having sex with all these married men?'

'D.C.O.L, darling,' Rose replied.

'What does that mean?' she asked.

'D.C.O.L., – Doesn't Count On Location.'

'Right . . .' she said. 'Y.H.A.G.B.A.'

'Eh?'

'Y.H.A.G.B.A. – Your Heart Always Gets Broken Anyway.'

Lulu had been a star at college, a student on the popular drama course that the school ran, tipped for success, but somehow she had not done very well in the outside world as an actress, so in her mid-twenties Lulu had retrained as a psychologist. Now she was very much in demand, she had her own busy private practice and was often called on to testify in the law courts, where her hammy acting skills were perfect in that arena of bad theatre. From what Harriet could see Lulu's job was to attest that clearly deranged killers were no danger to society and should be released immediately, or to affirm that obviously kind, loving parents must have their children taken off them by social services without delay. Like most psychologists, psychiatrists, therapists and counsellors that she'd met – and Harriet had met a good number, having been paying for various forms of therapy all her adult life – Lulu possessed no clue as to the reasons behind her own actions so she continually behaved in a manner well over the borders of sanity. Harriet reflected that Lulu was fortunate in respect of her career choice, since out of simple professional courtesy no other mental health care professional would ever agree to have her sectioned.

Then of course inevitably she felt guilty over thinking bad things about Lulu so decided to extravagantly praise the other woman's jacket (which was horrible). There was a chain of shops with branches in all the therapist-infested areas of north London – Hampstead, Muswell Hill, Crouch End – called Medina De Muswell Hill that seemed to sell clothes only to women psychologists – huge tent-like dresses, jackets made out of sacking and long scarves seemingly decorated with trails of acidic vomit.

As it turned out Harriet didn't get a chance to say anything to Lulu since as she sat down Lulu was staring with a furious expression on her face at a blurred woman right across the other side of the pub. 'That woman over there's talking about me,' she hissed, 'she's saying I'm a bastard.'

'Oh yeah?' Harriet said, having grown so used by now to

Lulu's outbursts that she hardly noticed them. She took a tobacco tin out of the pocket of her dungarees and began to roll a cigarette, before remembering with annoyance that she was no longer allowed to smoke in the pub.

She hoped they wouldn't talk about their personal lives tonight: Lulu was obsessed with a married Greek Orthodox priest whom she'd seen once in a shop and Rose was conducting a romance with somebody she wasn't quite sure was a man over the internet.

For a while she'd been planning not to turn up at the pub, to leave her friends wondering where she was and when they phoned to ask why she wasn't there to pretend to have forgotten about the whole thing.

If Harriet was mad at the neighbours for stealing her mother's brooch, she was also overcome with relief that they hadn't found her most secret shameful thing hidden in a secret compartment in the bottom of the sewing machine. It wasn't spiked nipple clamps or a signed Phil Collins CD but a small notebook. On one half of each page in neat, precise handwriting was a column headed 'I' for incoming calls and a column headed 'O' for outgoing. Beneath each column was a list of the same initials. 'R', 'L', 'P' and 'K' and next to each initial was written something like 'I txt, 2 pc or 4 ems'. This simple code was a list of her friends and a record of the incoming phone calls, text messages and e-mails they had sent to her and the number of the same she had sent to them. When the entries in the 'O' column vastly outweighed those for the 'I' column Harriet broke off contact until they more or less balanced out. (She was prepared to accept a twenty-five per cent imbalance in outgoing over incoming as being more or less an equality.)

The entry for 'K' was a man called Kevin Macardle who'd come into the shop two months ago to pick up a repair and had asked if she wanted to go out for a drink, maybe, sometime, whenever. The 'Outgoing' column read: '"K" 27 txts, 19 pcs, 46 ems'; the 'Incoming' tally read: '"K" 0 txts, 0 pcs 0 ems.'

Harriet thought there were so many ways now in which people were able not to get in touch with you. When she'd been a student there'd only been a payphone on the hall landing and it was easy to tell yourself that friends had rung and left a message with some drug-addled engineering student or confused African who'd forgotten it in the very moment of being told. Now, though, there was your mobile phone with message icons for both verbal and SMS Text to remain unlit, e-mail in-box that stayed empty and even the dear old fax that vomited out missive after missive about how you could buy a cheap panel van or go on the lemonade diet but never a kind word from a friend. And to make sure that absolutely nobody had called you at home while you were out there was always 1471 to dial up simply to check that you were surely alone in a collapsing universe.

Up until the night before there had been an imbalance of over thirty-six per cent in outgoing communications between Harriet and both Lulu and Rose but an hour and a half phone call from Lulu the night before during which the battery on her cordless phone went dead, she descended two floors to the shop in order to pick up the other handset, switched it on and found Lulu still talking, evened things out.

'So, you looking forward to the big workout?' Harriet asked.

'What?' queried Rose.

'The personal training with the guy?' she replied.

'What guy?'

'Oh shit, don't tell me you've forgotten.'

'Forgotten what?' enquired Lulu.

'The guy from the gym, you remember? You two were saying you really wanted to get fit, you were determined to do it this time and nothing was going to stop you. So I said I would book this kid from my gym to come round and give us some personal training next Wednesday afternoon.'

'I don't remember anything about this,' said Rose. 'Anyway

I can't come, I'm going to Wales to work on a film about Methodists.'

'And I can't go,' added Lulu, 'because it's the Greek Orthodox festival of Santa Kyriou and Constantine might need me to erm . . . to do something for him.'

Harriet knew better than to mention that Constantine was unlikely to need her to do anything, since he wasn't aware of her existence and mentioning that inconvenient fact would only provoke one of Lulu's rages. She was less certain whether Rose's excuse was true or not but again it would be difficult to challenge her on it since she would go to extraordinary lengths to back up the most outrageous lies, even producing forged documents and dragging out obviously bribed witnesses to back up some minor lie she'd been challenged on.

'Well, it's going to be bloody uncomfortable,' she sighed, 'with just me and him there in my big upstairs room. I'm just going to have to cancel the whole bloody thing.'

Except that somehow she never did cancel the whole bloody thing, so on the following Wednesday at exactly one minute to three, from her worktable, dressed already in her tracksuit, she saw Patrick walking rapidly alongside the park. Without seeming to look whether there was any traffic coming, he abruptly changed direction and swerved across the road towards the shop. Suddenly, seeing him outside the confines of the gym, she took in how slightly odd-looking he was, too pale and shiny, like a waxwork. Harriet got a touch of the Fear: she had thought she knew him a bit, that he was a sort of friend, but she realised that was only within the peculiar interior of Muscle Bitch; outside it he was just another odd-looking young man in sports clothes whom she had invited to come to her upstairs room to do things to her.

Observing him approach, Harriet thought to herself that he walked rather like a fly flies: with short little steps, his arms stiff by his side, he crossed the pavement in a dead straight line then, encountering her doorway, veered through it, disappearing from sight for a micro-second until, without slowing down, Patrick was in the shop taking another direct trajectory to her worktable.

'Where are your friends?' he asked, coming to a halt so suddenly that he swayed backwards and forwards on the spot until the force of his forward motion had dissipated.

Discomforted by the abruptness of his question and having no time to summon up one of the lies she'd prepared, Harriet said truthfully, 'They let me down, they said they wanted to do it then they pretended they didn't.'

Patrick stood at the counter not speaking, his face immobile, inscrutable, so she felt forced to babble on.

'Do you want to cancel? I feel like I've let you down, I have let you down, I'll pay for the session anyway, that's what I'll do, I'll pay for the session anyway.'

After a second's thought he said, 'No, I'm here and if I'm getting paid we should do it.'

'Right, OK,' Harriet said, unsure of whether this was the outcome she'd wished for or not; she wouldn't have minded a nice nap round about now and some pancakes. 'You'd better come upstairs then.'

Harriet's shop occupied the ground floor of the building: there was a space for the customers, then the L-shaped counter with the till on it, behind which were rails of repaired clothing on hangers shrouded in plastic and her worktable which she'd placed in the window with a strong bright industrial lamp on it made out of grey crackled metal. Harriet had thought when moving in that she would be able to look up from the scraps of cotton and shards of material and from time to time smilingly observe the activity of her neighbourhood, but in reality half the time when she did this there was something not very nice going on: a man shaking a crying girl, two uniformed security guards smoking crack in a parked car through a trumpet of silver paper or a one-legged pigeon stumbling about, constantly falling over and getting up again only to fall down once more. A door at the side of the shop set in the ancient tongue and grooved walls opened into a corridor with its own front door to the street and stairs that led up to her flat on the second and third floors, so that in the evenings and on Sundays she could come and go without having to pass through the workspace.

It was up these stairs that she led Patrick to the first floor and the big empty tobacco-yellow storeroom; at the front this room retained its original windows which ran almost from floor to ceiling, the ancient beige paint of the glazing bars splintered and cracked, while the frames, off-square from subsidence, jutted into the brickwork at an angle and they hadn't been able to be opened since the war in Korea. Through the dusty glass there was a vista of the road and the park beyond it. At the rear, metal-framed windows installed in the 1920s gave a view of her tiny yard and the blank rears of the houses and shops that ran away from the park towards Alexandra Palace up on its hill, resembling the château of a particularly mournful Fascist dictator.

At this level the vegetation of the park filled the floor-length Georgian windows and appeared almost pleasant if you didn't look too closely. Patrick stared around at the space deep in thought. Harriet assumed he was working out where it would be best to exercise but when he finally spoke he said, 'Carpet shop.'

'Eh?'

'Carpet shop. This used to be a carpet shop when I was a kid.'

'Really?' she replied, glad for a minute to put off the moment when she'd have to start exercising. 'You're from round here?'

'Yeah, the Watney Trust there over the way, still live in me parents' old flat. Y'know I actually worked in this place when I was fifteen, Saturday job. I remember one time the boss was out and a woman come in and she looked around at all the stock, took hours and she said to me, 'Oh that's a lovely shade of carpet that'd go great in my front room,' so she gave me all the measurements and I was real pleased with myself thinking how glad the boss would be that I'd done this big deal for him. I cut the carpet to shape while the woman went to get the money from the bank. When the boss come in and I told him he went mad with me, he said, "You idiot, she'll never come back . . ."' Patrick paused. 'And she didn't.'

'Why did she get you to cut the carpet then?'

The young man stared straight into her eyes. 'Because women are liars. They can't say what they want and they can't say what they don't want. That woman just wanted to have a look round but she couldn't leave without pretending to buy something. She didn't want to upset me by leaving the shop without buying something.'

'But she never came back and you got in trouble with your boss,' Harriet said.

'Yeah, that's right but she was out of the shop by then, she'd stopped thinking about me, she didn't feel responsible any more.' He paused. 'So shall we get started then, Harriet?'

'Yes indeed, I've really been looking forward to this,' she lied.

Patrick had brought along one of the yellow programme cards from the gym and on it he listed all the things she had to do to get fit. Harriet felt an immediate sense of disappointment; she had assumed somehow because she alone was employing him that he might now show her the secret personal trainer things that you wouldn't gain access to in the public press of the gym. The article in *Marie Claire* about the formerly fat woman had hinted that there was some mystical effect simply in having your own personal trainer person, that when you had one-on-one tuition the weight more or less fell off you of its own volition. Her feelings of disillusion continued when Patrick first took her through a series of stretches just about identical to the ones she'd done at Muscle Bitch, then sit-ups, press-ups and finally an aerobic workout precisely the same as any number she had bought on video, CD and DVD over the years. Harriet had hoped, even if she didn't learn secret things, that having Patrick doing the exercises in front of her might stir her to greater exertion but instead the disdainful ease with which he did all the movements – movements that were utterly impossible for Harriet – and the fact that he was clearly only using a twentieth of his energy, merely served to dispirit her even more, so that she felt she was actually performing even worse than she had done at the gym. On reflection, Harriet supposed she shouldn't have really expected any more, after all the same edition of *Marie Claire* in which she'd read about the formerly fat woman's weight loss had also hinted that avocados could cure Parkinson's disease.

After a painful hour it was over. He said, 'Now we'll do this every week, OK? But you've also got to do the workouts that I've marked down for you on your own. You'll never progress if you don't.'

'No, I understand that, I'm highly motivated,' she replied.

Harriet had expected him to leave after the session; her tracksuit was clammy and she longed to have a shower and then eat a whole packet of wholemeal chocolate biscuits, but Patrick simply stood tree-like in the empty room so that after an uncomfortable thirty seconds she felt compelled to invite him upstairs to her flat.

'This is lovely,' he said, staring at the light-up Madonna in a shrine of seashells that Rose had brought her back from Guadeloupe.

'Yeah, it's hilarious, isn't it?' she said.

'How do you mean hilarious?'

'Er . . . no, you're right, it's lovely. Would you like tea?'

He sat himself down tentatively in her inflatable pink armchair. Harriet could hear him causing it to squeak and squeal while she made them both Chinese tea in the kitchen. Returning with the tray, she set it down on the purple Formica coffee table and sat perched on her zebra-striped couch facing Patrick. He had been staring ruminatively up at the clouds painted on the ceiling but came back to earth focusing on the tea things – the porcelain pot and the two mugs celebrating the marriage of Princess Diana to Prince Charles.

'You have a beautiful flat,' he said.

'Thank you.'

'Painting clouds on the ceiling, I don't know how anybody thinks of that.'

'Well, you know . . .'

But then, like an interrogator on a cop show, he abruptly switched his gaze to her tiny black plastic television connected to an ancient VCR, both of them balanced on a small box ottoman, and stated in a sharp tone, 'I bet you rent that, don't you?'

'Er, yes, I do actually,' Harriet responded, feeling uncomfortable at being questioned like this in her own home.

'How much do you pay a month?'

'Twenty-five pounds,' she replied, automatically knocking off ten pounds.

'It's rubbish,' Patrick said vehemently. 'You could buy a nice big wide-screen plasma LCD TV, digital ready, with built-in DVD and nicam digital surround sound for what you're paying in a year for that crap.'

'Yes, but there's the . . . the, erm, free upgrades and the maintenance contract that gives you peace of mind,' Harriet retorted, trying feebly to stick up for herself. Even as she said all this she knew it to be a lie. Rose had been paying three hundred and eighty pounds a year for a TV that had broken down eighteen months before but she refused to call out the company's engineers in case she upset them. Harriet knew that if her television stopped working she would react in exactly the same way.

Patrick went on boastfully, 'A lot of the ladies at the gym are still renting their TVs as if they were students. Modern audiovisual equipment rarely breaks down. I tell them to buy new stuff and when they do they're always satisfied.' Less emphatically but still staring at her tiny scratched TV screen, he asked, 'You know that show that's on BBC 1 about movies, used to be presented by some bloke who liked cricket, now Jonathan Ross does it?'

'Barry Norman was the other bloke,' she said, happy to get off the subject of renting audiovisual equipment.

'Right . . .' Then he leant forward and staring into her eyes said very rapidly, 'Now quickly without thinking tell me what that show's called right now!'

'*Film 1988!*' she shouted, then was silently surprised at what she'd said.

'Exactly,' replied Patrick, leaning back, his air of wisdom slightly spoilt by the squeaking and squealing of the chair. 'But it's not 1988, is it, Harriet? It's 2006, isn't it? That's what the show's actually called: *Film 2006.*'

'You're right . . .' Harriet responded slowly then asked wonderingly, 'So why would I say 1988?'

'Because,' he stated, 'that's when you were happiest, in 1988. Everybody always shouts out the year when they were happiest. Do you know what year I'd say?'

'No,' she replied, though she could guess.

'Two thousand and six,' he said smugly. 'I'd say *Film 2006* That's what I'd say.'

'Because you're incredibly happy right now?' Harriet asked sarcastically. Then, attempting a joke, 'Because you're here with me?'

'No,' he said, 'of course not, not at all. But I live in the moment, do you see?'

'Right.'

'So what were you doing in 1988?' Patrick asked the fat woman sitting in front of him, sweat still sparkling on her forehead like industrial diamonds.

She thought about it hard, screwing her face up before finally saying in a wistful voice, 'I was twenty years old in my second year of college just outside London. You got a full grant back then, I lived on campus, in the hall of residence. There seemed so many possibilities and . . .' she trailed off.

'And what?' he asked.

'And I wasn't fat.'

'Now remember you're not allowed to smoke those filthy roll-ups,' Helen said.

'Of course not,' Harriet replied indignantly.

It was the night after her first session with Patrick. Harriet had walked to her sister's house, staying firmly on the pavement away from the threatening hulking gloom of the park. The route took her past rows of housing running away from the park on tree-lined streets. There was a smattering of spiky Gothic villas, Edwardian semis, artisan cottages, but mostly identical three-storey Victorian terraces built of London stock brick. Behind iron railings set in a low wall there was a huge, grey-brick, late nineteenth-century charitable housing estate called the Watney Trust Flats where Patrick lived. Then she arrived at her sister's house, a villa with twin bay windows facing the park.

Harriet's limbs ached horribly and she couldn't raise her arms above her shoulders, all of which she took to be a good sign. Helen and Toby were getting ready to go out, just as they did five or six nights a week.

Helen was worried they were going to be late but she forced herself to sit on the couch and let her sister talk about this strange Patrick, one of a long line of oddities she'd found for herself over the years. He didn't sound up to much but she always went out of her way to encourage Harriet to spend time with anybody who wasn't Lulu and Rose whom she considered a pair of unsuitable, drunken harpies. Her opinion of these two women was coloured by the fact that Toby had lived with 'that mad bitch Lulu' as she described her in a big flat above a vacuum cleaner shop in Enfield for all of their first two years of college.

'He's actually lived all his life round here and his parents and grandparents too,' Harriet said. 'Isn't that amazing?'

'Mr Sargassian's been here since the 1970s,' replied Toby, entering the room buttoning up his shirt.

'Yes, Toby, but not since the 1870s or whenever like Patrick's family,' she stated emphatically.

'No, I guess not . . .'

'I mean,' Harriet continued, 'look at everybody we know round here, none of them is even from London. They're all from the north like us, or Scotland or the States or Armenia, Toby, like Mr Sargassian is.'

'And you do your exercises together in that upstairs room?' Helen asked, to stop her going on at Toby.

'Yeah, it's brilliant, I've already lost pounds.'

'He's dead fit, is he, this bloke?' Toby asked.

'Yeah.'

'And a good teacher, is he?'

'Yeah, why?' she asked, unsure where Toby was going. 'Do you want personal training?'

'No, not exactly,' said Toby. 'I was thinking . . . do you think he'd do football lessons?'

'Football lessons!?' Harriet and Helen said at the same time.

'Yeah,' Toby said, blushing. 'It's just those guys I play five-a-side with on a Thursday night are pretty competitive; if I could improve my technique they'd respect me more. And, I dunno, maybe me and this Patrick might become mates, it'd be cool to know somebody from around here who was all fit and stuff.'

'I'll ask him, Toby,' his sister-in-law said, knowing as she spoke that she didn't want to be sharing Patrick with anyone else.

'Great. Thonks a lot, Hat Hat.'

'Now, we better get going,' Helen said in her busy fashion. 'Harriet, you got everything you need?'

'Sure.'

'Remember Timon's not allowed his fish fingers until he's eaten two plums and he can only watch half of his *Thunderbirds* tape.'

'Two plums, half *Thunderbirds* tape.'

'See you later, we'll be back about twelve.'

'You just have a good time.'

'Bye.'

'Bye.'

'Bye.'

'Have they gone?' Timon asked, coming out of his room where he'd been playing games on his computer. He was a stocky and composed six-year-old who to his aunt appeared to have very little to do with either Helen or Toby in looks or temperament. One of the many things she loved about him was that though both his parents strove energetically to transfer all of their many neuroses, vanities and anxieties to their son he seemed to remain entirely inured to their efforts.

'Yeah,' Harriet said, 'now what do you want for your tea?'

'Fried eggs and whipped cream from a can?'

'Sure,' she replied, taking out her tobacco tin.

Helen and Toby were making their way to the jubilee gala dinner of the Percussionists Licensing Society. Before Toby had taken the post at the Penrith Disaster Fund, straight out of college he had been offered a very good position at the PLS. This event tonight commemorated the founding of the organisation fifty years ago, to collect fees from concert venues, radio stations and record companies for the work done by drummers, timpanists and bongo players.

Every year the Percussionists Licensing Society threw themselves a big dinner at which various members of the office staff presented crystal goblets to each other and a list was read out of criminal prosecutions they'd brought against their own members who'd submitted false claims for royalties: no percussionists were asked to this event.

The regular dinner was held in a marble-lined room at the new I.M. Pei-designed Percussionists Licensing Society headquarters building in Mayfair but for this special event they had taken the big ballroom in a Park Lane hotel and as a valued ex-employee Toby had been offered four tickets.

In the taxi as they drove south into the city below them Toby sang, 'Whoo, whaa, whooo,' and Helen thought about her sister. Her hope was that in time maybe Harriet would start dressing a bit better for this Patrick fellow; she knew of course that there was nothing going on between them, but still at least there was a man coming to her flat regularly which was something. Before, in the house, she'd had to stop herself attacking her sister's clothes with a bread knife they annoyed her so much; force herself not to slash Harriet's hairy jumpers and her fat girl stretch pants, especially as she'd teamed them tonight with thick ribbed wool socks and walking boots, but Helen knew of course if she said anything out loud about the way her sister looked, even though she was just trying to be helpful, Harriet would go all silent and sulky. She had had to hold down one arm with the other to stop it snatching her sister's greasy spectacles off her nose and giving them a good polish.

As they'd been leaving the house, out of the corner of her eye Helen saw the businessman who hung around the area hurry past talking rapidly into his mobile phone, unable to decipher precisely who he was referring to; she only heard something about '. . . frizzy-haired midget thinks if a man doesn't fancy them he's gay'. Then, '. . . told you about him, he looks like one of those big Irish farmers, huge hands, failed suicide . . .'

To Helen it seemed nice that he had somebody with whom he could share these thoughts. The Easter when she was thirteen the family had gone on holiday to a rented villa in Lanzarote, a shabby breezeblock cube but with a swimming pool and everything. She'd found an old diving mask in a cupboard and had spent hours each day floating on the warm surface gazing down into the spangly turquoise-tiled depths, languorously twisting and turning for the eyes of her ever-present dad.

One day, as she drifted through the quicksilver chlorine-scented water, the shrivelled rubber of the mask's strap suddenly snapped, making her feel as if she'd been shot in the head, like the rooftop swimmer in *Dirty Harry*, and as she watched the mask beneath her dangling, pale feet tumbling down into the dangerous blue depths Helen lifted her head to look around and saw that her dad had left the poolside. She wasn't afraid, there was no risk of her drowning, but it just seemed there was no certainty any more and the loneliest thing in the world was to be by yourself in a swimming pool.

That sense of dislocation stayed with her until the last week of school before the summer holidays. She was in the school library, hanging around in there because this group of girls who the day before had been her best friends said they hated her and suddenly wouldn't talk to her any more. Seated at one of the long shiny mahogany worktables, sunlight streaming in thick tubes through the windows, she was pretending to work on a poem for the school magazine but instead was flicking through one of the old *Sunday Times* magazines that the librarian kept in Perspex binders. In an edition from September 1978 opposite a full-page advert for Ecko Hostess Trolleys there was a photograph, the black and white image so grainy that it seemed at first to be of bacteria or something; only slowly did it resolve itself into the sad face of a young man, a young man with long black hair parted in the centre. As Helen stared into his soulful eyes she felt an unfamiliar, warm sensation at the base of her stomach.

Flipping over the page she greedily dived into the story. His name was Julio Spuciek, the son of a Ukrainian father and an Argentinian mother; in the 1970s in his native Argentina he had been the country's fifth most celebrated poet, the reserve international goalkeeper and its most renowned puppeteer. For several years he had made fun of the authorities on his enormously popular TV and radio shows assisted by his puppets – Margarita, Tio Pajero, Abuela, El Gordo and Señor Chuckles. When, in a bloody coup and a wave of terror, the Fascist military junta came to power, his popularity and his socialism condemned him and he was swept up amongst the first wave of the disappeared into the notorious prison of El Casero. Yet even the terrible generals were reluctant to murder a man as popular as Julio Spuciek and in time they lit on another plan. One cold winter's day in the grey yard of the prison of El Casero Julio Spuciek's puppets were brought out, lined up one by one against the exercise yard wall and shot by firing squad.

In the magazine there were more blurred photos: of the splintered corpses of the puppets and further colour pictures of the mournful, sensitive bearded face of their puppeteer. Since that moment Julio had been inside her head, her constant companion, her special friend. Helen stood at the top of the stairs and, like a TV reporter, relayed the scene at the gala dinner of the Percussionists Licensing Society to him now.

She had carried this man around with her for over twenty years. Helen pointed out new things to him all the time and when she saw something wrong – the ugliness of a modern building, say, or some drunken boys behaving badly in the street – she would apologise to Julio on behalf of her country. He was with her for her first period, he sat alongside her during her A levels and he was watching benevolently the first time she sucked a boy's cock. Helen consulted Julio Spuciek on every major decision in her life and he always told her she was doing the right thing.

4

Harriet was trying to remember how much water she'd drunk – she knew she was supposed to walk ten thousand steps a day, eat five portions of fruit and vegetables, drink two litres of water and consume a minimum of three portions of oily fish during the week; the authorities seemed to have turned the simple business of staying alive into a full-time job. Also, if you drank the two litres of water then set out to walk the ten thousand steps as she had just done, then pretty soon the frantic hunt for the lavvy would begin. In the brief period when she tried to stick to the government's instructions Harriet was constantly being chased out of hotels by security men or in burger bars staff would bang on the the door of the stall she was using shouting, 'You no buy nothing, you gotta buy something to pee!' So she would have to purchase a giant flame-grilled bacon burger to pay for her use of the toilet, thus undoing all the walking and water drinking. In the end Harriet decided it was best if she stayed near her house and only drank tea, coffee and alcohol.

Since she'd become the sort of woman who had a personal trainer Harriet's visits to Muscle Bitch had ceased, though she hadn't of course stopped the direct debit that paid for her membership. During their weekly workouts in her upstairs room, with Patrick watching over her and urging her on, she put a lot of conscious effort into her exercises to show him she was sincerely trying to get fit, but when he wasn't there she couldn't find the motivation to do them at all. Lying on the floor with her toes hooked under the radiator fully intending to do twenty half sit-ups she would come to fifteen minutes later still lying on the floor having spent the time day-dreaming about wallpaper with the smell of burning trainer toe in the air.

So this act of taking on a personal trainer had resulted in Harriet losing what muscle tone she'd had, thus giving her sagging flesh the appearance of having gained even more weight. She also seemed to be spending a lot more of her time lying on the floor daydreaming about wallpaper, so some of her customers had begun to complain about repairs being delivered late. Harriet told herself that she couldn't afford to begin losing any business because of Patrick. The financial cost of employing him, forty pounds a week spent on nothing, was something she could just about afford but it was really starting to annoy her: she had plenty of nothing already. Sulkily she said to herself it wasn't as if Patrick seemed bothered whether he taught her or not; he took the money every week curtly without acknowledgement, then sat around her flat for hours expounding his bizarre theories, killing any shred of the mild excitement she'd first felt in knowing him. One day in the upstairs room as a gentle misty rain fell outside he said, 'Y'know, Harriet, what I wonder?'

'No,' she mumbled petulantly.

'I wonder what the Australians were doing fightin' in Vietnam. I mean you can sort of understand why the States was there and the Vietnamese of course . . . though they didn't really have a choice in the matter. But the Australians? They sent a boat to the Falklands as well and they're in Iraq of course.'

'Maybe they believe in freedom and democracy,' Harriet said in a sarcastic tone.

'I suppose they could,' he replied, taking what she'd said seriously, 'but I think they were just bored. Australia's a long way from anywhere else and they fancied getting out for a bit.'

'But don't you think that's a terrible thing: to fight a war in somebody else's country just to get away from home?'

'It's what men do,' was his answer. 'We must fight.'

'Really? How awful for you.'

'Yes, it can be.'

Another thing, it was starting to creep her out a little having him in her place every week, sitting there like a strange, unwelcome cousin from New Zealand.

The Booing Corporation was telling her that she might as well realise that she was never, ever going to lose any weight. All the little men at their morning conference told her to face it: if taking on a personal trainer didn't do it then nothing was going to, the nasty little men around the conference table all said. Harriet simply didn't have the moral character to stick to an exercise regime, she should get used to the fact that this was her now. A fat, useless, thirty-eight-year-old woman that nobody was ever going to love.

In mid-October, as the leaves on the trees in the park across the way began to turn red and in a few cases light blue, at the end of their fifth training session she said to him, 'Wow! Patrick, that was great.'

'So same time next week, is it?' he asked, opening the silver plastic case of the cheap personal organiser he used to record their appointments in.

'No, now here's the thing,' Harriet said quickly, 'I've just got a big contract to repair the costumes for the Welsh National Opera, apparently a tiger from a production of *Carmen* set in colonial India got loose and slashed all their costumes, so I've got to go and work . . . in Cardiff. I definitely won't be here next week at all so why don't I give you a ring on your mobile when the contract's over?'

'What, not the week after either?' he asked.

'Well, no . . .' His probing made her even more determined

to end it now. 'It's such a big job. I have no idea when it'll end but I'll certainly call the minute I've got further information and we'll start training again like before.'

'Well, I suppose so,' Patrick said, 'but you need to do your exercises every day on your own, or you'll lose all the progress we've made, you understand that, doncha?'

'Oh, I'll do it, don't you worry.'

There was one of the biggest film premieres of the year being held in Leicester Square: searchlights lit up clouds of starlings that circled in the orange night air and stretch limousines slid sinuously along the narrow side streets clipping pedestrians on the elbows with their wing mirrors. The movie *The Laughter of Eggs* was the first of Brazilian writer Paulho Puoncho's many successful novels to be filmed. Like a lot of Latin American fiction it heavily featured a talking bird that uttered all manner of wise and deep statements. Warbird had supervised the humane treatment of the talking bird while it was on set and during the promotional tour (during location filming the rumour was the bird had had a bigger trailer than Jeremy Irons), and now the European premiere was being held in aid of Helen's charity.

Toby and Helen had given their taxi driver a pass which allowed him to drive into Leicester Square right up to the entrance of the cinema down a high lane that had been carved out of yelling people. The cameras did not explode for them in a waterfall of light as they stepped from the cab, though a couple of freelancers penned outside behind barriers took a few shots of Helen since she was very pretty and might have an affair with somebody famous one day.

In front of the couple, capering in the entrance to the cinema, was someone they knew, an actor called Roland Malone who had co-starred in the early nineties with Lulu in her one hit, a TV detective series called *Bold As Bacon* about a father and son team who ran a bacon stall round the markets of the north-west and also solved crimes. The photographers called out to him, 'Roland! Roland! This way, Roland!' and he pranced and cavorted for them.

Toby and Helen, skirting Roland's flailing arms, mounted the stairs and entering the auditorium were shown to their seats; in the arm of each there was a free bag of popcorn and a bottle of flavoured mineral water of a new kind – carrot or something. The Odeon was separated into two halves by a long curving aisle that ran the width of the cinema. In front of this aisle towards the screen was the place where local radio competition winners and office staff from the companies who supplied bottled water and sticky labels to the film's producers were seated, overdressed in their ballgowns and rented tuxedos with red bow ties; a cloud of excitement and anticipation hung over this southern hemisphere of the cinema.

In the uphill part where Helen and Toby sat were the film's producers themselves, its distributors, various low-grade stars of television and radio and the senior executives of Warbird: there was no excitement here. Inside her head Helen explained all this to Julio Spuciek.

The couple had invited their friends Oscar and Katya to the premiere and they were waiting for them in the four-seater box that fronted the aisle. Oscar had once worked with Toby at the Percussionists Licensing Society, while Katya was a food writer and critic: at the moment she was working on a book of recipes for meals that were mentioned in the Bible; she reckoned this would be a huge hit with fundamentalist Christians who wished to eat only holy food.

Roland Malone, having been told by the photographers that they had enough shots of him now, thank you very much, had wandered into the auditorium; spying Toby and Helen he waved energetically and came over to stand in front of their seats in the aisle.

'Hi, Roland,' said Toby. 'How's it going?'

'Great,' the actor replied. 'I've just been speaking to my agent, he's got something really exciting for me.'

'What, the National job?'

'No, it's a memorial service at the actors' church for Tony Walker, big-time drama producer. Rumour is he died of a heart attack in the arms of a very good-looking Labrador.'

'I didn't know he was a big mate of yours,' Helen said.

'Me? I hated the bastard.'

'So why are you doing it?'

He looked at her like she was retarded. 'I'm top of the bill! If you do a telly or a play only the public see it but if you give a good performance at a memorial service for somebody really important then every bastard in the business is there to watch you breaking down in tears at the power of your own acting; can't fail.'

Helen said to Julio Spuciek in her mind, 'Roland! What a self-involved arse. Of course, Julio, you remember he was exactly the type I would have once fallen for, before I married Toby – handsome, creative, highly strung and a complete prick.'

'*Pajero* is the Argentinian slang for prick,' Julio said.

'Really, and isn't a Pajero a type of four-wheel-drive car?'

'Exactly, all these pricks are driving around with "prick" written on their car.'

'Oh, Julio,' she said, 'you're so funny.'

'And you are looking particularly beautiful tonight.'

Just about completing the fashion course, Harriet left college with an indifferent degree and none of her tutors, unsurprisingly, seemed willing to recommend an overweight girl who didn't look after herself as an intern at any fashion house. So, more or less at random, she took a job as a dresser on *Miss Saigon* at the Theatre Royal, Drury Lane. With her meagre wages she was able to move to a bedsit in the place that nobody calls Pointless Park.

When Helen left college she liked to think it was a complete coincidence that she moved there too, except she lived in a big house with the family of a lecturer from the college whom she was having an affair with. Helen gave dinner parties, she went to plays and the cinema and had lots and lots of boyfriends. If she fell out with one boyfriend there was always another waiting: one took an overdose because she chucked him, another became gay; one tried to join the French Foreign Legion but was turned down and settled for a fast-track management career at Waterstones. Sex was everywhere: in the same week as Cindy Crawford and k.d. lang were pictured kissing on the front cover of *Vogue* Lulu and Rose put their hands down each other's pants at a party and rummaged around as if they were looking for something. Even Harriet had a married man who slunk up to her little bedsit in the late afternoon.

Always in the background, almost unnoticed, there was Toby, hanging around without making any great impression except that he was generally drunk and there was often a crowd grouped around him looking down and asking, 'Are you all right, Toby?'

In 1998 the sisters' mother, who had suffered from ill health for years, suddenly became very sick. Helen was twenty-seven when this happened, Harriet thirty. Later on when they were in their mid-forties and they'd all begun to look like their own deranged elderly relatives, there would always seem to be somebody who was having to fly up to Scotland every weekend to comfort their father in a hospice or who was forced into making eight-hour train journeys to obscure mental institutions in Cumbria in order to visit their suicidal sister, but back then they seemed to be the only ones who had to endure this kind of crisis. When Helen told all her exciting lovers that she needed their help and support at a difficult time in her and her sister's life they all acted as if it was they who were having some huge crisis.

The men said, 'But I've got this meeting with a guy who might buy one of my pastry sculptures,' or 'My allergies don't allow me to go into or through the countryside,' or 'If I'm away who'll feed my iguana?' One particular boyfriend actually managed to develop all the symptoms of her mother's throat cancer including rapid weight loss, muscle weakness and coughing up blood whenever she saw him.

Only Toby emerged from the mist and would drive them up and down the motorway in the middle of the night, then wait patiently outside the hospital, would shop for them and cook their meals when they were too tired and upset to do anything for themselves.

All of the next week Harriet kept the lights turned off in the shop just in case Patrick was passing and happened to glance inside and see she wasn't in Cardiff. Unfortunately the door had to remain unlocked since she couldn't afford to be turning away customers. Just to be on the safe side though, her worktable was dragged out of the shop window and into the space behind the counter where it was mostly hidden from the street; the disadvantage of this was that there was less light back there so she needed to keep her work lamp burning simply to be able to do the repairs. On the day, at the hour when Harriet should have been having her sixth lesson with Patrick the sky was grey and clouded. Every few minutes, while working at her table in a pool of yellow light repairing moth holes in a tweed jacket, she would glance up at the window just in case he was there; in as much as she had a plan her thinking was that before Patrick saw her she could quickly turn the lamp off and hide motionless behind the hanging ranks of clothes. Though she told herself really she was being ridiculous even worrying about it.

When she looked up and he was standing right in front of her she didn't for a second take it in; Harriet thought a grey cloud had somehow come into the shop and was blocking her view. Once she realised it was him her heart gave such a lurch of fear it was as if a buffalo was loose inside her, careening around madly trying to smash its way out of her skin.

'You told me you were in Cardiff,' Patrick said.

She saw that his skin was completely white, even paler than it usually was. Harriet seemed to remember a medical student saying you shouldn't fear an aggressive person who was red in the face because they weren't going to harm you, all their blood was in their head thinking angry thoughts. You should really fear the white-faced since all their blood had gone to the extremities, their hands and feet, ready to do terrible damage.

'Oh well, yes but . . . they told me it . . .' she trailed off unable to think of a lie.

'But you're here.'

'Yes.'

'So as it turns out we can do our lesson.'

'Yes.'

'Lock the door and get up the stairs then.'

With uncertain legs Harriet rose, put the shop sign to 'Closed' and turned the lock on the door. She thought fleetingly of fleeing into the street but what would she say to people? 'There's a man in my shop and I'm afraid that he wants to give me a fitness lesson.' So instead she turned off the lights and walked into the hall. He followed close behind as they mounted the stairs up to the empty room.

Outside the big windows the sky was now a single shade of grey the colour of the sugarpaper that Harriet remembered they used to draw on in art class at school. Somewhere over Hackney lightning crackled.

Standing in the centre of the room she waited to be told what to do.

Patrick walked in tight circles around her and she tried to follow him with her eyes until he hissed, 'Look straight ahead.'

After some more pacing, out of her vision, he spoke again. 'We're going to try something different today. You're to stand as if you're riding a horse, do you know how to do that? Legs apart, knees bent.'

'Like I'm riding a horse?'

Suddenly he was right in front of her face. 'Yes, like you're riding a fucking horse, playing fucking horsey, do you know how to fucking do that?'

She thought to herself that she'd never seen her plumber angry, the postman had never sworn at her, Mr Sargassian, the old man from next door who came in to water her plants while she was away, had never stood in front of her, his spit flying into her eyes, telling her to play fucking horsey, so how had she got into this situation? This man who'd come to her house six times was now yelling at her to do weird stuff and she couldn't think of anything to do but to obey.

Slowly Harriet settled into the shape remembered from childhood, her legs apart, her bottom sticking out at a stupid angle. She felt the fat of her stomach creasing over itself and a single rivulet of sweat trickled down her back, suddenly making her want to giggle.

'Arms by your side, fists clenched . . .' He was directly behind her now as he spoke and though she desperately wanted to she was afraid to turn her head.

Then, more frightening than any angry words, there was nothing; for what must have been ten minutes Harriet stood in this posture; occasionally she thought she heard him move behind her, sometimes sensing he was somewhere at the back of the room, at other times feeling that he was right behind her, feeling his breath only a few inches from her spine. Soon her legs began to shake and she was considering asking if she might move when suddenly from somewhere out of the darkness he walked up and kicked her hard in the shins. Over the next few months Harriet would learn that each part of the body has its own kind of pain: head pain is like a bad fog, arm pain is like a stale sandwich, but she would always say that shin pain is one of the worst.

'Ow,' she yelped.

Immediately Patrick's face was centimetres from her own. 'Get back into your fucking stance, get back into your fucking stance.'

The agony was just beginning to subside when he suddenly flew from the opposite direction and kicked the shaking fat woman in the other shin.

'Ow, Christ!' she yelped again, but quickly stepped back into her stance without being told.

After he had kicked Harriet's shins three more times Patrick said, 'Right, follow me.'

In turning to try and follow she fell heavily and awkwardly to the ground, pain shooting into her palms. He did not wait, however, and as she lay twisted on the floor she heard his steps descending the stairs. Harriet could have let Patrick leave then and might have been free of him, but propelled by an indistinct fear she thrust herself upright and followed in a rush, bashing her shoulder on the doorway as she raced breathlessly down the stairs after him.

The front door was open and she could just see his feet disappearing over the road as she slalomed down the corridor and into the street.

Glimpsing Patrick disappearing into the park, Harriet was forced into a waddling, ungainly run in order to catch him up as he steadily pressed across the muddy grass and through the dripping undergrowth towards the centre of the greenery. Stepping straight into a laurel bush that wetly slapped her in the face she realised they had come to the very heart of the park, a place where she had not ventured for years.

It was strangely silent in this shallow bowl, the sides sloping gently down to the ancient oak tree right at the core soaking up all noise from the outside world, the only sound the delicate patter of rain on leaves. The edge of the bowl was ringed in an almost impenetrable tangle of bramble, dog rose, laurel, beech tree and scraggly pine. Looking down she saw that her stretch pants were torn and her legs were bleeding from forcing her way unwittingly through the thorns.

Patrick stopped by the oak tree and waited while Harriet staggered up to him. The first fork of the oak tree was about five feet above the ground. Patrick pointed to it and said to her, 'Climb up there.'

'What, where?'

'Climb up to that first branch of the tree.'

'I can't climb.' Despite what had just gone on between them she thought it still seemed particularly cruel of him to expect somebody as fat as her to climb a tree.

'I'll give you a boost.'

'No, no, no. I'll be too heavy.'

'No, you won't.'

He cupped his hands, Harriet tried to bend her leg to fit into them but couldn't get her foot high enough. With a sigh Patrick bent a little lower, she put her foot into his fingers and realised how strong he was as he more or less threw her into the tree. Harriet clung on desperately to the flaking grey wood as it dug into her stomach, knocking the air out of her as she hung over the branch.

'Stand up,' Patrick ordered.

With great difficulty she managed to lever herself upright so that she stood swaying unsteadily on the branch, forced to embrace the trunk of the oak tree like a lover just to steady herself.

Patrick's chest was now level with the woman's feet as he said quietly, 'Now jump.'

'Jump?' she squeaked.

'Jump,' he repeated quietly.

In Harriet's mind there suddenly appeared an image of the

shelf for tinned fish at the supermarket: there were so many different kinds of tuna that sometimes she stood for fifteen minutes trying to choose between tuna chunks in brine or tuna steaks in sunflower oil or tuna chunks in olive oil. She understood there was a sort of freedom in having no choice at all, so with her mind temporarily at peace and without further argument she stepped off the brittle branch and into the empty air.

Nothing happened then a lot happened. She struck the ground and her legs twisted beneath her as her body pitched forward, her glasses fell off and, stretching out her hands to protect herself tumbling forward, her soft pink palms scraped along the stony soil beneath the tree tearing the skin wide open, her chin hit the ground jarring the neck and her teeth dug into her lip splitting it open, blood spurting in an arc to land at Patrick's feet.

'OK,' he said, 'training's over for today.' Then he squatted down next to her fat exhausted body.

'Now here's your homework. Tomorrow I want you to get up at six in the morning and come here and climb to that branch and jump from there nine times. Nine times, do you get it?'

'Yes.'

'Yeah? I want you to do that every day. Now if you want, of course, you can not do that, you can not do that just like you've not been doing your exercises even though you promised you would, but next week, next week, I'm goin' to come to your shop and get you and we'll come here and you're going to jump from that second branch.' He pointed upwards to a cleft in the tree that was much, much higher than the limb from which she had so recently launched herself at such great cost. 'And if you haven't jumped nine times a day from the first branch then there's a possibility you'll die when you jump from that second branch, certainly you'll break somethin', leg or arm, nose or jaw, suffer terrible pain. Do you understand me?'

'Yes.'

'Good.'

Then he left.

Some psycho-dynamic therapist that Harriet had seen for a few increasingly unhappy and insane months in the late 1990s had suggested as part of her treatment that grown-up Harriet wrote a letter to 'Little Harriet', as she was encouraged to refer to her troubled teenage self back in 1982 when she had been fourteen years old. She wrote:

Dear Little Harriet,

I think you've got it into your head that you are unattractive to boys but you are actually a strong confident young girl, they are just morons who are frightened by your interesting ideas and your massive intelligence. You should just ask them out and see what happens and not be afraid of rejection.

You should be kinder to your mum when she gets sick because you'll feel bad about it later and your mum really does love you even though you are always being criticised and nagged and having your choice of clothes denigrated by somebody who dresses like a nineteenth-century gypsy herself.

Lots of love,

Your grown-up self, Big Harriet.

But then at the end of the letter she couldn't stop herself adding:

PS In 1985 Everton will win the Cup Final 1–0 against Aston Villa, 'Big' Dave Watson scoring in the ninetieth minute.

As Harriet lay on the moist ground peeling damp leaves off her face she reflected that maybe it was this sort of smart-arse behaviour, this inability to commit herself fully to anything, to turn everything into a joke, that had always sunk her attempts to climb out of the holes that her personality had dug for itself. But it occurred to her now that she had always refused to take anything seriously in the hope that if she didn't take things seriously then they couldn't become serious. Now, though, they had become serious anyway; this time there was never any chance that she wouldn't go to the park early every morning, climb the oak tree and throw herself from its lowest branch nine times.

All through the week the October weather remained stormy: gales swept in from the south-west stripping leaves from the trees, while the rain saturated the ground so that water lay in boggy pools all over the park sucking her trainers down into their clammy depths as Harriet walked each dark early morning to the oak tree, treading through the muddy, decaying flowerbeds and stepping around pyramids of damp cardboard that covered lumpy sleeping bags.

It was hard for her to describe her feelings even to herself during those next seven days; she thought the Germans probably had a mile-long word for it that translated as 'deathfearsexiness'. That was the closest she could come; she had given herself over to someone whom she was paying forty pounds an hour to to kick her in the shins and make her jump out of a tree.

She was impatient for what was going to happen next and at the same time terrified of it (how far would things go before she tried to refuse and what would happen then?). One minute Harriet would be giddy with exhilaration then the following one waves of humiliation and shame would sweep through her body. Yet, taking stock, she felt that over all these contradictory sensations was a feeling that she was more alive than she'd been for years. Somehow out of her lying and cowardice a special, secret thing had happened to Harriet: looking at her friends and her sister she thought to herself that whatever love, success or happiness they had managed to attain there'd never been anybody she knew who'd been caught up in anything like this, a matter both so dark and so dangerous.

The first day on her own she had to bring a small set of kitchen steps with her in order to get to the first branch; clumsily Harriet scrambled up into the arms of the oak tree, hesitated, felt sixteen different things at the same time and then flung herself from the branch nine times. First of all she fell very badly, scraping her knees and swallowing great clumps of damp earth, but by the middle of the week Harriet had dispensed with the steps and was managing to remain upright when landing, soaking up the impact with bent legs, until it dawned on her that she was landing in the horse stance that Patrick had shown her upstairs in the shop.

'Don't you want some more wine?' Lulu asked her as she sat in the pub on the Saturday night.

'No thanks, Lu, I'm happy with my water.'

'Nobody's happy with water.'

'I seem to be.'

'What's up with you?'

'Nothing.'

'Why have you stopped smoking?'

'Dunno.'

'Why have you only ordered a starter?'

'S'all I want.'

Her interrogation was cut short by the arrival of their dinner. Like many of the new-style food pubs the Admiral Codrington served sloppily prepared ingredients on cheap white plates plonked down on paper tablecloths, to be eaten with shoddy cutlery and brought to the table by an insufficient number of woolly-minded unemployed conceptual artists, while still charging prices that would have seemed quite steep at the swankiest hotel in Monte Carlo. In the toilets, instead of music they played the speeches of Martin Luther King.

'I didn't order the butternut squash,' Harriet said.

'My sea bass is cold,' said Rose.

'Don't make a fuss, it'll be fine, just eat it! Just eat it!' hissed Lulu.

'No!' Harriet suddenly said, slamming down her puny tin fork with so much force that it bent. She called out to the waiter, 'Cosmo, excuse me, excuse me but our food's not right!' Unfortunately the waiter wasn't able to hear her as he was doing a little dance for the barman and the other waitress.

However when the bill came she said to him, 'What's this?'

The waiter looked all confused. 'It's the optional fourteen and a half per cent service charge.'

'Well, take it off,' Harriet said. 'The service was poor, so I don't want to leave an optional tip.'

'What's got into you?' Rose hissed.

'I've been trying my best,' the waiter said with a quiver in his voice, 'it just, it just, you know, gets really busy in here.'

'Well, that's not my problem, is it? The service wasn't good enough.'

A woman who'd been eating silently with a young girl who had no eyebrows and a colourful bandanna on her head leant across from an adjacent table. 'Please, please,' she exclaimed plaintively, staring at Harriet, 'it's my daughter's birthday tomorrow and she's going into hospital for a cancer operation and you're ruining our night out making a fuss like this.'

'Oh, Christ!' cried the waiter, turning to the woman. 'I forgot to bring your cake, I'm so, so, sooo, sorry . . .'

'Please, please don't give it another thought,' said the woman. '*You* haven't destroyed our evening.'

'So tell me again why you wanted to make Cosmo cry?' Lulu asked as they walked to her house.

'I cancelled my television,' Harriet replied. 'I cancelled my television. Rang them up and said, "I don't want this crappy TV and video any more." They said I had a binding contract and they'd take me to court if I didn't keep it up. I said they could stuff their contract so then they said OK but actually they couldn't be bothered coming and picking their equipment up because it would cost them too much and so the guy on the phone sold me both the TV and the video for twenty-five pounds. I've been renting off them for ten years: in that time I've spent over four thousand pounds and they sold me both for twenty-five quid!'

'I still don't see what that's got to do with carrying on because you didn't quite get what you ordered. You knew that Cosmo was upset about what Michael said about Sasha's show and it's probably the last time that that woman's ever going to have dinner with her daughter.'

'I didn't get anything that I ordered from that idiot and I don't see why I should put up with it.'

'Well, where would we be if everybody behaved like that?' asked Lulu.

'France,' said Harriet.

Helen stood on the steps of the law courts and shook hands with Warbird's legal team, the nicely spoken, smooth-faced solicitors and the expensive, pointy-nosed barrister that they'd hired. The case these men had fought for them had been against the bereaved sons and daughters of an old woman who'd left her entire fortune in her will to Warbird; the sons and daughters had tried unsuccessfully to get the bequest reversed, telling the court that their mother was insane, wheeling a sick grandchild in from Great Ormond Street Hospital on a gurney and staging a rooftop protest dressed in bird costumes.

Refusing the offer of a celebratory drink at the stylish hotel across the Strand, Helen decided to walk along the Embankment then catch a train at Blackfriars to King's Cross where she'd be able to change on to another that would take her to the little station on the edge of the park.

The motion to dismiss the will was always bound to fail because those who had decided to give their money to her charity, especially the ones who were cutting out their families, were extremely systematic about making sure their bequests were legally waterproof.

Though she never met most of them she still felt great affection for the people who made donations to her organisation. To Helen they weren't like the morons who gave money to charities like the Penrith Disaster Fund – simple-minded idiots who made an impulsive on-the-spot donation because they'd just seen something sad on the telly or who bought a charity record and then wallowed in self-congratulation as if they'd done something noble, while in fact the only true beneficiary was themselves since they now felt free to carry on living their self-indulgent, unreflective lives.

She said to Julio Spuciek, 'Is it wrong if those of us who work at Warbird treat ourselves well? Is it bad if we eat nice lunches and sometimes travel about in limousines?'

'Of course it isn't,' he replied. 'Why shouldn't you? After all, you've dedicated your lives to doing good in the world, you are entitled to treat yourselves occasionally. You are behaving in exactly the right way.'

'But some of those animal rights activists despise organisations like mine, they see us as soft and corrupt.'

'No, those people have allowed themselves to be driven mad by the terrible cruelty they see all around. You do not allow yourself that luxury. You keep yourself a little detached and are more effective because of it.'

'*Muchas gracias,*' she said.

'*De nada,*' he replied.

The fury that swept over Patrick when he'd looked in the window of the shop and found out Harriet had lied to him had taken him completely by surprise. He really didn't know why he was walking past her shop right there and then anyway, but she appeared to be mocking him by sitting there under her yellow light, like she was saying he wasn't worth her lousy time, that he'd been wrong to like her even after all he'd done to try and help her get fit and after all the great chats they'd had together.

Oh well, there's no point in worrying about it now, Patrick thought, heading towards Harriet's shop for their next training session. As always he tried to walk as Martin Po had told him to: 'like water flowing downhill'.

When he saw her standing waiting for him in front of the counter a blush of agitation spreading upwards from her breasts, he was surprised to feel another rush of anger towards her so he simply said in a tight voice, 'Shall we go to the park then?'

'Yes,' Harriet replied, looking at the floor.

They skirted a drinking club of tattooed men and women hungrily guzzling cider from a big green plastic bottle and soon came to the bowl of earth with the oak tree at its centre.

'OK,' he said. 'You know what to do.'

'Aren't you going to help me?'

'No.'

With difficulty and a sulky look Harriet tried to scramble up to the second branch. She reminded Patrick of some sort of bulky animal that wasn't meant to climb trees, a kangaroo perhaps or an elderly overweight Labrador dog. He saw that she was opening some of the recently healed cuts on her palms as she climbed. Eventually Harriet reached the second branch and once there raised herself and stood gingerly balanced on the shaky limb looking at the ground, tears rolling down her nose. Patrick said nothing and after half a minute she simply stepped off. He remembered they'd told them at school about Galileo dropping stuff off the leaning tower of Pisa and how a feather and a cannonball would travel at the same speed, but, really, looking at how Harriet fell you had to believe that there was a different kind of gravity for fat people: she travelled at an extraordinary pace, smashing into the ground with a terrible thump that threw up soil like an artillery shell.

Harriet lay for a little while on the ground with her fat arse up in the air. He was almost tempted to tell her to forget it, her breath was laboured and she seemed to be crying properly now, certainly great snuffly sobs escaped from her face buried in the earth. Yet after lying there for a few seconds she slowly got up and, without a word, again climbed into the tree. As before she paused on the groaning branch, her face streaked with mud and tears running down her cheeks, before throwing herself once more into the air.

Eight more times she repeated the jump as she had been told, managing the last couple of times to land without smashing herself into the ground.

'I can do it more times. Should I do it more times? I can do it more times,' she said to Patrick, grinning madly with blood showing through the knees of her torn dungarees and snot running out of her nose.

'No, nine times,' he said, 'you always have to do a thing like this nine times or ninety times or nine hundred times, no more and no less.' He stared at her standing in front of him, fat and sweaty, panting and gulping with exertion. If he wanted to he knew it would be possible to leave her now, having done what was promised; Harriet had done the jump from the second branch of the tree nine times and that should have been enough but instead he stayed.

'For the rest of the hour we're going to do stone throwing,' he told the quivering mud-streaked woman in front of him. 'Stand with your back to the tree.' Walking nine yards away, Patrick picked up a small stone from the ground while she reeled towards the tree. Then he turned and threw it at Harriet not quite with full force but still causing her to yelp in pain and jump in the air as the stone snapped into her lower leg.

After half an hour and nine times nine stones bouncing off different fleshy parts of her body and her eventually managing not to flinch at each blow, he instructed Harriet to throw some stones at him.

'Throw stones at you?'

'Yeah. Here,' he said, bending down and handing her the small pebble he'd picked up.

She threw like a girl but worse, not even succeeding in hitting him from nine feet away.

'Throw harder and better!' he yelled, but she still didn't manage to get any shots on target until the hour was nearly up when with her last shot she caught the young man on the face, cutting his lip open.

'Yes!' she shouted with furious glee, jumping in the air with her fists clenched, arms aloft, before seeing the blood on his face and collapsing. 'Oh Christ, I'm so sorry,' she wailed.

'Stay where you are!' Patrick shouted. Then, 'You know what to do during the week?'

'What?' she asked, too distressed to understand the question.

'You know what to do during the week?' he asked once more.

'Er . . . Jump nine times a day from the second branch?'

'That's right.' Then he paused. 'By the way I forgot to get my forty pounds, you know with all that went on last week, so that'll be eighty with this week as well.'

Harriet pushed her glasses back up her nose and reaching into the tight back pocket of her dungarees with shaking hands brought out a clammy wad of notes; she peeled off four twenties and handed them to Patrick.

'Thanks.' Then he said to her, 'By the way you might want to get contact lenses, or have laser surgery instead of those glasses.'

Honestly! Harriet thought to herself that throwing the stones was nearly the most embarrassing thing she'd ever done, an untidy unravelling of her limbs that caused the pebble to travel about four feet before plipping to the ground. Then when she did hit him she was amazed to feel such wild exultation . . . well, that didn't even go halfway to describing it, it was like every blood cell in her body was doing a wild victory dance, then when she saw the cut on his lip she felt as terrible as she'd felt ecstatic a second before, so terrible that she wanted to fall to the ground to grovel all day at his feet and repair all his clothes and send him a whole smoked salmon from Canada but he wouldn't let her do anything.

She'd been feeling pretty good up to that point. Standing on the second branch she was at a negligible height, a height that was less than halfway up her stairs, an amount of feet and inches she disregarded twenty times a day but that was suddenly significant since she was going to jump it. Harriet thought to herself that this must be how an agoraphobic feels: where once perhaps they had taken underground trains without a thought, sailed on ferries and danced amongst seething crowds in clubs with inadequate fire escapes, now the trip down the hall to the front door contained too much terror for them.

The solution was the same, she thought: to face your fears.

Harriet stepped from the branch and into the void and experienced something for which she'd yearned all her adult life – weightlessness. Abruptly with that single step she had no body, no flailing limbs, no fleshy, demanding, restricting, smelly packaging – there was simply her and her mind in freefall through the singing air.

Like he told everybody, he was only trying to help. Toby had been sitting in a branch of the Pretzel Shed on the concourse of Euston Station because they have free newspapers in there when another customer, a young man of around thirty, suddenly started acting all odd, slurring his words, waving his arms about in an uncoordinated fashion before slumping in a faint on to the counter. Now because he was a keen watcher of medical shows on the television – *ER*, *Holby City* and *Casualty* – Toby had sort of got the idea that he had a basic grasp of medicine, so he said to the staff who were flapping about ineffectually in a variety of foreign languages over this passed-out man, 'It's all right, this chap's clearly a diabetic and he's become hypoglycaemic, we just need to give him something sweet to eat then he'll be fine.' So the boys and girls forced down the man's throat some of Rabbi Rabinowitz's Death By Chocolate, which it nearly turned out to be because the paramedics said that was exactly the wrong thing to give him in what Toby thought was an unnecessarily unpleasant manner.

Wandering north along Camden High Street he wondered whether Harriet had asked that guy about his football lessons. He'd gone into her shop to ask about it earlier in the week but she'd acted very odd when he'd mentioned him.

'What are those marks on your face?' Toby had asked. 'And on your hands?'

'Rough housing,' Harriet replied.

'Rough housing?'

'Rough housing.'

'Rough housing with who?'

'With Patrick; my personal training can be a little more physical than you might imagine.'

'Obviously.' He felt like a cop in a movie where he's standing on the doorstep talking to a woman and there's a gunman hiding behind the door with a gun to the woman's head so she can't ask for help but the cop's too thick to notice there's anything wrong so he goes away and the woman gets murdered or sorts out the situation by herself. Come to think of it, she had a sort of pleading expression on her face as well, a kind of mad, direct stare. Except there was no gunman; well, he supposed there might have been one hiding amongst the racks of clothing but he'd seen her since and if there was she hadn't mentioned it.

Toby wondered as he walked along whether somebody living alone could suffer from domestic violence.

All the next week Harriet practised jumping from the second branch and when Patrick came she was OK about throwing herself from the third branch even though it was really quite high. After the jumping they went back to her place and did the standing about like a horse thing again. Patrick didn't stay afterwards to chat any more like she'd hoped; she supposed he was still quite angry with her, but he did say as he was leaving, 'Do you know the community centre in the park?'

'Yeah.'

'I want you to meet me at the community centre café in the park at ten on Saturday.'

'OK. Yeah, I suppose . . . sure.'

'Good.'

Without another word he turned and stalked off leaving Harriet, the Mudwoman of north London. 'What was this – a date?' she asked herself. If so it was an odd place to go on a date. The community centre was little more than a large one-roomed wooden shed situated on the edge of the park directly over the road from Toby and Helen's house. Like the rest of the area the community centre was a battleground, part of the constant struggle for land going on in Pointless Park, a battle fought between on the one side the new arrivals – the families of the TV producers, bankers, lawyers and graphic designers who had bought houses in the last few years – and on the other the older community – a shaky alliance of the white unworking classes of the Watney Flats and the overseas immigrants. Recently the middle classes had seized control of the children's playground attached to the community centre; they had managed this coup because like General Zhukov's Soviet forces confronting Paulus's doomed 6th Army before the gates of Stalingrad their troops and their equipment were much better adapted to winter warfare. The flabby, exposed, tattooed, pierced, white flesh of the proletarian women was no match for the Berghaus anoraks and Timberland boots of the mothers and fathers of the new families. In six months' time the army of the poor, like the Germans at Kursk, would try and stage a summer counter-offensive but by then the situation would be irreversible.

The swings and the sandpit in the children's playground behind their low wooden picket fence resembled some playground of the Village of the Damned because silently playing inside it were so many pairs of spooky twins, laboriously produced by IVF and private medicine from the fragile sperm and damaged eggs of their over-achieving parents.

It was cold on the wooden bench in the children's playground. Helen was shivering with the cold despite her nose being buried deep in the collar of her North Pole jacket. To keep a watch on Timon she had to squinch her eyes up to see him through the fog that swirled over the park. Even so, from time to time he would disappear into the grey mist; fortunately it was easy to identify the identical blond triplets of indeterminate sex whom he was playing with, since from time to time their eyes would light up with a sudden eerie glow, like the brake lights on a truck. Helen liked to take her son to the playground on a Saturday: it was a treat for both of them to get out of the house; he could play with his mute replicant friends and she was able to smoke an illicit cigarette and, with a delicious squirm of guilt, read a particular magazine which she bought every week from a different newsagent to the one she purchased her *Independent* and *Guardian* from. The magazine was called *Have A Rest*. Often written as if translated from another language that didn't possess many verbs, the magazine detailed the lives of people who Helen knew must dwell around her, yet whose existence she would have been entirely unaware of if it wasn't for the stories in *Have A Rest*. Helen thought of the periodical as a sort of stargate which allowed her to gaze at a strange parallel universe that occupied the same time-space continuum as her but with which it would be impossible for her to intersect. In this universe people, nearly all of them fat and ugly, led the most extraordinarily complicated lives. They had sex with their drug-addicted ex-husband's sisters, they married Filipino grandmothers twice their age whom they'd met on holiday and took them to live on Sheffield housing estates naïvely expecting that things would turn out well; their mothers turned out to be their sisters, their uncles turned out to be their fathers and their fathers sometimes turned out to be their mothers. Judging by the photographs that accompanied the stories these people were of every shade of pink, yellow, brown and black, usually within the same family.

It was all such a contrast with Helen's own circle who were universally white (apart from Swei Chiang and even she'd been educated at Cheltenham Ladies' College), they married and stayed married, were good-looking and healthy, had only their own children and generally didn't commit suicide by hanging themselves in the garden shed. Sometimes she almost envied the people in *Have A Rest*: compared to the calm trajectory of the lives of her and her circle there seemed to be a mad vitality about what they got up to; she wondered what it would be like to be one of them, to live in such chaos.

As the fog closed in Helen became absorbed in a story about a woman who kept finding her underwear drawer disturbed so she installed a hidden video camera in the bedroom. Watching the tape back gave the woman a perfect full-colour Dolby stereo record of her husband having sex in her bra and panties with her own brother-in-law. The magazine had printed crystal-clear excerpts from the tape.

Suddenly with a start she looked up, remembering where she was; like all the mothers Helen was perpetually on the lookout for one of the five hundred different kinds of predator the local paper insisted were after their children. After a few worried seconds she saw with relief that her son was arm wrestling with one of the triplets who appeared to be hovering a few inches off the ground.

Nevertheless, feeling guilty, she swept the perimeter of the fenced-off area for suspicious men; looking in the direction of the park's interior Helen thought she saw through the fog her sister heading towards the café. This woman, if it was her sister, passed behind a man who was staring at the children – he was perhaps sixty with thinning black hair swept back from his forehead, a greying beard and a sad soulful expression on his face, he wore a dark suit and over his shoulders was draped an expensive-looking but clearly very old fawn overcoat. Her first reaction was that somebody with such a benevolent countenance could never be a threat to the kids; it was only on giving him a second glance that Helen realised with a thump in her chest that she was gazing into the face, now lined and grey, but still recognisable, of Julio Spuciek. She felt like a Mexican peasant girl who sees the face of Jesus in a potato.

On Saturday morning as Harriet headed towards the park café, even though an icy fog lay over the ground and the smell of sleet was in the air, there were some kids including a pair of twins and a set of triplets playing in the sandpit. It seemed cruel to her to expose your children to such rigours, though in all fairness they seemed happy enough. The twins sat upright and motionless in the sand communicating with each other in their own secret languages.

'Harriet immlich neem,' said one three-year-old redhead.

'Harriet treemput treek,' replied an identical three-year-old redhead.

'Seems to be losing weight and she's smiling to herself in a gormless fashion,' said the Tin Can Man as he stalked along the path shouting into his phone. '. . . no, no, she's not getting fucked, it's something else.'

The café attached to the community centre, being steamily heated, was still firmly in the hands of the old community of Pointless Park and since many of its clientele had served time in prison the food would have been familiar to anyone who'd done a ten-year bit in Parkhurst: the ciabatta and cappuccino revolution had not yet been able to reach this place. Until the new people could force themselves to find the terrible food or the unhygienic owners 'amusing' or 'charming' the locals were safe. The coffee came from a giant catering tin of Nescafé and the tea from a big, battered tin kettle. Trying to focus on the greasy chalked menu through her new contact lenses, Harriet realised there was almost nothing on there that she wanted to eat or drink, partly because it all sounded horrible but also due to the fact that her appetite seemed to have declined; in the past if she wasn't eating she was thinking about eating but now whole hours would go past before Harriet thought about food, so in the end she asked for a glass of tap water and some toast. When fat people like her ate in public they were used to getting angry glares from other diners; you could often see the people thinking, Look at the state of her! No wonder she's so fat eating all the time! even if all the fat person had in front of them was a small salad.

''Ello, Patrick!' she heard the woman call from behind the counter as the door opened and a shiver of cold air passed up her spine. The red plastic bucket seats in the café were bolted to the floor so they couldn't be moved and the edge of the sticky table was bisecting her stomach so she was in some discomfort and it took her a second to absorb his appearance.

He sat down opposite Harriet in his economical fashion like somebody folding a blind man's cane and immediately began talking.

Seeing him once more she was struck by how young he looked; in her mind, she supposed because he had power over her, he always appeared to be much older. The fat woman wondered to herself, not for the first time, how she had fallen under the control of this pale child.

'Your parents alive?' he asked.

And a bright good morning to you, Harriet thought to herself but said instead, 'No, no, they're both dead.'

'Me too. You know I sometimes wondered if God had invented sleep so people would know what being dead was like.'

'Except you wake up from sleep.'

Patrick's brow corrugated with annoyance. 'Yeah . . . still, without knowing what death was like people might not be afraid of it, they'd say, "So what's that like then?" And step in front of buses and stuff. Well, people who'd been knocked out by a punch or something might have some idea of what death was like but not the others. But there is no God so it was a stupid question to ask myself.' Patrick paused, confused as to what he'd been talking about. 'You know I'd always sort of vaguely assumed that I wouldn't be that upset when me parents died, so when they passed away so close to each other I was . . . I was really surprised to feel . . . well, I dunno what you call it . . . depression I suppose. Only nineteen years old but suddenly I knew there was no purpose to life, that everything was point-less and when I died there was only . . . nothing, nothing forever.' He stopped then after a second resumed. 'I dunno, the nothing-ness thing might have occurred to me at some point in me life but if Mum and Dad hadn't gone so suddenly it might not have hurt me as much. I left me job at the shoe shop and used to go looking for busy crowds, I'd wander through them straight ahead without moving me shoulders and do you know? Other people just sort of bounced off me.

'One day I was in the West End and turned off the Charing Cross Road into Chinatown. I went into this big Chinese restaurant, I think my mind was sort of searching out humiliation so it could feel even more miserable, I think now that misery needs more misery to feed itself. As soon as I was through the door a Chinese waiter saw me and though there were loads of empty tables on the ground floor he shouted at me, 'Upstair plee!' I did what he said and trudged up a narrow greasy staircase to the first floor where this other Chinese waiter yelled at me, 'Upstair plee!' On the second floor again I was ordered to go 'Upstair plee!' even though up there there were more vacant tables on that floor than full ones. At last I reached the almost totally empty roofspace of the building where there were just a couple of diners and as soon as I came into the room another Chinese waiter saw me and shouted, 'Downstair plee!' and because I didn't move fast enough, he bellowed again right in me face, 'Downstair plee!' On the second floor again it was, 'Downstair plee!' 'Downstair plee!' until finally I was in the basement that really was full and another waiter shouted at me, 'Upstair plee!' 'Upstair plee!' and I just froze. You'd think they'd feel sorry for me but I know now that's not the Chinese way; rather than having any sympathy I was suddenly surrounded by a crowd of the restaurant's managers in their black jackets screaming abuse at me in Cantonese. Until suddenly they all went quiet, a small middle-aged waiter with shiny, dyed black hair, wearing one of those plum-coloured waistcoats, pushed his way through the crowd. The funny thing was that although he was clearly an underling the managers fell back as he took my hand and led me back upstairs to a big table in the window where he brought me that stuff they call congee-rice porridge and barbecued meats free of charge.'

Patrick paused for a few seconds then continued.

'Not that I felt any better after that, in fact I stopped going on those long walks. They say exercise can help with depression but you need energy to get yourself up to take the exercise and I didn't have it, I was slipping down. A lot of the time I came here to the park and sat on a bench; it was here one day I saw that same waiter in a T-shirt and shorts standing motionless and barefoot in a patch of brambles starin' at me. The waiter made a gesture for me to come to him.

'"Why don't you take your shoes off," he said to me. Somehow, Harriet, it seemed natural to do as he said, so that I took off me shoes and wandered into the briar patch as if I was stepping on to the beach at Brighton and stood next to this small Chinese man. The thorns hurt like hell, puncturing my flesh like little curved knives. "It hurts," I said to him. "Yes," he said, "it hurts," and I realised this pain was the first real thing I'd felt in months.

'Afterwards he brought me here to the community centre café. When we were sat down at a table the Chinese man introduced himself. He told me his name was Martin Po. I told him mine was Patrick O'Reilly.

'Then just like I told you my story he told me his. He said he was born in 1949, in Hong Kong. His family lived in a place known as the Walled City, it sounded like a strange place. When Britain beat China in the Opium Wars they leased the New Territories for ninety-nine years. Somehow in the agreement the Old Kowloon Walled City got left out, so that afterwards it was claimed by both the Chinese and the British as their territory.

'It was like a big council estate on a rocky hill where everybody had built their own apartments without any kind of regulation you might get a bit of the idea. Everyone's flat was on top of everyone else's flat, their living room jutting into your kitchen, your bedroom on top of their toilet. The buildings were connected at all different levels: there might be a door in the floor of your bedroom that dropped you into a narrow passageway, or a panel at the back of the living room behind the TV giving into a dark alley with water dripping down the walls and piles of garbage everywhere. Electricity was tapped from outside mains, wells were drilled to get water. Mixed in with the apartments were sweatshops and factories. The place was lawless, the Hong Kong police rarely entered and the Triads controlled a lot of the day-to-day life.

'Nevertheless Martin's family though poor were honest and, for the Walled City, well educated. His father was a clerk in the colonial customs house; his mother a teacher. They wanted the best for their only son but couldn't afford an academy, so they sent him away, aged seven, to Blue Cloud Monastery, on a high mountain in the New Territories, run by Taoist monks. There he learnt mathematics, the Chinese classics, calligraphy, acrobatics, meditation, herbal medicine and a style of Wu Shu boxing known as White Crane kung fu.

'He missed his family but studied hard and became one of the most promising students the monks had ever seen. At the annual rice pounding festival it is said that he ground more rice than any boy of his age. Yet Blue Cloud Monastery was a cruel place. The monks earned money for its upkeep and recruited new converts by touring their students in a troupe around villages and towns and sometimes to Hong Kong itself. The youngsters demonstrated their hard Ch'i Kung skills by being beaten by iron bars, jumping through burning hoops and making six-layer human pyramids. Many children were injured, but there was no hospital or sympathy from their Taoist masters, only bitter herbs.

'Aged thirteen Martin became disillusioned with this hard life and deserted the circus on a trip to Hong Kong. Shorn of discipline, he said he entered a dark period. Under the influence of one of the many Triad gangs in the Walled City, the Black Singlet Cobra 13, he smoked opium, listened to jive music and almost ruined his internal chi. He also developed a fondness for ballroom dancing.

'Martin Po's family were worried that their only son would

ruin his life hanging round Locarnos and chasing the dragon, so for his sake they gave up everything and together emigrated to England in search of a better life. Unfortunately, they were misled by relatives and his educated parents found themselves owners of the Happy Garden Chinese Takeaway in Kettering, Northamptonshire.

'In 1965 at the age of fifteen, he was in a foreign land, with no friends. Ballrooms were unknown in Kettering. Though he heard there was a Mecca in Northampton, adolescent Chinese were not welcome there. He refused to help his father, instead spending his time in the flat above the Happy Garden watching the television, all-in wrestling on Saturday afternoon and his favourite shows, *Robin Hood* and *Come Dancing*.

'The new towns of Kettering and Corby were not the best places in Britain to open a Chinese chip shop. The area around Kettering was known as Little Scotland in the 1960s. There was no work in Scotland so men and their families came down to work in the steel mills, the Aquascutum factory and the famous Corby trouser press factory.

'Most of the Scots were Glasgow Rangers fans, fanatical Protestant Christians. Many nights he watched his father taking terrible abuse from these huge drunken men. One summer night in 1967, when Glasgow Celtic won the European Cup, a gang of drunken Scots got the idea that his father was a Catholic Christian, a rival sect. They jumped the counter and held his hand in the fat fryer whilst urging him to say, "Queen good, Pope a bastard." Hearing his father's screams, Martin rushed downstairs. He tried to save his dad but he had neglected his training. Martin's rusty kung fu had no effect on these giants; their pain receptors had been dulled by huge amounts of drink and they merely laughed at the boy before them, battering him to the ground and kicking him unconscious. His father's hand was completely crippled, and they had to sell the Happy Garden. Social services provided the family with a council flat on an estate in Corby but his father now had a total breakdown and wouldn't leave the house.

'Martin swore revenge on those who had mutilated his father, but how to do it? He calculated that while the methods of Chinese boxing taught by his old academy had many valuable elements, dealing with enormous alcoholic Scotsmen was outside the experience of the Shaolin monks and required something more suited to the modern world of the 1960s. But how to devise it and what to call it? It was almost unknown to see Asians on the TV but one night his mother called him to say there was something on about a mighty Chinese warrior. It was a piece on the BBC programme *Panorama* about Lee Kuan Yew, the first leader of independent Singapore. The programme was not favourable because in Singapore long hair was banned, chewing gum was outlawed and people were sent to prison for crossing the road at the wrong time. But Martin thought any man who could corral and unite the disputatious Malays, Han Chinese, Indians and the Straits Muslims must be a mighty warrior indeed, so he named his fighting method Li Kuan Yu in tribute to him.

'Now it had a modern name what would be its foundation? Of course Li Kuan Yu is rooted in his training at the monastery, but where would its modern influences come from that would help him defeat the giant alcoholic Scotsmen?

'He thought of Richard Green's *Robin Hood*, which he had watched so avidly, recalling the scenes where the merry men regularly jumped out of trees on to their enemies. This gave him the inspiration for the Li Kuan Yu signature form, Anaconda Tree Jump Vine Strike. He spent hours hiding in trees and jumping out of them in order to perfect this art. Another move in Li Kuan Yu is called Broom Staff Pike Stance which, while it may resemble an Aiki Jujitsu Jo weapons form, is also influenced by Little John out of *Robin Hood*. From his other favourite show *Come Dancing* he took many examples of fancy footwork and complicated turns.

'Out in the wider world to make money Martin took work as a waiter in local Chinese restaurants, but even here he got more inspiration: the drunken customers of these places led to him inventing Roll Eyes Fall on Enemy which involved deceiving your opponent by staggering around pretending to be drunk then falling on top of him; some of the inspiration for Roll Eyes Fall on Enemy, also came to Martin from a Big Daddy/Giant Haystacks body slam.

'It took four years before Martin felt he was ready to take revenge on those who'd attacked his father. The leader of the gang was a steel worker called Scots Billy, who lived on the Glenfiddich council estate. Martin silently watched from the shadows as Scots Billy and his fellow gang members spent many evenings drinking in the local pubs. On the night chosen for revenge he raced ahead of them to the estate and arrived in time to see the three cackling drunks heading for one of the entrances. Martin ran silently up the opposite stairwell. The estate was built on eight deck levels. He went up three flights then leant over the balcony; he could hear Scots Billy singing and chanting below. Martin hung from the railings in Anaconda Tree Strike preparation form, suspended in the blackness. As Scots Billy rounded the corner on to the landing below, he launched himself down, wrapping his legs round the head of the startled steel worker.

'Scots Billy fell forward with the young Chinese man on his back like a rodeo rider. He dug his fingers into Billy's ears and wrapped his thumbs round the big man's temples, digging into his eye sockets. Expanding his chi from the chest, he pulled the skull apart, exposing for a second the fontanelles which had closed six months after Billy was born. He twisted the head for good measure and completed with Knuckles to Temples Big Headache, a deadly pressure-point blow.

'Scots Billy fell forward like a Sherwood Forest oak. The second man was next, another Scot called Big Barry. Swooping upward from Snake Creeps Down into Golden Cock Stands on One Leg, Martin hammered his fingers firmly into the big man's groin, twisted and pulled; that did for him. The third made to run, but Martin sidled alongside and tangoed him down the corridor before dipping like Victor Sylvester. Scooping up, he flipped the man over the balcony where he was impaled on the railings below. Then,' Patrick finished, 'he ran to London.'

'You mean he ran away to London?' Harriet asked.

'No, he ran to London. Down the A43, A15 and the A5. Running all the way using his Tibetan Lung Pa stride, he arrived in Stanmore eight hours later, feeling only slightly breathless.'

As Patrick finished talking Harriet had been thinking of Roland Malone, recalling the time when he'd been on tour and had found a book in some provincial dressing room called something like *Mysteries of the Universe Revealed*. The actor had gone through a phase where after reading this book he could provide banal and tedious explanations for every mystery or enigma that anyone ever mentioned. He'd say, 'You know Cézanne painted like that after he was kicked in the head by a horse in Pamplona and started seeing everything in funny shapes.' That was his explanation of post-Impressionism.

Harriet had never thought for one second that the things she'd been doing these last couple of weeks had any kind of explanation; if she had considered it at all she'd sort of assumed that Patrick had invented the tree jumping and the stone throwing right there and then because her lying had annoyed him so much, that it had all come out of his feelings for her even if those feelings were mostly extreme annoyance. That it had been something unique to the two of them.

She felt desperately sad that it wasn't special after all. She tried to hang on to the fact that whatever they'd been doing the past couple of weeks at least it had made her feel better and, for the first time in her adult life, she'd lost a bit of weight.

'So what do you think?' he asked.

'About what?'

'About becoming a student of Li Kuan Yu. My dojo, the place where I teach, is in the community centre, from eleven to one. I thought you'd like to join us.'

'I dunno . . .'

'Li Kuan Yu is more than martial arts, Harriet; many refer to it as "the Grand Ultimate".'

When she looked at Patrick he reminded her of a kid showing off his paltry collection of toys to another richer more spoilt kid.

He said, 'Martin told me everybody had to find their own way to Li Kuan Yu, that's why we don't advertise or anything. I think you lying to me was your way to it.'

It seemed to Harriet that in fact the whole thing had been more about him than her and she really didn't want to get caught up in this new entanglement, but the look of puppyish desperation in his eyes made her say, 'Yeah, fuck it, why not?'

'Great,' Patrick replied, with a little moue of irritation at her swearing.

Brilliant, she thought to herself, I'm being taught kung fu by my mother.

They left the café and walked on the foggy, frost-crunching path round to the entrance of the community centre. He led her across the small foyer, seemingly papered with fluttering notices and messages, then through cheap wooden double doors into the large main space; this was a low-ceilinged, all-purpose hall, stacking chairs pushed back against the walls and a jumble of stage lights dangling from the roof joists. Though it wasn't yet eleven there were a group of people wearing kung fu-style outfits stretching and limbering up in the centre of the wooden floor. With his hand on her shoulder he presented Harriet to the others.

When he spoke they all stopped stretching and turned towards

Patrick. She noted that even though several of them were much older they listened to him in reverential silence as if he was reciting interesting poetry rather than simply introducing them to a fat woman.

'Now, Harriet,' he said, once he'd given everybody her name and told them she was joining the group, 'I'm going to get changed and you need to talk to Ali' – he gestured towards an Asian man in his thirties – 'about what your outfit's going to look like.'

'I'd have thought you martial artists wouldn't care what clothes you were wearing,' she said to Ali once they were together.

'Why would you think that?' Ali replied. 'Harriet, have you ever heard of the novels of Paulho Puoncho? You know *The Pharmacist*? *Marion Decides to Buy a Hat*? *Forty-eight and a Half Seconds*?'

'I think my friend Lulu read one once, she said it was sh—'

'You shouldn't listen to what other people think,' Ali said, telling her what he thought. 'He's sold over twenty million books worldwide, Paulho Puoncho has, and many people say his novels have saved their lives, think about that. These books they're all about the choices we make in life, about listening to our hearts and most of all about following our dreams. So, yes, it is important what outfit you choose.'

'Right . . .'

He produced a number of catalogues from different outfitters and, pretending to care, she finally selected a grey outfit with two black stripes down the leg and shamefacedly gave her measurements.

'There's a fifteen pound supplement for Super XXL,' Ali said, reading from the catalogue.

'Right, that's OK,' Harriet replied, her blushing unseen by Ali.

These measurements were to be sent off to a place in Leeds

and the suit would be ready for her to pick up on the next Saturday.

While she had been consulting with Ali, Patrick returned wearing a fighting suit of extraordinary whiteness and called them all together. He announced that because there was a new student they were going to practise Anaconda Tree Jump Vine Strike, the centrepiece of Li Kuan Yu.

He said to a tall women in black pyjamas, 'Helga, can you get the ladder?'

She returned a few moments later with a dented aluminium stepladder, then one student stood on it while another held the legs. Patrick in his bright white outfit explained to the group that the student on the ladder should wait with what he said was 'full tension and intention focused in thighs' while the rest of them ran in a line past the ladder. With full kiai, which was apparently a sort of shout, and focused chi, which was a sort of energy, the person on the ladder was supposed to choose their victim then jump feet first and wrap their legs around the opponent's neck, making sure their groin pressed into the back of the opponent's neck so that they couldn't turn and bite what Patrick called 'the secret place'. When Harriet watched a football match on the TV and she saw the footballers tackling each other or embracing after scoring a goal she was often distracted by the thought of their 'secret places' rubbing and banging against each other and when she went to the hairdresser she always kept her arms squeezed tightly into the sides of the chair so the hairdresser's 'secret place' wouldn't inadvertently touch her, yet now she was going to have one of them tucked into the back of her neck. Harriet thought to herself that in a short time she'd come a long way, though in what direction she wasn't sure.

As it turned out it was considered too dangerous for Harriet and a couple of the newer students to jump off the stepladder so they were were told to practise Anaconda Tree Jump Vine

Strike by sitting on a partner's shoulders and walking around. Patrick handed out grubby foam neck braces to be worn by the training partners but it was clear that even with them on nobody was willing to carry Harriet about, so in the end she found herself on Patrick's shoulders with her secret place tucked into the back of his neck.

After two hours' training the group went back next door to the community centre café. Apart from Harriet there were seven other members. Seated next to her at the Formica table was Ali, an accountant; next to him was Helga, a large German woman in her forties, an aromatherapist. There was Paul, a BT engineer; squeezed next to Paul was Langley, a Jamaican cabbie; opposite him Gill, a housewife; and next to her there was Jason, a teenager who'd been sent along by social services. Lastly there was Jack, a small compact man who, though extremely fit-looking, Harriet guessed to be in his early sixties, a retired engineer. She found it odd to see a man of that age dressed in short leather jacket and light blue faded jeans; like Patrick he too was Old London from the Watney Flats and was also the only person apart from Patrick who had actually been taught by the Founder – Martin Po. Jack was a devotee of everything Chinese: he spoke Cantonese, spent his holidays over there in strange industrial cities nobody had ever heard of that possessed two million inhabitants and had even gone so far in his Sinophilia as to join an extreme Maoist group in the 1970s.

There was also something of the Politburo apparatchik about Jack in that he played the wise old adviser to Patrick's more impetuous temperament, advising caution and offering sage interpretations of some of Sifu Po's more confusing and contradictory statements.

It wasn't until later in the afternoon when she was back in her shop, dizzy from the strange day she'd just had, that it dawned on Harriet that she hadn't just been told some ancient tale of monks or Samurai: Patrick had given her explicit details of a thirty-six-year-old unsolved triple homicide. She decided that maybe Martin hadn't really split Scots Billy's skull or killed Big Barry by twisting his testicles or tangoed the other one on to the railings: it was just some sort of parable.

5

Nearly two months went by. Northerly winds blew the remaining leaves off the trees in the park. The contractors should have come by to collect them for compost while burning those that were diseased, but they never arrived, as if they had a plan that in the summer there should be virulent outbreaks of many different and varied plant contagions. Halal Meat and Videos became Azerbaijan Fried Chicken. The Tin Can Man appeared for a time without his sardine tin looking mute and distressed until he managed to steal a new one from the Valueslasher Mini Market. He then had to catch up on his calls, talking for hours, up and down the shopping parade, mad insults, comments on people's clothes, deranged observations on their lives pouring from his mouth.

Late one still, windless night, practising on the unmarked punchbag she'd recently bought, Harriet heard him begging from beneath her window, 'Please, Lynn,' he cried, 'no, darling, you know there's no one but you. I just lost my phone for a while . . . baby, no . . . please don't . . . please don't . . .' To drown out his sobbing she punched harder and harder until she made her first dent in the shiny plastic of the swinging bag.

Harriet's life until meeting Patrick had resembled owning a rare kind of horse: it needed constant tending, feeding and maintenance in order to try and prevent it from dying limply in a field. Phone calls had to be made, people needed to be tracked down and forced into meeting for drinks or reluctant visits to see things. They couldn't be ordinary things either. You couldn't bribe people to go to something simple like the theatre or the cinema these days, so she had constantly to be finding new and exciting events to visit – physical theatre performed in disused ammunition factories, low-flying balloon trips across safari parks, walking tours led by a comedian off the TV around Brent Cross Shopping Centre. Birthdays had to be remembered for which presents needed to be bought so offence wasn't caused and feuds had to be taken into account so two or more people who weren't speaking didn't end up spending an evening together.

Now, though, with Li Kuan Yu her life had taken on a life of its own, needing no attention whatsoever. Patrick told her firmly that if she wanted to make progress then attendance at the dojo two nights a week and all of Saturday morning was the bare minimum; he added that as a special favour he was also prepared to give her private lessons three times a week in the room on the first floor, so there was suddenly very little time for Harriet to do anything else except work, sleep and exercise. When she wasn't at the dojo or in her shop she went on long, huffing half-walk half-runs, wearing out the crotches of two pairs of dungarees in a fortnight with the unaccustomed friction below her secret place. As she walked and as she exercised her body twisted and creaked and protested like a suspension bridge in a high wind but there was the definite feeling that there was a tiny bit less of her every day and what remained was a tiny bit firmer.

She said to Lulu and Rose in the pub, 'I dunno, I was so disappointed at first when he told me what it was, this ridiculous nonsense. But y'know something's made me stick with it and the odd thing is I am losing weight so I'm sort of beginning to think there might be something to it.'

The day before Lulu had phoned her. 'Didn't you notice we

haven't been talking to you for nearly a month?' she asked in a querulous voice.

'How do you mean?' Harriet replied, confused. 'I've talked to you both loads of times on the phone.'

'Yeah,' said Rose, jumping in, 'but we've been sniffy and distant.'

'Is this on speakerphone?'

'Cutting and abrupt,' added Lulu.

'Churlish and unpleasant.'

'Why?' she asked, trying to sound like she'd noticed.

'Don't you remember? That terrible scene you made last time we were in the Admiral Cod, making Cosmo cry and acting all crazy.'

'You reminded us of Hitler, but not in a good way.'

'Oh that, well, you know it's . . .' Harriet mumbled.

'Apology accepted,' Lulu said.

That night they all went to the pub to make up. Right away it was clear that Cosmo the waiter was completely transformed; he shivered with an almost sexual delight when she came in, he whispered to Harriet that he was so glad she'd decided to return after 'our upset' as he referred to it, and that evening he was attentive and kept slipping them dishes from the kitchen free of charge so that if that had been the pub's general policy it might almost have been good value.

Harriet's attitude to the other people at the dojo also underwent a slow change. When sitting amongst this odd assortment of people she realised something about her old group of friends, the ones she had had all her adult life. It dawned on her that they were more or less the same: they were more or less white, they were more or less educated and what held them together was a weak thing. A vague hatred of Tony Blair, burnt-out love affairs, the thought they might need each other one day when they were old and incontinent, the fact that they didn't know anybody else: that was pretty much it. Now it seemed to her that at the dojo she was sitting amongst a group of people who were bound to each other by something much stronger than the coincidence that they'd all discovered couscous and New Zealand wine at more or less the same time.

One big thing that she started to think about was what it would be like to be able to fight. Up until then like most women she'd thought of physical violence as an almost exclusively male pursuit, like yachting or exposing yourself to schoolgirls, but now sometimes she found herself fantasising about what it would be like to get people to do what you wanted because they were frightened of you or respected you rather than because they felt sorry for you or because you'd gone on and on at them.

Patrick said to Harriet in the upstairs room one afternoon as light snowflakes drifted like parachutists to the cold pavement, 'An important part of learning to be a fighter is getting used to being hurt, that's the point of all that stone throwing and the shin kicking. What confuses the average civilian,' he went on, 'is just the act of gettin' punched, they're standing there thinking, My God, I've been punched! Being punched is the worst thing in the world! Then you punch them again and bingo! They're down and out. But if you get used to being punched, it's no big deal, no shock, so you're ready to shrug it off and take action back.'

She nodded vigorously at this, knowing for once exactly what he meant because she'd discovered that she didn't much mind being hurt in this way; maybe her nerve endings weren't as sensitive as most people's or something. While it wasn't pleasant being hit or punched, in a way she sort of welcomed the sting of the stones against her skin; sometimes she wondered to herself if because of her tolerance for pain she was maybe already halfway to being a really good fighter.

When she told Lulu and Rose about the punching and the hitting thing Lulu asked, 'So in this barmy new upside-down world of yours are battered housewives really good fighters because they get punched all the time?'

'Is this you still being cutting and unpleasant?'

'No, it just sounds a bit odd is all.'

'We worry about you, darling.'

'Is this some sort of cult you're getting yourself involved in?'

Harriet had told them emphatically, 'I'm fine, don't worry.'

Last time she'd seen Patrick, she'd asked, 'What are you going to be doing next Monday?'

'Monday?' he replied thoughtfully. 'Well, Mondays I usually start with Frog Jumps into Lily Pond. I wake at dawn and start my exercises while still in bed with the frog stretch exercise. I touch the soles of the feet together and flatten the knees to the horizontal position; assuming this triangular shape I attempt to bring the heels, keeping the soles of the feet together, up to the base of the mei lo chakra point, situated midway in the perineum. I repeat this at least ninety times. Then moving to standing position, I stretch skywards, extending fingertips and moving on to tiptoes, again at least ninety times. Next I bring arms to shoulder height extended horizontally and commence to make small circles, moving to wider circles then full wind-mills, counter-clockwise then clockwise. I perform nine hundred revolutions "until your arms rotate like roundabouts at Wicksteed Park" as Sifu Po says. Then I go for my nine-mile run. Why? Why do you ask?'

'It's Christmas Day.'

'Oh.'

'It's just my sister and her husband always make Christmas dinner for anybody who's still around in London; they're always going on at me to bring someone, I never did up to now but I thought, I dunno . . . I thought you might like to come.'

Underneath the flashing red chilli peppers lights, which were Harriet's sole contribution to the day, Martin and Swei Chiang were talking about their children's education. Swei Chiang said, 'Of course we'd love to send the kids to the local state school but it's a jungle down there, there's a shooting most days . . .'

'Well, actually, somebody was squirted with a water pistol,' Martin corrected.

'But it had acid in it.'

'Diet Doctor Pepper.'

'Stop correcting me, Martin!'

Facing them across the table Oscar and Katya weren't listening but instead were arguing in hissy whispers.

'I can't drive home, I've had too much to drink.'

'Well, I can't drive home, I've had too much to drink.'

'Well, I can't drive home, I've had too much to drink.'

At the far end of the table was Roland Malone, his hair sticking up in clumps, wrapped inside a ratty torn anorak with a fur-lined hood that he wore up so it covered his head completely. He had just been offered a part in a gritty new British film and was refusing to come out of character, so his family had gone on holiday to North Africa without him. He was speaking to nobody in particular at high speed in a strange nasal 'northern' accent.

'The trees are full of spiders, right? Waiting, hiding from the light, the fist-in-the-face Nazis that vomit up car jack neutral spinsters – it's all in the Bible, man – St Paul's letter to the National Car Parking company complaining about a scratch on his Nissan Micra that some clown . . . Coco? I'd rather have Horlicks if it's all the same to you . . .'

Bored, Harriet got up from the table unnoticed and went into the kitchen where her sister was preparing the meal. Helen had decided to have a Slovakian Christmas this year and her arm was halfway up a large carp, stuffing it with walnuts that she'd already cooked separately.

'Hi, how's it going out there?' Helen asked, reaching for more nuts.

'The usual: Swei Chiang's explaining that although she's still a rampant socialist they've just got to send their three-year-old to military academy because there's regular outbreaks of cannibalism at the local comprehensive. Oscar and Katya are practising for the European bickering championships and Roland . . . well . . .'

'It's better than the time he was playing an SS officer in that mini-series with Cybill Shepherd.'

'Yeah,' the older sister agreed. 'He said if we didn't finish the chocolate mousse he'd made then he'd force us to dig our own graves and shoot us. Honestly, though, it's the same every time we meet, we could put our conversation on a fucking tape loop then we could just eat our dinner and flip through magazines while the tape played.'

'I thought you liked our Christmas dinners?'

'Oh, I suppose I do but, you know, Christmas is always a bit of a pain.'

'I don't know where you're getting this sudden bad temper from, you've always said you had a good time on all the other Christmases. I burnt my finger on the carp, you know.'

At college those on Harriet's fashion course interested in designing costume for the theatre were required to take a subsidiary drama course. Though unwilling and shy at first she had found herself rather enjoying the workshops she took part in.

One of the exercises the teacher set their group was to take a page from a foreign language phrase book and for them to try and dramatise it, to attempt to make logical sense of the unrelated phrases. '*Estoy enfermo*, I'm sick,' one would say.

Another student would reply, '*Estoy bien*, I'm well.'

'Where is the hospital/ambulance/doctor's surgery?' a third would ask.

'I'm going to be sick/faint/give birth.'

'Where is the bus station?'

'*Nos divertimos mucho*, we had a lot of fun!'
'*Voy a verle otra vez*? Am I going to see you again?'
'I have been bitten by a dog!'
'My car has a flat battery/engine fire.'

With their abrupt switches of topic and sudden dives into self-pity, conversations with her sister reminded Harriet of these workshops fifteen years ago. Helen had drummed into her older sister since they were kids that the idea of anybody having a bad time at an event that she'd organised made her deeply uneasy. She knew Helen hated the very idea that she wasn't enjoying herself now and hadn't enjoyed other Christmases – that's why she'd let it slip; siblings know how to push each other's buttons, because they installed them. Or rather Helen didn't care whether Harriet was having a good time or not but she couldn't stand her showing that she was miserable. In the past Harriet would have been too intimidated by the scene Helen might make to let her boredom show but she suddenly didn't want to put up with it any more; after all, this insistence on everybody acting hysterically merry was simply another facet of her sister's egotism. Helen felt that her very presence in a room made it sparkle, so she assumed if somebody was having a bad time it implied that there was some flaw in her loveliness. Harriet decided it would probably be good for both of them if in the future she didn't try so hard to placate her sister.

It was all right for her, Helen thought, Harriet didn't have her responsibilities: Helen was a wife, she was a mother, Harriet didn't even look after her own appearance, never mind a husband and son and all the distressed talking birds in the world. Plus looking as good as Helen didn't happen without her doing a huge amount of work while her sister went out looking like a bag of potatoes. She knew now that Harriet would never stick to this latest fitness regime any more than she'd stuck to any of the others over the last fifteen years despite all the support and the expensive equipment she'd given her. Helen had been glad when Harriet had become friendly with this Patrick but she still didn't understand why she had invited her personal trainer weirdo to Christmas dinner.

Helen would sometimes think after a particularly good night out or a pleasant weekend that time should really stop now, since everything was perfectly balanced, through her efforts all her friends were getting on, because of her constant vigilance everybody was in good health. She would say to the universe while dropping off to sleep, 'OK that'll do now, let's stop it all, everything's perfect,' and would be genuinely surprised to wake the next morning and find that time was still grinding onwards. 'I thought I told you to stop,' she would say grumpily to the universe, aware that her memories of the perfect night out were already fading.

She asked Harriet, 'What time's your friend coming?'

'Two forty-four.'

'Two forty-four? Not two forty-three or two forty-five?'

'No, he said two forty-four.'

She glanced at the clock on the wall. 'Well, it's two forty-four now and—'

The doorbell rang.

'I'll get it!' Toby shouted from the bedroom.

They heard the cannonade of his feet running down the stairs then the door opening, muffled conversation and the door closing.

'Harriet, your friend's here!' Toby shouted.

'Two forty-four,' said Harriet as she left the kitchen.

In the hallway Helen heard Toby ask, 'So what can I get you to drink then, Patrick?'

'Just tap water, please,' Patrick said.

'Ah, "Pointless Park Pop".'

'No, tap water, please.'

'That's what I said.'

'What did you say?'

'Oh, ah, I . . .' Normally Toby would stubbornly stick to his name for something in the face of everybody's confusion but there must have been some quality about this Patrick that sapped his confidence so he said, 'Tap water, yes . . .'

'No, didn't you call it something else?'

God, Toby! Helen thought. Stop being so pathetic.

'Hi, Patrick,' Harriet called out.

'I'll get your water,' Toby said, scuttling into the kitchen.

'Harriet's friend's here,' he said to his wife.

'Come and sit down next to me and meet everyone,' Harriet said to Patrick, considering taking him by the hand or arm but not daring to do so. Eventually she just sort of poked him with her finger in the direction of the big living room where everybody was sitting around the dining table. Patrick sat down in Toby's chair: to Harriet his straight-backed posture made a powerful contrast with the slumped, weak, caved-in bodies of all the rest of them.

'Everybody, this is my friend Patrick.'

Patrick stood up again and shook hands rather formally with them all. She could see they were all confused by having somebody who wasn't exactly the same as them in their midst. So, trying the most obvious way to work out his place in the hierarchy, Martin asked, 'Hi, Patrick, and what do you do?'

'Well,' he replied, looking all serious, 'I met Harriet at the gym. I'm an instructor there but now we've been doing personal training together and I hope become friends,' and he gave a shy little smile.

They'd never actually had a discussion about whether Li Kuan Yu was to be mentioned to outsiders; clearly it wasn't.

'And what do you all do?' Patrick asked in turn.

'Percussionists Licensing Society.'

'I'm writing a book of recipes of food mentioned in the Bible – I made the unleavened bread flavoured with bitter herbs that we're having later.'

'I plan conferences for dentists,' Katya said, 'and Martin's at Birkbeck College University of London, professor of modern languages.'

'What, all of them?' Patrick asked.

'I'm sorry?'

'All of the modern languages does he teach?'

'No, just French and German obviously.'

'Right, so he's a French teacher.'

'Well, no, well, sort of . . .' Katya decided not to pursue it. 'Of course you know Roland, he's a—'

Roland Malone spoke up for himself. 'Neck monkey!' he shouted.

There was an embarrassed silence during which Patrick stared levelly at him for several seconds. 'No you're not, you're an actor,' he finally said. 'I know that because I've seen your picture a lot of times in the local paper.'

Though Patrick seemed as far as anybody at the dojo could tell completely uninterested in watching television, never went to the movies and didn't read books, he faithfully read the local paper every week. From it he would extract stories of knifings, rapes and robberies (of which there seemed to be many), cut them from the paper and read them out to Harriet in her room or to the dojo as they practised. Then Patrick would ruefully explain exactly how the victims of these assaults would have been able to beat their assailants if only they'd been adepts of Li Kuan Yu.

'That woman whose bag was snatched, she could have used Shin Strike and Elbow Strike to the Side of Head on the bloke who did it. That bus driver could have used Split Fingers Cobra Eyeball Strike on the man who showed him his penis on the N19 night bus, and if that other man had known Li Kuan Yu he wouldn't have driven into that elm tree in the park because he wouldn't have been drunk.'

Patrick said, 'What interesting jobs you all have.'

There was a self-satisfied murmur of assent at this.

'I bet you all went to university as well and got firsts or something.'

Another hum of happy assent.

'Well, a good 2:1,' said Katya.

Toby came back in and handed a glass to Patrick. 'There you go, Patrick, there's your . . . water.'

Patrick took one sip of the clear liquid and immediately gagged. 'Dear God!' he said, looking at his drink in an appalled fashion. 'What's that?'

Everybody else stiffened with embarrassment; everyone in their social circle knew better than to ever ask Toby for a soft drink at home. One of his most prized possessions was a machine called a ColaJet: this contraption of pipes, gas cylinders and nozzles was advertised as making carbonated drinks, supposedly 'as good as the real thing' from a mixture of tap water and a selection of disgusting syrups Toby kept in labelled bottles. Guests at Toby and Helen's were always being offered 'tonic water' that tasted like sump oil or unpleasant-looking brown Cola the consistency of glue. They learned rapidly to take their drinks straight or to bring their own mixers with them, but if he did somehow slip them a drink from his machine the last thing they would do would be to complain about it, since another rule of dinner at Harriet's sister's house was that you didn't upset Toby by confronting any aspect of his alternate reality. There was an unspoken agreement that you didn't do it since there was a generalised fear that his fragile world might crumble like a computer-generated parallel universe in a dystopian science fiction movie.

'It's fizzy mineral water,' Toby said.

'Well, it tastes disgusting,' Patrick replied. 'I asked you for tap water which is perfectly fine to drink as it is. So could you get me that?' Then he continued with what he'd been saying, ignoring Toby who drifted back to the kitchen looking as if he'd been punched in the face. 'I left school when I was very young me but it amazes me all the different sorts of things educated people like you do. I look around and see all these incredible things – did you know there's a new kind of salmon-flavoured waffle coming on the market? Somebody who went to college must have thought of that.' Harriet knew Patrick and the ways of Li Kuan Yu well enough by now to discern that the smiling, slightly confused dinner guests were being led blindly into a trap just as the great Samurai Musashi ensnared the three brothers of the Yoshioka Shogun at the Sanjusangendo Temple, home to the thousand statues of Kannon. He pressed on, 'But when you think about it all these people are wasting their time because there is only one thing in the world they should be working on.'

'How do you mean?' asked Martin.

'Well,' Patrick replied, 'let me ask you, what's the greatest crime you can commit?'

Swei Chiang spat, 'Parking in a bloody bus lane according to Islington bloody Council, though how else are you supposed to get your child to its piano lessons on time? Tell me that.'

'Murder,' Oscar said.

'Murder, exactly, that's right, Oscar. So we believe the worst thing you can do is to kill somebody, because we think death is the worst thing that can happen to a person. Yet at the same time we're all going to die, aren't we?'

'S'pose so . . .' mumbled Oscar.

'But not for a while,' said Katya.

Patrick ignored her. 'And yet we meekly accept it. This terrible thing is going to happen to you all.' He pointed at them as he spoke. 'And to all your children and to all your pets and to everybody you've ever met and still you people with all your talent and your brilliant minds you just shrug your shoulders and you spend your time administering estates or sending dentists to the Great Barrier Reef or teaching French or being in films when if you think about it you should all be working on a cure for death twenty-four hours a day! Or at the very least trying to make life longer for people until somebody else comes up with a cure for death! So really, looking at the situation in the cold light of day anything else you do is a complete and utter waste of time.'

'I say! Everybody's very quiet in here!' shouted Toby, as he entered carrying a big soup tureen he'd had specially made for him by Spode of Derby.

During Patrick's speech Harriet had felt herself glowing inside like a toaster. Usually her sister was the star of these Christmas dinners, everybody cooing over her fantastic food and how lovely she looked and the funny things Timon said, but here this year was her guest and he was saying all this brilliant, fascinating stuff that had completely derailed the usual boring stream of tediousness.

Added to that there was the way he looked! Though it was winter he wore a simple white T-shirt, its semi-see-through material stretched tight over the swelling muscles of his arms and outlining the sturdy rippling contours of his body. Patrick's hair was cut close to his skull and his pallid blue eyes under long pale eyelashes glittered with ferocious life so that he made everybody else seated round the table seem waxy and inert by contrast.

Harriet caught Katya running her eyes hungrily up and down Patrick's torso, as well she might, she thought, given the crumpled, stove-in posture of her own man; in fact come to think of it there was a certain wolfish longing in Oscar's own gaze towards Patrick.

Toby placed a steaming bowl in front of Patrick and said,

'There you go, Patrick, lovely soup, swoop, loop de loop.'

'What did you say?' Patrick asked.

Later that evening she walked with Patrick along the edge of the park, back towards the Watney Flats where he lived.

'Thanks very much for that, Harriet,' he said.

'Yeah, Christmas dinners like that remind you of what you haven't missed.'

'No, no,' he replied, 'it's good to mix from time to time with people. There's always something you can learn from them and it was nice to have home-cooked food.'

Over the road the Tin Can Man passed them rapidly walking south. Perhaps because it was Christmas Day, rather than commenting on other people he was having one of his anguished conversations. 'Please, Lynn,' he was saying, 'you might at least allow me to see the kids today. I've got everyone these really great presents . . . a rocking horse . . . a Nintendo . . . a Ninja Turtle game . . .'

Even Harriet knew the Ninja Turtles hadn't been popular with kids for years.

'I told you I lost my phone for a few days . . . yes I know, Lynn, but if I could just come and . . . no, Lynn . . . yes, Lynn . . . but please, darling, if I could just . . .' His desperate entreaties faded as they stopped at the flinty gateway to the Watney Trust Flats.

'Harriet, I wanted to say . . .'

Suddenly she wasn't paying attention but was staring beadily over her friend's shoulder. 'Excuse me a minute, Patrick,' she said.

A number of seconds before, a battered whitish van with ladders on the roof had pulled into a parking bay a few yards further along the pavement. The driver, a large burly man, was locking the rust-streaked door as she reached him. 'Excuse me,' she said, 'in the cold my fingers go white and then blue, do you think I've got thromboangitis obliterans?'

'Eh what, love?' he asked, staring at this wired-up bulky woman in confusion.

'See, I'm asking you this question because you're a doctor, aren't you?'

'No, I ain't a doctor.'

'Well,' she said in a quiet voice, pointing to the white-painted space in which the van was parked, 'you're parked in a doctor's space.'

The builder stared back. 'It's Christmas Day, love,' he said with a smirk, 'the doctor won't be needing it.'

'How do you know?' she spat. 'They might be called out on an emergency to help a seriously ill asthmatic refugee child and when they get to the surgery they'd like to park, all tired and weary as they are since they've been on call for the last thirty-six hours, in their own damned space.'

The big man seemed inclined to argue but something in her manner made him reconsider. 'I'll move it,' said the builder, climbing back into his vehicle.

Harriet skipped back to Patrick who'd been watching motion-less and tense.

'I hate people who park selfishly like that in disabled spaces and such, I've always wanted to tell one of them off. And now I have . . . a little Christmas present to myself. Now, what were you saying?'

Patrick smiled and uncoiled his fists. 'Would you have done that a month ago?'

'What?'

'Spoken to that guy like that.'

She had acted without thinking; now forced to reflect on her actions, Harriet said uncertainly, 'Well, I've thought about it loads of times but I've never . . .'

'Acted?'

'Yes, you're right.'

'So what's changed?'

There was a pause in which her new self caught up with the small alterations that had already happened with her body. She said, 'Li Kuan Yu?'

'Li Kuan Yu,' he repeated. 'It's a sign that we need to work harder than ever then you will be ready to move to a whole higher level of understanding. You have this anger which could turn you into a really good fighter, Harriet.'

6

In the park for most of the month of January the strong winds switched direction and now blew from the east, though just as intensely as before. Snow fell heavily and froze over the ground for nearly two weeks. When the park had been first laid out there had been a municipal paddling pool built for local children to wade in. It lay about twenty yards across the grass from Harriet's front door, in the north-western corner and within sight of her upstairs room. The pond was constructed as a concrete oval (corners being considered hierarchical at the time) and was half a metre deep. Of course she wasn't there at the time since this happened in the sixties but she knew what would have happened next: within a week of its installation the shoddy concrete begins slowly to leak. Though employees of the parks and gardens department are supposed to attend to it the water is never changed or filtered or topped up so that after a month no children will venture near its foetid surface and when in late autumn the water finally all drains away into the surrounding soil the pool is not refilled. This is not the end though – over the next two winters leaves from the trees blow into the empty stained bowl and lie there, rainwater falls on them and they rot down until a thick mould effectively seals the cracks in the concrete. Further rainwater falls and refills the pool and thanks to the base of leaf mould it is constantly oxygenated making it a much purer liquid than the chlorinated acid with which the paddling pool had originally been filled. Nevertheless, while the water is pure and clear the rotted vegetation lining the bottom makes it appear black and sinister, especially since clutching tendrils of floating sweet grass curl beneath the surface: the result is that it is still shunned by the human population.

The silt had built up over the years so that now around the edges of the pool couch grass and ferns had seeded themselves, fringing the margins; beyond that cracked willow formed a further barrier to the curious human. Some days while on her way to the oak tree Harriet would force her way through the willow and jump over the pond at its narrowest point before climbing to the oak's highest branches and throwing herself to the ground nine times.

Two mornings a week at 6 a.m. Patrick would come to her place to train and – especially if the weather was bad – he would insist they went to the park. Sometimes as they tramped through a hollow or along a grey tarmac path they would come upon prone figures lying on a bench or sprawled across the dank earth inadequately wrapped in cardboard and newspaper; usually these homeless were asleep, though from time to time they were dead. These corpses were part of the ever-changing population of drinkers and drug addicts in the park whose poisoned systems had given out on them, yet despite this there always seemed to be new recruits whose intended career path was that they planned to die alone during the night under cold and unfriendly trees.

One morning Patrick said to her, 'Harriet, you know that guy who talks all the time about people into his sardine tin?'

'The Tin Can Man, yeah.'

'Did you know he lives right here in the park, in a secret burrow in the ground? It's quite clever really, seeing as he's nuts. He digs air shafts, storage rooms, sleeping ledge, a system of channels to drain away rainwater, all kinds of stuff like that.'

'Really? Have you seen it? Is he, like, a friend of yours?'

'Naww,' Patrick replied, 'the guy's a loser otherwise he wouldn't be living in a hole in the ground in the park, would he? No, I know all about him because I stalk him. See, the martial artist is a hunter as well as a warrior, Harriet, and man is the most dangerous animal of all and the most exciting to hunt.

'When I find his hiding place what I do is I trash it. He had a couch in the last one and photos of his kids – I pissed on them to show I was marking his territory, like a male lion would. He's moved again since and I'll give him that – he learns. His place must be really well camouflaged 'cos I've looked all over and still don't know where it is but I'll find it one day.'

'That must be a lot of effort for him digging it out time after time,' Harriet said.

'Oh, I'm sure he enjoys the hunt as much as I do,' Patrick asserted blithely. 'Another time,' he continued, lost in happy memories, 'I stole his sardine tin, his phone, reckon I did him a favour, at least it shut him up for a few days. You know, Harriet, what I wish more than anything else?' he asked wistfully. 'I wish that I'd been sent to an English public school. They really break a kid's spirit there, you're pretty much impervious to torture if you've been to an English public school and you have lovely manners.'

It had been a hard winter and February was the coldest month that year; afternoon temperatures often didn't rise above freezing point. Though the sun tried to shine, its watery light failed to reach the ground. In March the rays began to grow stronger and out of the wind it could be quite warm. Men who exposed themselves to schoolgirls and young mothers began to return in growing numbers to the park.

During this same time Harriet's appearance underwent a slow and subtle change. It was as if a lazy but talented sculptor, trained in the classical style, was carving the statue of a striking woman from the misshapen, pink, wobbly block of Hattie. He didn't do much each day, in fact sometimes the sculptor didn't turn up for work at all, but when he did his craftsmanship, though minute and leisurely, was assured and confident. In the morning now to get to the shop she would jump down the stairs: she'd started with three steps and had now worked up to the full flight. Falling through the air she imagined, as Patrick had told her to, that she was flying like a cormorant with a fish in its mouth away from the surface of a placid lake disturbed by a single ripple; this led to a lightness of spirit and body and a great deal of plaster falling off the walls and ceiling.

Her attitude to the world around her also began to change. After all, she thought, the purpose of all the work on general fitness, the stalking, the breathing techniques, the philosophical discussions, the history lessons on Tönpa Shenrab, the founder of Bön, which pre-dated Buddhism in the mythical land of Olmo Lung Ring, was to teach her how to cripple or kill another human being effectively. No – not another human being – *a man*. The people who did the crimes that filled the local paper, the torn clippings that Patrick showed them, were always men; no women lurked in the bushes of the park with knives, wire and silver duct tape in a sports bag. It occurred to her that as a woman she had always acted in a certain way, constantly, subconsciously on alert since she was a child. And who or what had she been on the alert for? Men, men and boys. Endlessly vigilant for single men walking the streets at night, constantly listening for their footsteps behind her on the pavement, crossing the road to avoid groups of boys and ceaselessly having to deflect their drunken attentions in the pub without enraging them.

This was the way it had been. These days she no longer worried about the danger before walking down a dark street or entering a rough bar, going exactly where she wanted to go, down alleys, across trading estates; she drank alone in the saloon bars of the few remaining old man pubs and even travelled the broken paths of the park at the dark of night. Because now Harriet had no reason to fear anyone, her new-found strength, her knowledge of the secret killing points on the body, her ability to drop silently out of trees on to anybody who annoyed her, meant she was a woman who to all intents and purposes lived as a man.

On becoming a part-time male Harriet began to feel a degree of sympathy and understanding for her fellow men, dispensing with the default anti-man disdain she'd previously hidden behind. Most of them weren't so bad really, she thought to herself, at least in the Western countries. Considering they had this physical power over women, most of them struggled really hard against their natures, they strove literally manfully not to use their force on women, they allowed women to boss them around, to stop them seeing their kids, to take their money and their houses off them and a lot of men took it. Of course, she said to herself, a good few of them didn't take it, they used their fists and their feet all the time or they got the address of the battered women's shelter from friendly police officers and went round and killed everybody with a shotgun, or they said they were taking the kids to Alton Towers for the day then drove the family car into a canal thinking, Ha, ha, that'll show her . . . But still and all when she considered it she was surprised by the number of males that did put up with not getting their own way. Now that she knew how to punch and kick better than most of them she wasn't sure that she'd put up with a lot of what a lot of men put up with.

As the weight dropped away Harriet also began to think again about sex: for years she had suppressed her desire but as her new body tingled with sensual life it was impossible to prevent a desperate yearning for another's touch seeping back into her mind. Each day at some point, often in the afternoon, she would go up to the bedroom, take all her clothes off then look at herself in the full-length mirror. She would run her hands down her torso and over her hips, staring at this woman who was slowly being revealed like a complicated picture being sent over the internet.

*

Helen and Toby were attending a supper party in the ruins of Oscar and Katya's home. Nine months before, the couple had got a builder in to do some minor redecorating of their dining room, and this small project had somehow turned into a massive remodelling of their entire house. In a sort of builders' Stockholm syndrome, rather than get angry Oscar and Katya had fallen completely under the spell of this man. They appeared to find him wise, exciting and hilarious while to everybody else he was the exact reverse of these things. If Oscar and Katya invited their friends round for a meal you could never be quite sure whether the builder would be there or not and consequently whether the evening would be completely ruined or not.

He was there tonight, a thin sallow-skinned man with a voice as flat and dull as Luxembourg. And it was worse: the builder's one interest, outside wrecking people's homes, was the Rio Carnival with which he was totally obsessed. He saved all his money so that he could go every other year to Brazil for a whole month and a half, to take part in the preparations and even to serve as a judge in some of the local competitions for junior samba bands. Tonight he had brought his slides of the carnival along to show everybody. Kerclick. 'That's a fellow called Paulho Harvihad,' he said in his nasal drone, 'and' – kerclick – 'that's a fellow, a friend of mine, called Paulho Herviho.' Kerclick. 'That's a fellow called Paulho Hohahivo. He's a funny fellow, Paulho Hohahivo is.' Kerclick. 'That's the stadium, the Sambodromo, where the parade ends and the judging of the . . .'

The flickering lamp and the builder's droning voice sent Toby into a light trance. He found himself drifting off and thinking for some reason about Harriet, his sister-in-law. He reflected that she certainly wouldn't be sitting there pretending to be all interested in these awful slides. With half his mind he heard Helen asking the builder, 'So does each favela have its own samba band or is there more than one?'

Toby smiled to himself; he knew that if she'd been there

Harriet would be shooting him secret looks under her eyelids, that they'd both be struggling to repress muffled laughter at the crappiness of the situation, especially as . . . 'Dear God!' Kerclick. A slide came on the screen of the builder standing with his hands on his hips at night on some steep cobbled street, wearing high heels, a sparkling green high-cut thong, jewelled emerald-studded bra and feathered green and gold headdress. 'That's me in the . . .'

As rapidly as possible Toby sailed away again in his mind but the happy place had gone. Instead, with a shiver of nausea, he recalled the strange pale psycho Harriet had brought along to Christmas dinner. What was she doing with him? Well, she'd said he was her personal trainer but Lulu had told him they went to the park in the middle of the night and did some strange kind of martial art together. What was that all about? Was something more going on there, some electricity between them and why did he, all of a sudden, care what she did? Toby abruptly wondered if Patrick was having sex with his sister-in-law. No, it wasn't possible, he thought to himself, that Patrick was really good-looking. Then he understood why he'd been thinking about Harriet in this new way – somehow now she was becoming really good-looking too.

'Crikey, Hat,' said Toby, opening the door when she called round one evening to babysit, 'you look . . . I dunno, different.'

'Well, you know, it's doing my training with Patrick, all that exercise is really starting to pay off.'

'Right,' he said.

'D'you like my new body?' she asked, stretching her arms above her head and turning slowly so he could inspect her.

'Yes, I do,' he said. 'I do like your new body. Yes, I do.'

In Harriet's first year after college, though beginning to put on proper weight, she'd still been sort of pretty, in the way that nearly any young woman is pretty but even then she had a sense that she was nothing special. Yet somehow underneath the rippling flesh there seemed to have been incubating all through her fat years a woman of truly startling appearance. Maybe keeping her out of the light all this time had allowed the woman to ripen unblemished. Her hair that had once been limp and an unvarying sweaty flat black was now, due partly to all the time spent in the open air, shot through with iridescent coppery highlights. Harriet's skin, formerly pasty and white, was these days lightly tanned and had acquired a healthy blush beneath the surface thanks to all the blood that was now pumping madly round her system. Her breasts had reduced and taken on a pleasant springy shape, so much so that she was constantly genuinely surprised that they belonged to her and was able to contemplate them for a long time in the mirror, marvelling at them as if they belonged to some other woman. She wondered in a languid sort of way whether it was a sign of lesbianism if you were getting aroused at the sight of your own tits.

When customers came into the shop she also noticed a change in their attitude towards her: saying something perfectly ordinary that she'd said a thousand times before caused them to laugh or smile as they'd never done before; customers would tell her to forget the change or say that it didn't matter that she hadn't got their repair ready even though she'd said it would be done a week ago. Harriet would think to herself, Why are they suddenly being nice to me and why are many more men coming to me with repairs? and it would come back to her that she had accidentally become beautiful.

Having never looked exceptional before, she was completely unprepared for how other people's attitude to her would shift, simply because of a change in her appearance.

This must be what it's like to be my sister, Harriet thought wonderingly to herself.

All kinds of visions, images and memories that had formerly been suppressed began to force their way to the surface of her mind. She recalled that due to Helen's overall loveliness and soppy, gentle manner people constantly assumed that naturally she would be a vegetarian and even those friends who knew her well were repeatedly shocked when she ordered a rare steak or some raw smelly kidneys in a restaurant. By contrast, with Harriet, in the past, people would phone when they were taking a trip to the freezer centre to enquire whether she wanted them to pick up a couple of ten-kilo bags of liver while they were down there.

Toby and Helen's gala benefit that night was for a charity organisation called Plumbio; it had formerly been the Lead Miners Benevolent Society but lead mining and lead miners had died out many years ago, yet the society continued with its name changed to collect funds, hold benefits and mount celebrity polo matches. Plumbio served a very useful function in that it enabled people to hold decadent champagne parties in marquees in Mayfair squares in the name of charity without the money actually going to anyone unpleasant such as the poor or Africans.

'Now Timon's got to read the front page of *El Pais* to practise his Spanish before he can have any of the aubergine dip and he's not allowed to play with his light sabre until he's taken all of his echinacea,' Helen said to her sister.

'Sure, don't worry.'

'Hey, Timon,' Harriet said, once the boy's parents had gone, 'how would you like to see what the inside of a pub looks like?'

When the two of them got to the Admiral Codrington, the little boy's hand in that of his auntie's, Lulu and Rose were, as usual, already there seated at a table with Roland Malone between them. Two empty wine bottles were on the table and the trio were halfway through their third. Roland was in the middle of telling the two women all about his latest acting role. He'd recently become involved with Fathers 4 Fathers 4 Kidz, a group that militantly campaigned for disgruntled divorced and separated fathers. The day before he'd dressed up as the Norse god Wotan and climbed a crane on the new Terminal Five construction site at Heathrow.

'Some planes coming in from the Middle East had to be diverted to Frankfurt,' he was telling them proudly, 'and the Duke of Westminster's private jet had to circle for three hours till it was nearly out of fuel and had to land on the M4. I was on all the UK news channels and Al-Jazeera because of the planes from the Middle East.'

'But, Roland,' Rose said, 'you're not actually divorced or separated, you and Inga are perfectly happy together though God knows why, and you can visit your kids whenever you want seeing as they're at home with you.'

'Yeah, but if we did split up she'd probably stop me seeing them.'

'No, she wouldn't.'

Lulu said, 'The men in those groups, the genuine ones, not you, Roland, are a pack of self-justifying creeps who can't believe anything's their fault.'

'Yikes, Hattie,' said Roland, who hadn't seen her for a while, 'you've lost a lot of weight.' Then a theatrical look of concern crossed his face. 'Do you have cancer?' he asked, tilting his head sideways like a confused dog. 'Because I reckon I've got cancer of the—'

'No, Roland, you idiot,' Rose interjected, 'she hasn't got cancer any more than you have. Haven't you heard? Harriet's become a Mutant Ninja invisible mender.'

'What?'

'Our Hat could pull your spine out of your body and you wouldn't notice,' Lulu added.

'Poke yer eyes out,' said Rose.

'You bitches! I told you about that in confidence.'

'We wormed it out of you really.'

'Well, I still said I didn't want to talk about it,' then, turning to Roland, 'I've been doing a lot of fitness training but I've also been learning a martial art called Li Kuan Yu. That's why I've lost so much weight.'

'Oh yeah? And you're good at it?' Roland asked.

'Don't sound so surprised.'

'No, it's just you've never seemed . . . I dunno . . . sporty.'

'I guess I just never found the sport. But, yeah, my sifu says—'

'Your what?'

'My sifu, my teacher.'

'Oh, is he that weird pale kid,' Roland asked, 'who was at Christmas dinner?'

'Patrick, yeah.'

'What's his surname, by the way?'

She blushed. 'It's O'Reilly Po.'

'O'Reilly Po?'

'What kind of a name's O'Reilly Po?'

'It's part Chinese. In martial arts circles it's a common thing, apparently, he took the surname of his sifu. Who was called Martin Po.'

'You certainly look good on it,' Roland said, then asked, 'Do you think learning a martial art would help with my depression?'

Harriet was silent. She had discovered with Li Kuan Yu that she wasn't a proselytiser: in the past she'd been eager to recruit others to her many short-lived enthusiasms, signing them up to subscriptions for magazines on literary theory, dragging them along to performances of obscure puppeteers, but with her fighting art there was no urge to share it at all.

Harriet was spared making any reply by Lulu saying with professional disdain, 'You're not depressed, Roland, at the most you're just a bit fed up. If you want to see depressed you should come with me round the wards. Those people are much worse off than you.'

'No, they're not,' the actor replied.

'How do you figure that out?'

'Well, it's easy, you see, their depression is happening to them but my depression is happening to me so it's clearly much worse.'

Rose said, 'Christ, Roland, you're an arse.'

Whenever Harriet watched a movie in which the hero was a wild, authority-defying free spirit who lived life by their own rules, her enjoyment was always spoilt by her inevitably wondering what they'd be like to have as a neighbour. She'd be happily submerged in the film then suddenly find herself thinking, Well, that's all well and good you having wild sex in the jacuzzi to the sound of rock music in the middle of the night, but what about the people next door? They've probably got to get up for work in the morning. You could bet Billy Bob Thornton's character in *Bad Santa* might ultimately be a life-enhancing force for good but he still wouldn't turn down the music if you asked him to or be conscientious about only putting his rubbish bags out on the correct night, and if you lived downstairs from him he'd never be there to water your plants (not with water anyway) or feed the cat when you went on holiday. And she doubted whether the folks in the next apartment to Keanu Reeves's character Neo in *The Matrix* would appreciate him smashing through their wall pursued by computer-generated replicants, or indeed be grateful to him for showing them that their entire world was an evil illusion – they might have been happier living in ignorance hooked up to a feeding tube full of nutritious mush.

When Harriet got back to the shop at 1 a.m. after Toby and Helen had finally returned from their Plumbio function, a pyramid of black rubbish bags and the frame of a bicycle had been piled against the street door to her flat.

'Why does Timon smell of beer?' her sister had asked in a nasty voice as soon as she'd come into the living room, while

Toby had seemed to be acting even odder than usual and now there was this crap all over her front door.

'Enough of this,' Harriet muttered to herself and stepping over the garbage hammered on the door of her neighbours' house, the Elderly Namibian Women's Housing Association Home. She felt the flimsy wood beginning to shift and splinter under the force of her blows. Soon there was shouting from inside and heavy steps descending the stairs before the door was yanked open by a dark-skinned Namibian youth with bulging eyes, sharp features and zigzags carved into his haircut. He was dressed in a shiny turquoise and pink tracksuit, a cigarette hung from his lips and as the woman watched embers from it dropped on to the oily material where they caught fire and burnt little black circles.

'What you want?' he queried in a thick accent.

Struggling to control her runaway breathing, Harriet said in a rush, 'You might recognise me – I'm your neighbour. I live next door and you keep piling your bloody rubbish against my step.'

'It's not our rubbish, mate,' he replied, making to close the door.

She blocked it open, locking her arm in such a way that it was impossible to close and at the same time bent down and tore open one of the rubbish bags: inside on top of other garbage was a lustrous blue and gold tracksuit, the jacket half of which was burnt into black cindery tatters. Harriet picked it up in her free hand and held it in front of the youth.

Looking at the tracksuit jacket the young man said, 'You better come up.' Suddenly uncertain but committed now, she followed him into a greasy mirror image of her own home. Standing uncomfortably close to the youth in the hall, Harriet expected to be led up the stairs but instead, keeping his eyes locked on hers, he sat down on a top-of-the-range-looking pink-padded chairlift that took up most of the hallway. The Namibian pulled back on a joystick built into the arm of the chair, there was a loud beeping noise and after a second the young man slowly began to grind upwards. His ascent was so slow that she waited until he was halfway up before climbing a couple of steps and it was only when he turned the corner and disappeared out of sight that the woman followed him up to the landing.

Like her big upstairs room this matching floor had been retained as one big space. Presumably it had been intended as some sort of meeting room for the Namibian grannies since there were grab bars at waist height screwed into the walls for them to hang on to, light switches had been placed at the level of a wheelchair and panic button alarms had been fitted beside the doors; the only thing that was missing from this picture was the grannies themselves. In their place various young men, their features ranging like their grandmothers' from white to deepest black, dressed in the uniform cheap tracksuits, lounged about on council-supplied velour sofas. In one corner there was a huge flat-screen TV on which was playing a shaky DVD of a fat woman yelling out a hysterical song against a rapidly changing background of forests, rivers and mountains with writing in Arabic running backwards on a crawl along the bottom of the screen.

In the centre of the room on one of those brown leather reclining armchairs that extend like a club-class seat on an aeroplane sat an older bearded man.

Unlike the youngsters this man was not wearing a tracksuit but instead was dressed in well-cut dark brown Italian moleskin trousers, a white poplin cotton shirt and a beautiful knitted cardigan that looked Spanish to Harriet's experienced eyes, and on his small feet were embroidered leather Moroccan slippers. Though his skin was dark mahogany his features seemed Arabic rather than African, the smart clothes combined with a small pepper and salt beard and the reading glasses worn on a chain round his neck gave him the air of a successful American jazz pianist popular in Sweden and France but ignored in his own country due to his radical political views on class and race and his controversial marriage to a beautiful blonde woman. Though smaller and more slender than the muscular young men around him it was clear they deferred totally to the older man. Since obtaining a little of it, Harriet had become interested in the exercise of power, reflecting that maybe you didn't need to learn how to punch and kick and jump on your enemies from trees if you could get others to do it for you.

She had always had the feeling that only creepy people such as Oscar and Katya's weird builder got on well with foreigners, not all foreigners of course, not sophisticated architects from Madrid or painters from Los Angeles but rather primitive foreigners, goatherds, tribal foreigners, foreigners like this lot. Toby had told her once that he reckoned the people in the slums of Rio – the favelas – whom the weird builder stayed with, were just nice to him because they were after his money, but she wasn't so sure, feeling that they really, really, truly liked him for who he was. Though of course they still took as much money off him as they could. In her experience foreigners often responded to the bogus, the fake, the untrue in other nationalities.

But then it occurred to her that Martin Po was a foreigner and Patrick had got on with him so well that he'd saved his life and become Patrick's sifu. Well, Harriet reasoned to herself, Martin was Chinese and somehow they didn't count as foreigners: Chinese people managed to be both really alien and familiar at the same time.

The young man who had answered the door crossed to the older one and spoke in a low voice. He listened then bade the woman come and sit facing him on a leather footstool. She considered remaining standing but in the end sat down.

'You wish to speak to us?' the older man enquired in a treacly accented voice.

'Yeah,' she said. 'I live next door to you and I'm getting really sick of you people leaving your crap outside my door.'

The head man didn't appear to be listening. 'So,' he said, acting all cunning and vague like a wily wolf in a cartoon, 'you say you are the woman who lives next door.'

'Yes, that's right I do, I am.'

'Then explain me this if you can, the woman who lives next door is a big fat woman. How can that be you? You are not a big fat woman.'

'I've lost weight,' she replied.

This seemed to throw him for a second but then he came over all wily again. 'I see, then explain me this. She seemed also to be a frightened woman, the woman who lived next door. We used to see her from our window, pulling angry little faces at our front door then running inside her house as if angry parrots were pursuing her.'

'Well,' she said, lapsing into his portentous way of speaking, 'it seems that I have lost my fear along with my fat.'

'That is unusual . . .' There was silence as he mused on this for half a minute then he began again. 'So now tell me this, when you were fat and fearful and you saw rubbish on your step what did you feel?'

It was her turn to ponder in silence before saying, 'Angry, powerless, humiliated, it was like you were insulting me.'

'And now you've come up here and you've faced us, told us of your righteous anger . . .'

Harriet thought for a further few seconds then laughed, raising her arms and letting them flop to her side. 'I don't care any more.'

The old man smiled too. 'Of course you don't! Because it wasn't the rubbish that was making you angry but your own weakness. Now you've faced us without fear, you've done what you can and we are no longer a faceless enemy – you know us now a little. I hope in future you can come and visit us many times, neighbour, and tell us of the many ways in which we are annoying you.'

'And does that mean, now we're friends, that you're going to stop piling your rubbish across my door?'

'No, of course not.'

'Oh.'

'Let me introduce myself, I am Mr Iqubal Fitzherbert De Castro; my name reflects the polyglot nature of our beloved Namibia. The names of these others,' he said, waving his hand vaguely in the direction of the young men, 'do not matter.'

'Harriet Tingle,' she said.

'Wait a second, Harriet Tingle . . .' He spoke in what she thought must have been Swahili to one of the young men who immediately left to return a few seconds later clutching something small which he gave to the head man.

'Here, now we are good neighbours, I have a gift for you.' Then, leaning forward, and taking her hand in his own he placed something in Harriet's palm then folded her fingers over it. When she looked down she saw that they now held her mother's brooch.

Toby typed 'surplus computer leads' into his Brother P-Touch 2000 Label Maker then pressed the 'Print' button. He watched as the slender label spooled out of the machine, next he chopped off the label with the built-in guillotine and peeling off the sticky back stuck it on to the front of a drawer in his office desk filled with leads for various obsolete computers that would never ever be used again.

Then he sat back wondering what to do next. One thing about being a drunk, empty hours had never been a problem when he drank because of course you filled them with being drunk. You never had to think what to do when you were out of your head and every decision you made seemed brilliant at the time though not necessarily afterwards. Sure his life was better in many ways now: he had his Brother P-Touch 2000 Label Maker for a start which he loved more than nearly anything else. He loved the Brother P-Touch 2000 Label Maker so much that he kept one at home and another here in his office, though he'd never told each about the other's existence in case they got jealous. Toby loved to figure out exactly what a thing was, then label it – already that morning he'd done the separate shelves in his cupboard, 'Rejection Letters' he'd printed out in rather nice black on silver, then switching to black outline on white he'd typed 'Refusal Letters' and 'Lost Research Application Form Letters'.

Then just as suddenly his fragile, happy mood dissipated; it occurred to Toby that if he could just figure out what precisely his feelings were for his sister-in-law and label them, then maybe he'd feel a bit less miserable such a lot of the time. He had no doubt that his recent agitation was connected with the sudden and unexpected alteration in Harriet's appearance: who'd have thought Big Fat Hat was a stunner underneath all that blubber? Then perhaps the label should read 'Confused Feelings Created by Relative's Sudden and Unexpected Beauty'.

Looking back, Toby realised that he'd succeeded for quite a long time in deliberately not noticing what was happening to Helen's sister but when she'd come round to the house to babysit the other night, when she'd done that little turn in front of him in their hallway, turning and twisting her wonderful body, he could no longer ignore the fact that over the last few months his sister-in-law had gone from being a huge fat ugly blob to someone who was on their way to looking absolutely ravishing. He'd genuinely thought he was going to faint in the hall like a Victorian lady.

So maybe the label should be 'Sexual Desire for Close Relative Like in Family on Leeds Council Estate'. It wasn't just her appearance though. That was only a part of it, though certainly her features were beautiful – her caramel skin flawless, her eyes sparkling and bright, her black hair lustrous – but more than that there was a wild brave energy about her now so that it seemed as if her whole body was lit up from inside with a powerful lamp.

Toby thought mournfully to himself that you could say he'd been uniquely unlucky: 'Unique Situation – Not Your Fault At All' might be a good label for the situation. What he meant was that he loved the way his wife looked, it was her remarkable beauty that he'd fallen for in the first place, but then that was sort of the problem because suddenly he'd been presented with a taller, fitter, less smug, more amusing, more intelligent replica of his wife. How many times did that happen? It was like when Porsche brought out a new car that sort of looked like the car they'd been making before but was better in every way: bigger engine, twin turbos, electronic traction control, fifty airbags, MP3 player. He'd often thought that if you'd bought the old car just before the new one came out you'd be really pissed off. Well, that's what had happened to him: he'd been stuck with last year's Porsche and the payments would last for another fifty years.

It occurred to Toby that Helen's beauty wasn't her, it wasn't her nature, it was just a thing she possessed. Her beauty had made her seem wonderful to him but now he wondered whether he'd been looking at his wife for eight years without actually seeing the personality underneath it. All of a sudden he wasn't sure whether she was a nice person or not. The way when she came into a room she acted like she was doing it a favour, for example. Harriet didn't do that. Harriet was like Helen but because she hadn't been pretty all her life she wasn't so extraordinarily full of herself. Harriet didn't feel that people should just pay attention to her without her saying or doing anything the least bit interesting ever.

Then his emotions did a handbrake turn and his mind was flooded with what he thought was a sudden and overwhelming love for his wife and what certainly was a great pity for himself.

How could he say these terrible things to himself about Helen? She was the loveliest thing in his life, she was a brilliant mother and a devoted wife, a successful career woman. Instead, massive feelings of resentment towards Harriet engulfed him. What was she doing suddenly changing like that? He'd been happy before and now he wasn't and he could date his unhappiness from the point where he'd noticed the difference in Harriet's appearance, so that proved him being unhappy and mad was his sister-in-law's fault.

Toby knew he was definitely unhappy and mad because the voices, the tics, the mannerisms had got worse. He wasn't sure but he was worried that he'd started yelling stuff out without knowing he was doing it. On the tube or somewhere else public he'd drift off on a train of thought about his problems, trying to figure out what was bothering him and what to do about it, then suddenly he would sort of return to his body to find all the other passengers staring at him and the faint echo of a demented sound ringing in the air.

He'd started to see sex everywhere too, struggling to hide sudden erections in a way he hadn't since he was a teenager. The few centimetres of flesh that girls began to expose at this time of year sent his mind boiling. In his calmer moments he feared that there was going to be a generation of young girls who were going to have terrible kidney problems in later life due to the delicious little slivers of skin on their rounded stomachs and curved lower backs that they showed off to the frigid air. Not to mention a generation of sexually deranged middle-aged men.

In addition he feared he might be revealing the turmoil going on inside his head to Helen. The previous evening they had been watching television.

'*Allons enfants de la Patrie . . .*' Toby sang as usual as the theme music for the main news bulletin faded then abruptly he couldn't stop himself shouting, 'Another bloody pregnant weather girl!'

'What?' Helen asked, looking up from her magazine.

'That girl there doing the weather, she's pregnant! Lots of them are, newsreaders, traffic women, weather girls, they're always up the duff one after another. I bet there's all these satanic orgies once they're off the air. All these young dollies naked, spread out in an X shape and Michael Fish going round dressed as a goat impregnating them.'

'I think Michael Fish has retired.'

'Well, some other weatherman then!'

'What's the matter with you?' Helen asked.

'Nothing, well, I dunno, maybe I do feel a bit funny.'

She said, 'Maybe you need to get more exercise, like my sister.'

'Yeah, exercise!' he gurgled. 'That's the thing! Like your sister!'

Finally alone in his office he picked up his Brother P-Touch 2000 and slowly tapped into the keyboard, 'Bloke – Completely Fucked by Impossible Situation'. Then he printed out the label, peeled off the backing and stuck it to his forehead.

7

Years ago in her late twenties, Harriet had owned a little Morris Minor convertible car. That's who she thought she was back then, a big fat girl, huge tinted brown glasses, crocheted poncho, knitted hat on her head, driving around in a comedy clown car with the pram top down, parp! parp! Had loved that dumpy little car though. Since it was a fragile classic, unsafe on the streets, 'Marcus' had to be kept parked in a lock-up garage, one of about ten built around a square on a piece of land alongside the railway tracks on the other side of the little railway station. One day, intending to take a drive to Suffolk to attend a concert at the Henry Moore sculpture centre, on turning into the garages she found her way blocked, disorientatingly, by a big caravan with net curtains and pottery shepherd and shepherdess figurines in the window. What had happened was that during the night several families of travellers had parked their caravans on the square. Every metal door of the garages had been ripped open and the cars inside had already been gutted down to their entrails. As she came to where her Morris Minor was parked a traveller child was crouched defecating inside it.

Staring open-mouthed at this violation of her property, she was filled with the familiar feelings of impotent anger and rage that she felt most days but she was also surprised to detect a hungry sense of envy that fizzled alongside it. She thought that to be so careless of the feelings and property of others must be a wonderful thing – such freedom! Harriet imagined that nobody in those caravans kept a list of all their friends' and acquaintances' hat, shoe and ring sizes so they could buy them the perfect anniversary present, none of those travellers had ever biked anybody over an extra large muffin basket, not one of those tinkers had ever spent all day carving a birthday card out of a potato. Of course the travellers didn't have friends and acquaintances: they only had their tribe and anybody outside it could go get fucked but they seemed happy enough with that. In the past she'd been obsessed with not upsetting not just the people who were important to her but total strangers as well. That situation was changing – since starting Li Kuan Yu Harriet seemed to care a good deal less about the opinions of others: she wasn't yet with those travellers ripping open people's lock-ups and shitting in their cars but sometimes she thought she was getting there.

Remembering her little Marcus (whom she'd never been able to look at again no matter how many times he'd been steam cleaned) made her think that it was time to get a new car. Up until then, Old Fat Harriet had owned a bland little beige hatch-back made in Malaysia and called something like a WeeWee One Point One SPLX, which she always drove as if she was taking her driving test right there and then. This sad, self-effacing little vehicle did not in any way suit New Thin Harriet, so one day in March she part-exchanged it for a big silver Japanese 4 x 4 pick-up truck with a crew cab. She wasn't sure how she'd be able to manage the finance payments on this enor-mous thing – but New Thin Harriet put the problem out of her mind. Being careful with money, paying off your credit card every month, watching the pennies, buying reasonably priced food down the street market rather than grabbing expensive deli-cacies in tiny jars and tins from all-night delis, seemed like the sort of thing a big, ugly, fat girl would do.

The truck she drove as if she was a character appearing in a film, swiftly and with confidence, often not looking for a parking space but simply leaving it outside wherever she was going just as they did in the movies. One day in north London picking up some material for a repair, Harriet parked her truck on a patch of waste land, a decommissioned petrol station awaiting re-development, conveniently sited opposite her destination. Returning twenty minutes later she found a battered green metal clamp attached to the front wheel along with a sticker demanding one hundred and fifty-eight pounds for somebody to come along to remove it.

In a fury she called the mobile phone number on the sticker, a man's voice told her to go to a cash machine and get the money, then to wait for somebody who would be along to release her vehicle sometime within the next month and a half.

After returning from the money machine, unable to contain her frustration, she phoned Patrick. It struck her as she was punching in the numbers that she'd never called him before except on dojo business but seeing as most of Helen and Toby's friends spent a huge amount of the time at dinner parties whinning about speeding tickets and traffic lane cameras and getting clamped she expected him to do what she'd been forced to do hundreds of times – that is to half listen to her moan on and on about the terrible iniquity of it all and throw in the odd sympathetic comment.

Instead, after she'd explained what had happened, he said coldly, 'So you parked on this private land and got clamped?'

'Yeah, that's right and it's so unfai—'

'So what are you complaining about? You were drawn into a trap by your enemy and you were defeated.'

'But it's not fair.'

'Did the Founder moan about it not being fair when Scots Billy crippled his father?'

'No, but . . .'

'Did the great swordsman Sasaki Kojiro complain when the Samurai Musashi defeated him in a duel?'

'Well, he had no head so he couldn't but I suppose he wouldn't have, no . . .'

'So I want you to go to a place called an HSS Hire Centre where they will rent you a thing called an angle grinder; with it you can cut the clamp away.'

'But won't they have a record of my car's number plate so the police can track me down and do me for criminal damage or they can find out my address and send the bailiffs round or worse?'

'True. You could attack the man as he's taking the clamp off, wait until he bends down then use Panda Bear Breaks Neck on him, but then you'd be in even more trouble with the police. See, I wouldn't have that problem because I don't exist.'

'What do you mean?' Harriet asked, suddenly panicked. 'You're not my imaginary friend, are you?'

'No . . .' he laughed. 'I mean I don't exist to the authorities. My car's reg is a clone, I don't have a bank account, the flat's still in me parents' name, I don't exist, so my enemies can't find me.'

'That's not much use to me, what am I supposed to do? I can't disappear myself in the next half-hour.'

He was silent for a second before asking, 'How many times did Sifu Po say we should jump from the branch of a tree?'

'Nine.'

'And how many branches are there on the tree that we jump from?'

'Four.'

'Four, that's right.' Then he rang off.

Eventually an old white Ford Escort van pulled into the petrol station. It parked blocking the exit and a bulky man of about fifty-five, shaven-headed and gone to fat, climbed out. Hitching up his sagging jeans, he crossed to where she stood, a big bunch of keys in one beefy, scabbed hand.

'You got the money?' he asked.

'This is a rip-off,' Harriet said.

'Yeah, yeah,' he replied in a bored voice used to hearing a thousand complaints and excuses. 'It's clearly notified that you risk clamping if you park here.' It struck her that his voice was the same as the one she'd heard on the phone.

'Where?' she asked, looking around.

'There,' said the man, pointing to a sheet of plywood with some writing on it screwed halfway up a brick wall some distance away and half concealed by a bush of wild buddleia.

Harriet walked over, stared at it hard then returned and said, 'That sign is written in what I think might be Tagalog, a language that is only spoken in certain remote parts of Malaya, Micronesia and Papua New Guinea.'

'Yeah, well, that's your multi-cultural Britain for you, innit?' the man replied. 'Still means you have to pay up, love.'

She angrily handed over the cash but as the man bent to remove the clamp she saw a stained, streaked length of aluminium pipe lying on the ground. Harriet walked over to it, picked it up and began, slowly at first, to practise Broom Staff Pike Stance.

As the pole tumbled and swished through the air inches from the head of the clamp man kneeling by the front wheel of her truck, he began to look uncomfortable and confused, dropping the big bundle of keys as he fumbled with the brass padlock. Then, to her mind, he began to look a little afraid.

As the man finally straightened to his feet, holding in both hands the separate bits of his money-making slabs of metal she, continuing with her stabs and sweeps, suddenly said, not looking at him, 'I want thirty-six pounds back.'

'What?' he asked. The man was pinned back against the front of her truck and unable to reach his van without walking into the orbit of her swirling metal pipe.

'I want, four times nine, thirty-six pounds back, to erm . . . buy a friend some flowers.'

'Eh, what?' he asked again, his eyes distracted by the pole hissing inches from his face.

'C'mon,' the woman said, moderating her tone a little but not discontinuing the ferocity of her movements, 'it's your firm, isn't it? It was you I spoke to on the phone so you're getting one hundred and fifty-eight pounds for basically nothing and you can afford to give me thirty-six pounds back.'

The man was forced to duck as she swiped the pole through the air behind him.

'Are you happy with your life?' she asked.

'Is that a threat?'

'No, no, no, I'm just asking, is this the way you imagined things turning out, is this what you thought you'd be doing and are you satisfied with it?'

'Yes. No, well, no, I have suffered a couple of bouts of moderate to severe clinical depression.'

'So maybe you should change your life. Do you think your life might be to blame?'

'Possibly. I've done some things . . .'

'So perhaps you should change it, not totally at first, but gradually in small pieces, a little at a time . . . to show that you are in charge of events, in charge of your life.'

'And I could start by like giving somebody thirty-six pounds back from their fine?'

'Yeah, if you felt that that was the right thing to do.'

'To buy flowers for a person in hospital?'

'That's right.'

Harriet did not immediately lower the pike to her side but continued lunging and poking for thirty seconds then stopped. The man took out a wad of notes from his back pocket and handed back to her some of her own money with a sigh. Returning, she thought, wearily to his vehicle he threw the separate bits of clamp in the back where they crashed on to a pile of others. As the man squeezed himself into the driving seat of his van Harriet felt a sense of exultation sweep through her.

The clamper started up the Escort then drove in a big sweeping circle to exit the petrol station. As he passed her he slowed down and said out of the window, 'You want to be careful with that stick, love, you could hurt someone with it.'

'I will be,' she called after him.

When Harriet had left college in the early nineties and taken her first job working backstage on *Miss Saigon*, one of the male dressers had been in a band called the Sissy Robots. At that time, making one of her vain attempts to break away a little, to forge new friendships outside those she was related to or had been at college with, Harriet went along to a few of their performances. On Sunday nights, taking unfamiliar tube lines and buses with strange numbers like the W 564 and the K6 N, to scout huts and Oddfellows Halls in distant suburbs, she discovered that the Sissy Robots were pretty much as bad as any band could ever be. Really it was unlikely that a trio of drums, xylophone and vocals singing songs inspired by the poetry of Mario Vargas Llosa were going to be any good. Yet as she sat in three-quarters-empty basement theatres in Wood Green and eighth-full town hall function rooms in Lewisham, an amazing fact struck her: the band, appalling as they were, actually had a following. There was a married couple call Rex and Marion who would drive in from Colchester to every one of their performances, there were three girls all called something like Lucy who followed them from place to place and were planning one day to run the Sissy Robots fan club and there was a futures trader from the City called Robert who went so far in his dedication as to hire the band to play at his wedding where they were so bad that his wife left him on the honeymoon. The intensity of the clique's interest in the Sissy Robots, the late-night talks on the phone discussing their preferred track off the band's cassette, the comparing of favourite gigs and also the sneering dismissal of competing musicians allowed these few fans to imagine that the world outside their little circle was almost as taken as they were with the band, instead of utterly indifferent.

The S Robots as the fans referred to them even had a record out with posters that the illegal flyposters plastered over all the streets in the neighbourhood of the record company headquarters but nowhere else. The three Lucies bought a hundred copies each and Robert made everybody at Citibank phone in to Steve Wright on Radio 1 to try and get their single on the playlist, but even with all this effort the song only got to number eighty-five in the charts so the record company dropped them and the band split up.

The lesson Harriet took from her brief period following the Sissy Robots was that people seemed to need something, anything, to believe in and that more or less anybody could have a following. Any ideology no matter how mad could attract disciples, any leader of anything could have themselves a small band of devout believers. She thought at that time that she would never fall completely for anything herself – all right, she might attempt all kinds of diets and miracle cures for fatness but there was a tiny part of her that always hung back and she had been proud of that part. What she hung on to (along with the fat and the high blood pressure) was the idea of herself as Harriet the Sceptic, the big fat girl who no matter what else was wrong with her you couldn't fool.

Even with Li Kuan Yu, even though it was transforming her appearance, she still couldn't quite become a true believer: unlike the others at the dojo it was impossible for her to completely swallow all the stuff Patrick told them about the triple-burner chi-raising techniques of Tummo Tibetan monks who would test their powers by sitting naked in the snow, covered by freezing wet sheets, mastery being demonstrated by the number of sheets that could be dried solely by the internal heat the monks were able to generate. All the others seemed to believe this story was true and that it actually happened, while Harriet just found herself thinking if it was feasible she'd be able to cut down on her laundry bills. To her it was just a story, a fable, an illustration of a hoped-for sort of martial arts fairy world where such things were truly possible.

All the same, she was beginning to think that maybe it was time to give up this long-held scepticism. 'Right, Harriet,' she said to herself, 'it's time, for once in your life, to let go of all these doubts and quibbles that have been holding you back. It's time for you truly to let them all go.' While going through her Li Kuan Yu form, during freezing early mornings in the park or late at night in her echoing upstairs room, dust exploding from the floorboards as she stamped and turned, her dreams were of what it would be like when she became finally a true believer. There was no knowing what wonders awaited her on the other side of cynicism.

Unfortunately she had to admit to herself there were going to be casualties. There had always been one big area of disagreement that had existed from the earliest days between her and Patrick. Though he was immensely pleased with her progress and proud of his new student, the single grain of discord dividing them had been her continuing friendship with Lulu and Rose: Harriet's sifu couldn't understand how somebody who was proving themselves to be so adept at Li Kuan Yu would still choose to hang round with a pair of drunken harridans like those two. He told her time and time again that the true martial artist only mixed with others who were totally dedicated to their training. 'Stick with the winners, win with the stickers,' he told her. Patrick was also constantly hinting that for those who went deeper into their fighting style there were all kinds of magical things that would be revealed, so maybe now it was finally time for her to cut Lulu and Rose off and become a true disciple.

A few years after stopping work on *Miss Saigon* Harriet had bumped into the dresser in Brent Cross Shopping Centre. He'd gone bald, amazingly had a wife and son and told her he was now in a band called Metal Negro. But she hadn't ever seen any posters for Metal Negro anywhere.

'Isn't Southport all posh people and multi-millionaire footballers playing golf?' Toby asked Helen the first time he drove the two sisters to their parents' shabby little terraced house in the dull flatlands behind the railway station.

'Not all of it obviously,' Harriet mumbled from the back seat where she was lying sprawled out, her legs twisted into the backs of the front seats.

'But this is just like Swindon where I come from.'

The Percussionists Licensing Society had given Toby a very smart black diesel Saab as part of his job package. The front wheels sizzled over the sand in the gutter as he parked in the frosty, salty, seaside night air amongst the papery, dented Hyundais and Protons lined up along the narrow pavement.

The three of them had met four and a half hours before, at closing time, outside the Admiral Codrington. Harriet had spent the three and a half hours before that inside the pub with her two horrible cronies but Helen had been at home reading so just needed to walk round the corner from her flat. Together they'd driven north.

The phone call from the next-door neighbour telling Helen that Mum had been taken to hospital had come a little while before. In the shiny grey leather front seat of the car, as blacked-out England slithered past, Helen was so upset that everything felt sort of weirdly disconnected and floaty, but oddly there was still the air of an outing hanging over their trip. At a twenty-four-hour petrol station, after he'd filled up the car, Toby bought two big bottles of Tango, a supersize bag of Skittles and a CD of the number one hits from the eighties. As they hissed up the dark motorways the two of them sang along to T'Pau, Culture Club and Duran Duran while Harriet slept sprawled out, snoring, in the back.

Somewhere near Stafford in a comfortable period of silence Julio Spuciek said to her, 'You know, fifty years ago you would not have had to make these terrible journeys – a girl of your class would have lived round the corner from her mother, married a man from the neighbourhood, cooked a roast dinner for her aunties every Sunday, had few decisions to make and been nearby when a crisis arose. Or, on the other hand, you might have lived in India or somewhere else colonial with your husband who was a sergeant in the sappers' (Julio got some of his ideas about England from the works of Rudyard Kipling) 'and the trip home would have taken six weeks by steamship so the whole emergency would have been resolved by the time you got there.'

Either way she wouldn't have had to endure these trips. There were times when Toby couldn't drive them and then they had to submit to the human rights violation that was inter-city train travel. The railways had been privatised a few years before and at the same time as the carriages of the many companies were being painted in gorgeous colours they began to rot from inside like the tropical flowers they had come to resemble. Helen remembered one train they were on, its heating going full pelt though it was a sweltering summer's day so that Harriet was cascading with sweat, locked wheels outside Crewe Station and stayed there for three hours. Out of the window Helen and her sister were able to examine in detail the Co-op supermarket car park, the weird train-spotters looking at them looking at them and the hulking red-brick hotel like a pirate ship with jolly flags flapping and cracking from its round medieval towers.

Whenever Helen saw a movie in which the happy ending was that the super-intelligent working-class girl received the letter telling her she'd been accepted for the swanky academy, she always wondered whether that really was a happy ending. The likely outcome of the girl getting her education would be that in the future even if she loved her parents dearly she wouldn't be able to stop herself being bored and petulant with them and though she struggled against it she wouldn't be able to resist finding her home town tedious, tiny and peculiar.

She and her sister had hardly returned home at all until their mother got sick so that now, after London, Southport reminded Helen of a model village in the window of a toy shop, with its neat flowerbeds and fountains that actually worked and the little electric trains that ran to and from the not-at-all toytown of Liverpool.

When they weren't visiting the hospital she would take Toby into town or to the beach or the pine woods; she showed him the Art School which Marc Almond had attended and Lord Street where, standing by the war memorial, she told him how the Protestant Fanatics – the Orange Lodges – from Liverpool, Londonderry, Belfast and Glasgow would parade every July 12th, marching pipe bands and pallid slum boys dressed up as King William precariously balanced on white cart-horses.

As they wandered the wrought-iron-canopied streets of the northern seaside town and looked out over its grey sands Helen wasn't sure then what she felt about Toby; certainly intensely grateful to him for all his help, but unsure whether there could be anything more between them. She'd had men crazy about her before, but his level of looming devotion could sometimes verge on the disturbing.

Mostly she took Toby out in order to get away from her parents' uncomfortable furniture. Every time she sat down on Mum's couch immediately there would be a terrible and familiar pain running across her shoulders. It became automatic for Helen to wonder at this point where working-class people like her parents managed to buy their furniture. In the homes of her friends in the big city there were big comfy couches that you sank into as if falling into a delicious sleep, whereas all the sofas and chairs in their parents' and their aunties' homes seemed to contain hidden pointy bits, like mantraps devised by the Viet Cong, that forced the sitter's spine into all kinds of uncomfortable, sometimes permanently damaging, contortions. The couch in the living room of their childhood home had an upholstered ridge that ran along the back of it that forced anyone sitting on it into a hunched simian posture. Maybe, Helen thought, that was some marker of the difference between her generation and her parents'. For Helen and her friends, their furniture was like their lives: it was there to look good and be lounged on, to be enjoyed in a sensual fashion, while for Mum and Dad and everyone they knew their couches and armchairs were uncomfortable and full of hidden pain and would eventually leave you bent, broken and in great physical distress.

In the big upstairs room above the shop, as hail battered on the windows, eager to begin her new life as a devoted disciple and thirsting to know more, Harriet said to Patrick after practice, 'We never really talked about it but you said you came to Li Kuan Yu because of your fear of death.'

'That's right,' he replied, only half concentrating as he had been balancing in Golden Cock Stands on One Leg for the last twenty minutes.

'So I assume meeting Sifu Martin Po and learning Li Kuan Yu helped you conquer your fear of death, did it?'

Her expectation had him replying that he had learnt some great, marvellous calming wisdom from Sifu Po but instead he said, 'In a way, yeah, you could say that.'

'So can you tell me how?'

'Sure, because quite soon I'm not going to die.'

'No, well, hopefully you're not, especially with all this

exercise and healthy living, you'll live a long life, so no, you won't die quite soon, no.'

He look directly at her for once, before putting both feet on the ground and stating, 'No, that's not what I'm saying, Harriet. What I'm saying is that in five months' time I will be immortal.'

'Really, immortal you say?'

'Let's stretch our tendons,' he suggested. So they squatted down facing each other (rather like a traveller child crapping in a car) while he went on, 'Yes, there's nobody at the dojo knows this, not even Jack.'

'No, well, I can see why you wouldn't want to tell them.'

'At first in the early days as I worked with the Founder my depression felt a little better but I was still haunted with thoughts of death. The idea that when I died all my memories, all my thoughts would be gone, I still couldn't take it. That Patrick would be gone as if he'd never existed and if Patrick was gone and nothing remained of him then what's the point of doing anything because it would all evaporate. Everybody dies and nothing remains. Death was coming to get me.

'Even with the help of Sifu Ma Po for three months some days I thought of nothing else and it was all I could do to lift me head off me chest. Finally, as I say, I began to feel a tiny bit better with all the exercise, better chemicals getting into my system and so on. Yet the Founder could see without being told 'cos he was that wise that there was still a great fear of dying at the heart of me. So one day he brought me to the oak tree in the park and told me more of his story.

'After Martin Po killed Scots Billy and ran to London he took many jobs, working in the laundries of lots of smart hotels, a waiter in the Won Kei restaurant in Wardour Street known to have the rudest waiters in Chinatown, runner for the illegal bookmakers controlled by the 44K Triad. In the free time he had he worked solely on perfecting the form of Li Kuan Yu. When two years had gone by Martin had saved a little money, not wasted it on drink and gambling like so many other Chinese. For some time the Founder had, he told me, been thinking about his time when he had been a child growing up in the Walled City.

'Sifu said he was thinking about a place all the kids knew – and avoided – a red door with a curved yellow portal, temple style, at the bottom of a dead-end corridor on the fifth level at the very epicentre of the Walled Citadel. Even the Snakeheads left its inhabitant alone. There were a pair of porcelain guardian dragons on either side of the studded metal door and a pot burning incense. Behind this door was supposed to live a Master. Some said the Master was an Immortal – over one thousand years old – who lived on the blood of young virgins and grave-yard herbs, both of which he picked up at night by adopting the shape of a Flying Fox. Others stated he was a much younger Taoist priest – only a hundred and twenty years old – who owed his longevity to a yin/yang alchemy of breathing techniques and T'ai Chi Ch'uan which also gave him limitless fighting powers. Yet others claimed he was himself the leader of the most powerful Triad group in Hong Kong, the Tyan T'ai Pitchfork Clan. Some swore the Red Door became invisible during police raids. Others told the tale of five youths from the notorious Jonny Swords Triad gang who tried to rob the Master and were found blinded, with massive internal bleeding and insane with terror.

'In 1976 Martin Po, the Founder, returned to the Walled City, found his way to that door, knocked and asked the Master to teach him how to fight.

'The Master had heard of Martin from his time as the best student ever at Blue Cloud Mountain but he still had to take a test; he was forced to hang upside down, bat-style, suspended by his insteps from a beam inside the Master's temple for twenty-four hours, and only then would the Master agree to take him on.

'For the following three years Martin spent most of his waking hours at the feet of the Master or standing on one leg in a corner. He learnt Taoist breathing, the reverse of the normal inhale-exhale cycle, cat-walking on burning coals, a hundred and twenty-two deadly and semi-deadly pressure points, the ancient five animal exercises, hurling anathemas and a lethal cookbook of poisons made with readily available herbs and spices. These were things Martin had expected to learn but one November morning the Master showed him a copy of a book called *The Jade Monk's Doorway of Light*. The book was written in Mandarin and contained many odd diagrams, but the main text was concise and talked of Ching which is essence or sexual fluid, Chi which is breath and Shen which is spirit. At its core was a poem which the Master told Ma Po to "memorise and recite nine times a day".'

Then closing his eyes Patrick recited:

Listening not to me but to the account
It is wise to agree all things are one
They do not comprehend how in differing it agrees with itself
A backward-turning connection like that of a bow and a lyre
Unapparent connection is better than apparent
But of this account which holds forever men prove
    uncomprehending
Both before hearing it and when they hear it.
But nine hundred times nine the morning recitation shall rise
Nine years shall see the release of the spirit
Rising above the accounts of men

The immortal shall be mortal
The mortal immortal
Living their death
Dying their life
Soul has a self-increasing account

Holding its jade in special esteem
If you do not expect the unexpected you will not discover it
Cold things grow hot, the hot cools, the wet dries, the parched
    moistens
Souls are exhaled from the moist things
For souls it is death to become water
For water death to become earth
But from earth water comes into being
From water soul

Keep close to yourself the moisture of your body
Neither depleted nor injured
In your fastness shall come life
The cure is within you
In a nine-year spirit shall fly.

Then Patrick opened his eyes and, his voice returning to normal, he said, 'Do you see what it's saying, Harriet?'

It didn't seem to be saying anything as far as she could tell but then many Oriental things were a mystery to her, she was never sure whether their poetry was deeply profound or just stupid stuff broken into short lines. 'I think so a bit,' Harriet said, 'but just explain it to me a little better.'

'Martin told me that basically this poem means that if a man doesn't spill his fluids for nine years – you understand what fluids I am talking about here? The Ching fluids – and does the breathing exercises and all other exercises and becomes wise in the fighting arts then it will lead to a reversal of the ageing process and to immortality.

'He said that Taoists believe that when a human is born they acquire a hun spirit and a p'o spirit. Hun is yang which is heaven, immortality, and p'o is yin, which means earth and mortality. If we have lived within the nine emotions of the desire realm – that's all the stuff I was talking about – then at death when hun and p'o separate our spirit will leave through the top of our head and we will return as one type of ghost which is called kuei. That's the the hun type which is immortal. If we have spilt our seed and not lived within the nine emotions of the desire realm we will become a p'o spirit. This type doesn't survive very long and soon becomes a dead ghost which is no good at all. If you are a hun spirit after some time you can locate a p'o spirit which has just died to unite with to return to earth and try again.

'You can't believe the effect this had on me, Harriet – at that instant all my fear of death disappeared because I was being told of a way not just to live a longer time in this realm but a way to be immortal. It was eight years and seven months ago that Martin Po told me this. If I can hold on to my fluids for five months more then I will never die. I will live a long, long, long time and even if I'm killed by somebody my spirit will be hun. At the moment of death it will leave through the top of my head, I'll hang around for a while then return to earth.' He paused for a few seconds, his brow rippled with thought. 'Of course what Martin Po told me means I can't have sex ever again or you know . . . do anything else along those lines because I can't spill my seed. Still, on balance I'd say it's definitely worth it.'

Harriet asked herself what was that familiar sensation she felt? It was the plummeting feeling experienced the first time she'd launched herself from the branch of the oak tree, except this time there was no excitement, only the sick sensation of falling. She said to him, 'But you won't be able to have children or anything.'

'Oh,' he replied nonchalantly, 'that's not a problem. See, I've got a kid. By a girl in the flats, we were married and everything but Martin told me I had to leave her as she was getting in the way of my Li Kuan Yu.'

'So,' she enquired, 'erm . . . if I keep doing my Li Kuan Yu and stuff, after nine years will I achieve immortality then?'

'Oh no,' he stated, smiling in a patronising way she'd never noticed in him before, 'you women don't have fluids, do you? Fluids like men? All the adepts agree the only way women can live forever is through having children. That's why they're always trying to steal men's vital fluids so they can make babies and become immortal themselves.'

'Oh, right . . .' Harriet said, nodding. It figured. Apparently immortality, at least according to the laws of Li Kuan Yu, was one of those things, like being an ayatollah, a chief constable or a football commentator, that men had reserved solely for themselves.

Before she had known anything about martial arts she'd sort of vaguely assumed that if you became an adept then there was naturally a calm serenity that came with it, like that guy on the TV show *Kung Fu* or Jackie Chan who seemed like a happy sort of bloke despite all the injuries he'd picked up in his career, but her experience had shown her that that wasn't the case – if anything it seemed to make people more angry to know that they could pulverise most others in the world.

In Harriet's case her feelings of calmness towards her neighbours had not continued; as promised they had carried on leaving their rubbish on her step and instead of learning to live with it in a state of serene acceptance as she'd hoped she might, she'd taken to stuffing it back through their letterbox, sometimes dousing it in petrol and setting fire to it first. The Namibians next door didn't match her escalation but they didn't stop leaving their garbage piled against her front door either.

During all the things she had been through, all the wasted, sorry, bitter years of her fatness, it had always been a massive consolation to Harriet that at no point had she been dumb or desperate enough to turn to religion. No matter what comfort other people took from their idiotic illusions at no time had she

sought to believe angels were looking after Mum and Dad, not
for one second had she trusted that everything happens for a
reason and God was smiling down on his creations. Harriet
swallowed none of that shit. Nuns with their silly smiles,
Christian politicians with their simpering certainty, mullahs with
their stupid hats and their absurd conviction that they were
going to some sort of theme park in the sky because they avoided
eating pork sausages and got up and down five times a day
pointing east ('Excellent aerobic exercise, being a Muslim,'
Patrick had said), to her these and any other religious believers
were simply cowards, trembling curs terrified to look into the
black void that awaited all of us.

She'd found it really moving when Patrick had told her about
his despair, she'd thought, Here's a person like me. Now to
discover that he believed this crap about his spirit leaving
through the top of his head and not spilling his fluids made her
feel furious towards him. Harriet had trusted him, let him make
her jump out of a tree, turned to him for advice and all the time
he'd been someone who'd put his faith in the existence of ghosts.

She told herself to calm down, that whatever nonsense Patrick
had in his head at least Li Kuan Yu had wrought a huge change
in her and she should be grateful for that. In turn this idea cast
her down again as the thought struck her that she was stuck
doing it now forever, knowing for certain that without her
constant training the fat and the fear would be back within
hours.

'So, slut, you were going to dump us, were you?' Rose said.

'I might not have done it.'

'Throw us out like a used dishcloth,' Lulu said.

'Well, I didn't do it, did I? So everything's fine. Except I'm
stuck with a loony for the rest of my life.'

Lulu said, 'It's not just the religion shit though, is it, darling?'

'How do you mean?'

'Well, nobody gets as angry and hurt as you're getting over somebody turning out to be not quite what they thought or believing something they don't agree with. The truth is you're all bent out of shape because Patrick was telling you that he was definitely unavailable.'

'Don't be stupid. I've never fancied him.'

'I don't know how much fancying has to do with why we fuck anybody. We've all done it out of politeness, loneliness, power, because he told you he had a KitKat in his pocket that he said he'd let you have half of. It had been one thing for you to choose not to do anything with him but for him to say he can't have sex with you or he'll lose his magical powers – well, I'm thinking that might have been all right for some big fat bird but that isn't you any more, is it, darling? You're beautiful, Harriet, now and nobody tells you they can't fuck you or they'll die.'

Harriet wasn't prepared to grapple right now with the truth or not of what she was being told so instead asked, 'Do you think it's easy for him?'

'Not doing it?'

'Yeah. I mean we spend a huge amount of time at the dojo grappling with each other and I have to admit that's making me horny such a lot, all the healthiness and the constant touching and that.

'I mean that's another difference between the average civilian and the martial artist, as if they weren't weird enough already: your ordinary person gets touched maybe by their partner in just a few places a couple of times a week but at the dojo we spend such a lot of the time with our noses in each other's armpits and our legs wrapped round each other's heads.'

'And don't forget the danger,' Lulu said, 'that always makes people want to fuck, to reproduce before they die.'

When Patrick told her about not spilling his fluids she had actually asked him, 'Don't you find it a strain? You know, being certain that you'll never—'

'No, no, no,' he replied a bit too quickly, 'after all, when the prize is immortality it's easy to bear.'

But she didn't care what Patrick said, she was certain he found it a strain. She knew she did and at least she was able to attend to her own needs when the pressure became too much. He couldn't even do that.

8

Though it was early April north-westerly winds blew and they generally brought sleet with them. The skies remained cold and grey and Azerbaijan Fried Chicken became Kennedy Fried Chicken. When Harriet practised in the park the air above her remained as featureless and mute as a switched-off television screen.

This was when Toby's behaviour usually began to calm down a bit because they had come to the end of the time of year he hated most, what he referred to as 'Static Season'. None of his friends and family had ever gone into the meteorological reasons for it, only that from late December to the end of March people would hear him yelling, 'Christ! Shit! Cripes! Bugger!' as he touched virtually any object and got a vicious belt of static electricity from it: balls of blue sparks would leap across the gap between the lock and Toby's key as he tried to get into his house; stroking a cat could result in him being jolted like a suspect in a South American prison and he told Harriet that he'd once managed to get a very nasty electrical shock from a loaf of bread. From Christmas until Easter Toby approached hand-shakes with a strange limp-wristed, mincing skip and a hop which convinced those who didn't already think it that he was gay. In the many restaurants and bars of the new chromed metallic sort that he and Helen frequented he always tried to open the doors using only his shoulders, causing many angry exclamations, buffeting aside creative directors, publishers and commissioning editors. Luckily these were not the sort of people who started fights simply because they were hit in the face and quite badly injured by a swinging door barged by a big mad-looking man's shoulder. Large department stores, with their nylon carpets and central heating, were Toby's particular Abu Ghraib prison; shop assistants were constantly jarred from their daydreams by his yelps of pain as the metal racks and the nylon clothes threw jagged shards of lightning at him. Harriet had once heard him plead with Helen not to force him to accompany her when she was buying clothes during the early months of the year but she couldn't understand what he was going on about. 'I get shocks too, Toby,' she said, 'I just don't make a fuss about it.'

This year although the balls of blue lightning had gone away there still seemed to be some other thing deranging him. Harriet wondered what it was. She thought that she'd read somewhere that when medieval peasants got static electric shocks they thought that they were being stung by invisible bees, but she didn't think that was what was bothering Toby.

The green plastic pitch next to the community centre in Pointless Park on which Toby was playing football could at the wrong time of the year be particularly bad for static. Under the hot white floodlights, every time he made a tackle in the winter months there would be a flash of electricity between him and the other player and he would feel the familiar sharp stab of acidic pain. Fortunately that period was now over and he was able to play with his usual giraffe-like abandon. Over the years his team mates had come to realise that Toby's form improved dramatically in the later part of the football season though they didn't know the reason why. Suddenly as the game went up to the other end of the field he noticed Harriet watching him play. Her fingers were laced through the chain link fence that surrounded the pitch and her body pressed against the sagging barrier so that the plastic-coated wire cut a diamond pattern into her breasts and stomach.

Toby became so confused at the sight of his sister-in-law that his play became erratic and finally he got given a yellow card and had a penalty awarded against him by the referee for fouling two players on his own team.

'Toby, you twat!' his team captain shouted at him. 'You're playing as if it's February!'

Harriet was waiting for him at the gate after he'd showered and changed out of his football kit and into his street clothes.

As he walked towards her with a team mate Toby said, 'See that girl over there on the other side of the pitch waving to me?'

'Yeah.'

'Don't you think she's the most fantastically, unbelievably beautiful creature that you've ever seen in your entire life?'

The other guy took his team mate's question as a serious enquiry between men so he stopped and, staring hard at Harriet, looked her up and down. Finally he responded meditatively, saying, 'Well, she's got a nice body, obviously fit, decent-sized, shapely tits and all that, nice face, but I'd have to say on balance no, Toby. I mean she's very pretty, I'll give you that, but to me a woman's got to have . . .'

'Why was that bloke staring at me like that?' Harriet asked when he reached her.

'He thought he knew you from a camping holiday he went on in Cornwall last year.'

'By the look he was giving me it was a Turkish brothel he thought he knew me from.'

'Well, he did say it had been a very nice holiday.'

As Harriet embraced Toby he gave her a kiss on the cheek and there was the feared crackle of static on his lips.

'Ow, bastard!' he shouted.

'Sorry, Tobes,' she said, 'static?'

'Yeah. Should have stopped by now.'

'But you're shivering as well. Why are you shivering?' she asked, rubbing his arm. 'It's not cold.'

'I'm OK, maybe a bit of a chill, that's all.'

'So anyway,' Harriet said, 'I just thought I'd come and say hello, see how you're doing and take you for a drink, maybe have something to eat at the Cod. I don't seem to have seen so much of you lately. You used always to be dropping into the shop with tears you'd made in your clothes. What's happened? Judging by those flying tackles you made, your physical co-ordination hasn't improved any. Aren't the players wearing the same shirts as you supposed to be on the same side?'

'That's it,' he replied, 'you women never understand the rules of football.' Then Toby said, 'Look, can we go somewhere else, not the Admiral Cod?'

'I suppose so,' she replied. 'Are there other places?'

'One or two. Let's walk for a bit.'

She linked her arm through his and they strolled out of the neighbourhood of the park. Crossing over the bridge that spanned the railway line they walked up a hill lined with Turkish greengrocers and bakeries, their open shopfronts strung with light bulbs throwing their light on to high piles of colourful fruit and vegetables. To Toby it seemed strange to be able to buy a melon this late into the night. Next they passed through an area of dark and silent Edwardian villas until finally they came to another parade of shops facing another park almost identical to their own neighbourhood amongst which there remained an old-fashioned Italian restaurant: a restaurant that served food that was authentically Italian in the same way that a Swiss roll was authentically Swiss.

The restaurant's manager had written some samples from its menu on a chalk board outside on the pavement and had put a little circle before each of the dishes, making it appear as if the board was singing the praises of the food in a Puccini opera:

'O Seafood Salad,' it sang, 'O Spaghetti Pomodoro, O Veal, O Tiramisu.'

Normally a restaurant of this type would be completely invisible to people such as Toby and Harriet, their senses being tuned to stripped floorboards, metal lamps and exotic floral displays – that said 'food' to them. It was only perhaps because his perceptions were in a heightened, disturbed state that the pink tablecloths and breadsticks of this place were visible. 'Let's go in here!' Toby shouted.

'Where?' asked Harriet, looking around.

'Here, this place, here,' he said, indicating the Italian restaurant.

'S'pose so,' replied his sister-in-law. Then, deciding to treat it as a lark, she said, 'Yeah, why not?'

A waiter who'd been standing in the doorway looking mournfully up and down the street darted inside as they approached.

'Have you booked?' the manager asked as they came through the door though the place was almost completely empty except for some elderly couples and two old men in blazers eating alone.

'No, but if you could fit us in . . .' Harriet asked, smiling winningly at the man.

He simpered back at her and the couple were shown to what Toby imagined was the best table, in the window overlooking this other park, where they ordered pâté from a tin and then pasta with sauce that came from a big jar while they drank nasty red wine.

'This should really be in a flask wrapped in straw,' he said of their drink.

'I think the straw's on the inside, in the wine,' Harriet replied. Then she asked, 'You drinking again then, Tobes?'

'Oh yeah,' he said casually, 'I can take the odd drink, you know, it's not a problem for me or anything.'

'Really?' she asked, sounding unconvinced.

'No, I don't think drink was my main problem.'

'I dunno – you were pretty mental when you drank.'

'What, more mental than I am now?'

'Differently mental, it was like you drank to dissolve yourself.'

'Well, I've got it under control now.'

'OK, if you say so.'

'Yeah.' Then he suddenly said, 'Hat?'

'Yes?'

'I've been thinking about being tested.'

'What, like doing your GCSEs again or a degree from the Open University?'

'No, not that. See . . . last week I was at one of those dinner parties we go to all the bloody time and found myself staring one by one at the people there and wondering who the hell they were. Do you ever get that?'

'No, I don't think so. Everybody I know seems a bit too real if anything.'

'No, right . . . So anyway, I dunno, before I married Helen I'd had my own gang of mates, great mates like Tom Tom Culshaw.'

'The one who's now the life and soul of a Zimbabwean prison?'

'That's the fellow. But I let them go, my good mates, and allowed Helen to drift me towards this crowd. Do you know, over dinner they spent nearly three hours moaning about the number of parking tickets, speeding points and fines for driving in bus lanes that they'd picked up in the last week or so?'

'You'd think they'd stop doing it seeing as they get fined all the time.'

'No, that never occurs to them. But all this moaning, Hat! They acted like getting a parking ticket was the worst thing that had ever happened to them. Then I realised – it was! The shock of getting their car towed away after they'd parked it outside the American Embassy was the worst thing that had ever happened to them! How can you have a sense of proportion if that's true? It made me think how people in the past had such tough lives: wars, disease, strikes, those stiff celluloid collars.

'These days we aren't tested . . . well, men mostly I'm thinking about. I suppose women still have childbirth, but in the past men grew up through being proven in conflict. Hundreds of years ago, right? Life was really short. A man's life expectancy was something like fifteen. There were admirals in the navy who were nine years old yet they still thought nothing of setting off on a trip to Australia that took four years just to look for a particularly interesting kind of grapefruit. Four years which was maybe a fifth of their life! Nowadays we expect to live until we're a hundred and yet we go mental because the tube train stops in a tunnel for five minutes – and we try and sue the authorities for compensation for the emotional distress they've caused us. In times of conflict a man can find out exactly who he is. So I got to wondering whether there might not be some way in which I can test myself, find out what I'd do if faced with a crisis. Is there some war or something I could go to? There must be some sort of adventure . . .'

'Like what?' Harriet asked. 'I mean all that stuff like rollerblading along the Great Wall of China for charity is a major cause of third world debt, you know.'

'Er, right,' Toby said. Really, he had only told her all this stuff to make himself seem more exciting. He had perhaps had a distant sense that some day he might go off on an adventure but not any time soon, yet her taking it seriously made it seem real.

Harriet reached out and took his hand. 'I think that's great, Toby,' she said. 'You find your adventure.'

'Well, you've been an inspiration to me, Hat, you've turned your life around so why shouldn't I do the same?'

'Yeah, you go for it, Tobes,' and she reached out and embraced him, getting tomato sauce on her breasts as she leant over their food. Toby would have liked to order another bottle of wine but decided he couldn't in front of Harriet. Looking across the empty tables to ask for another bottle of mineral water instead, he saw the entire waiting staff of the restaurant clustered in a greasy-jacketed clump in an alcove by the dumb waiter smiling fondly at him and his date. In the 1960s when it had first opened, a new and exciting venue of previously unimaginable sophistication, this restaurant had regularly been the location for such scenes, agitated handsome men and beautiful women holding hands, suddenly embracing and talking wildly about important things. It gladdened the hearts of the elderly Portuguese who ran the restaurant to see a young couple re-enacting such a romantic scene now, making them wonder whether their doomed restaurant might not be coming back into fashion.

In the last couple of years a plague of street furniture had broken out around the park: there were at least four pedestrian crossings around the boundary road each with its own set of flashing, beeping traffic lights, zigzag lines either side of the traffic lights, black and white stripes traversing the road, nasty little fences around the crossing and uneven red pimpled tiles for blind people to trip over on the pavement facing the crossings. There were speed bumps of random height down the centre of the road with white triangles painted on their lumpy surfaces, on poles at the roadside there were signs saying the many things you weren't allowed to do and the times when you weren't allowed to do them and there were so many more lines, yellow lines, double yellow lines, red lines and more white zigzags painted on the road surface. The disruption in Harriet's field of vision was such that sometimes, like now, it made her feel as though she was in the first stages of a migraine, there was

a foggy pressure in her head and a fuzziness around the edges
of her vision. She'd walked Toby back to his house and was
now heading home herself. Reflecting on their conversation, she
reckoned it had been safe to encourage him to seek adventure
even though the idea of Toby going on any sort of expedition
would be catastrophic. Luckily there was no chance of him
giving up his easy comfortable life and looking for any kind of
dangerous test that would stretch him: she loved Toby but had
no illusions that he was the kind of man to go on an adventure and, more than that, her sister would never let him.

To get away from the fuzzy lines Harriet crossed the road
and cut through the north-west corner of the park, heading
towards her building. She wondered whether Toby fancied her
– maybe he always had done and that was why he'd spent so
much time in her shop, but right away her mind, snapping shut
on this disturbing thought like a mousetrap, told her she was
probably making it up or he maybe only had a little crush on
her that would fade in a few weeks. Temporary relief swept
through Harriet and the indistinct terror that she might have
caused Toby to fall in love with her receded. It was as if a plane
had suddenly dropped with a thump and a peculiar high-pitched
noise had come from the engine and then the cabin crew rapidly
began putting stuff away even though they were in the middle
of serving dinner. Yet after a few tense seconds level flight
resumes and slowly the cabin crew recommence serving dinner
but their faces are like wax and their smiles are printed on.

Dark trees in the attitude of preying insects hung over her
path and through their budding branches she fancied the
welcoming lights of her upstairs room could be seen, the
battered punchbag hanging from her ceiling like a tubby suicide.
From the brittle undergrowth there came a rustling and sibi-
lant voices that whispered foul obscenities but she didn't feel
the least bit afraid.

*   *   *

As well as great financial wealth donated by rich, bird-loving patrons, Warbird also owned a good deal of property. Indeed, though Helen kept it quiet, they held the leases on a number of shops in the parade facing the park, including the hardware store. Recently that lease had come to an end and the general improvements in the area coupled with the new, wealthier people moving in meant that the charity was in a position to raise the rent considerably. Unfortunately this was more than the old tenant could afford to pay so, after a brief fight, they were sadly forced to evict him.

Hauling Timon in her wake, as Helen passed the boarded-up shop and the tattered remains of a defiant banner Mr Sargassian had made, she heard that funny businessman who walked around the neighbourhood shouting into his mobile phone.

'The bastard landlord's turfed the old tenant out even though he's been there thirty years. They say it's going to be a Starbucks,' he yelled, 'or one of those places that sells sandwiches made in India the day before and then packed into triangular little packs by people with cholera.'

'I have a responsibility to raise as much money for the charity as I can,' she told Julio Spuciek in her head. 'If Starbucks pays us more than Mr Sargassian I have a duty to the talking birds to evict him.'

'Of course you do,' Julio replied.

She then continued just so he understood, 'But sometimes do you think people who campaign for things can have too narrow a view? That while we might set out with good intentions our vanity and competitiveness might occasionally take over?'

'No, no, you mustn't think like that, Helen. There may be others in your field who act like that but your motives are pure, you are a good person doing good work.'

'You're right of course, Julio, you are such a comfort to me.'

The reason Helen was dragging her son towards the community centre was because it was half term and the local mothers – well, the middle-class ones who cared about such things – had demanded that the council pay for a puppet show to be put on in the playground. They paid their taxes so the least the council could do was to occupy their children for a couple of hours.

At one end of the playground a tall thin stage made from faded fabric had been set up. It was a bit like the Punch and Judy tent she remembered from the seafront at Southport but wider and with a very un-Southport painted backdrop of sinister forests and mountains. There was already a fair-sized audience of expectant kids gathered there, wriggling about on folding chairs, eager to see the show. Helen heard one pale, six-year-old triplet in perfect imitation of overheard adults say to the child next to him, 'How post-ironic, a puppet show.'

The other replied, 'I was thinking if I like it I might option the film rights. My godfather's chairman of British Screen and . . .' The child never finished the sentence as its tentative attempt at adulthood fell away and childish terror returned, its silent mouth hanging open, because to the accompaniment of strange discordant accordion music the first of the puppets shambled on stage. Helen thought she had not seen a more malevolent wooden figure since the time she'd asked a market stall owner in Port au Prince, Haiti, to show her her best, most authentic voodoo dolls, the ones that the tourists didn't usually get to see.

'This might not be so bad after all,' Timon said, smiling.

The wooden figure turned in a jangly way to the front of the stage and began screaming at the audience in a high-pitched voice about the environment and the end of the world. By the time it finished its first speech several of the formerly sophisticated little ones were weeping in terror. Helen too was staring, suddenly realising where she had seen the puppet before. Though one of its glass eyes was splintered and milky, its mouth torn back to the jaw and one of its legs was little more than a splintery stump, it came to her that she was looking at the wooden face of Señor Chuckles, beloved marionette of Julio Spuciek.

At one point in her twenties Harriet had gone to see a proper old-style Freudian psychoanalyst with a place in Hampstead, a couch, substantial wallpaper, African sculptures on the shelves and everything – she thought there was probably a place like a pub outfitters where they bought this stuff, so identical did their consulting rooms seem. Following her first consultation the fee he'd asked for, written out with a fountain pen on thick creamy paper, was breathtakingly high. He also told her she was supposed to visit him three or four times a week. When Harriet asked this man why it cost so much to sit and talk to him he said it was part of her therapy, that in order for her to take her treatment seriously the fee 'should sting a bit'.

It seemed very convenient that these medical men had actually managed to work it into their ideology that they not only got to charge her a huge amount of money but they could pretend it was part of her treatment. She imagined if it was proved conclusively that her mental healing would be helped by them giving away treatment for nothing they wouldn't be so keen to promote that theory.

A little while later the psychoanalyst, accurately spotting Harriet's dogged reluctance to commit herself unquestioningly to anything, suggested that the best way for them to overcome this crucial, crippling inhibition might be for her to dress up as a jockey and ride him around the consulting room.

Patrick didn't charge as much per session as the Freudian but it still stung a lot. He continued to charge one hundred and twenty pounds a week for her three private lessons, plus another 'general fee' of sixty pounds as he called it for all the other work they did together. She'd hinted at a possible reduction but with echoes of the analyst he had said that an important part of being a disciple was making a financial contribution to what he called 'the cause'. Harriet felt a twinge of suspicion but had to admit he didn't seem to be spending the money on himself: apart from his little red hatchback car he appeared to own virtually nothing. The few clothes Patrick possessed were worn in strict rotation and a number of these items had visited her shop for mending on several occasions, for free of course. The one time she had seen inside his flat, though it was incredibly clean, it appeared to contain only a solitary office chair, a television, a computer balanced on a milk crate and a single mattress on the floor serving as his bed and it smelt rather horribly of what seemed like sour milk and turpentine.

Harriet felt spending so much money wouldn't have seemed as bad if her business had been going well. Certainly more men and a few women seemed to be coming through the door with holes in their clothes but this was balanced by her losing several big contracts with West End theatres due to late delivery. The truth was she just found it harder and harder to repair holes: whatever therapeutic purpose it had served seemed to have gone. Harriet hadn't realised how important her work had been in keeping her sane. Once invisible mending had been a refuge for her; when the world had been full of fear she had been able to submerge herself into her work like a diver sinking down to the ocean floor so that as she drifted deeper the anxiety floated away.

Now she no longer felt fear, the urge to invisibly seal up holes had evaporated. Not that fear had been replaced by serenity as she'd hoped. When she had been Fat and Ugly Harriet she had found consolation through telling herself that there were many things in the world that clearly weren't for her. Now, however, there was a terrible hunger for nearly everything.

*　　*　　*

Helen stood fidgeting in the playground as a stream of nannies and au pairs collected the weeping children and Julio Spuciek was shouted at by the unnaturally thin woman who organised children's events in the borough. In the weeks since seeing his face Helen had more or less convinced herself that she'd been mistaken. But now the thin, bearded man, at least thirty years older than the person yelling at him, who turned his unhappy brown eyes to the ground as the angry woman's words ripped through his ancient overcoat, could be none other than the person who'd lived inside her head since she was a young girl.

'I've never seen the children so frightened!' the council's children's entertainment officer bellowed. 'And some of them have been to *Shockheaded Peter* four times.'

'I'm sorry,' Helen heard Julio whisper in accented English, his voice sounding almost exactly as she'd imagined it would – sort of sad and smoky. 'It's not me, it's the puppets, they have their own minds. Señor Chuckles is angry because of the destruction of the forests and . . .'

Feeling breathless, on unsteady legs, she approached the council woman and touched her lightly on the arm. 'Melanie,' she said, 'would it be possible to have a word with you?'

'Oh, hi, Helen, yes I suppose so . . .' Then she turned back to the puppeteer. 'I haven't finished with you. Honestly, some of those kids have never heard such swear words even though a number of their parents are stand-up comedians . . .'

The two of them walked a few paces off. They had met a number of times at functions and for a while Melanie had worked for another talking bird charity. They knew each other to be professionals in the world of public service and as such were always happy to perform little favours for each other – speed up planning applications or jump waiting lists for serious operations, that kind of thing.

Melanie asked, 'What can I do for you, Helen?'

'The puppeteer,' she said, 'you shouldn't be so hard on him, Melanie; he was tortured.'

'Not by the children he wasn't,' Melanie replied unforgivingly. 'Well, maybe those Yentob twins, they're capable of anything but really it's not the little ones' fault.'

'Still, he was a political prisoner.'

'Oh, they all say that when they get into trouble . . .'

'No, I know he was genuinely, it's Julio Spuciek. The Edge wrote a song about him, don't you remember?'

'Not Sting or Bono?'

'No, the Edge. But please give him a break.'

'Oh all right . . . I suppose so.' She gave a testy glance towards the old man still standing head bent. 'I'm only doing this for you though.' The two of them returned to the old puppeteer.

'Mr Spuciek, Helen here has asked me to go easy on you because of your . . . past but I have to tell you that if I have anything to do with it you will never be employed by this council again.'

There was a pause while the man nodded, then raising his eyes he asked, 'Do I still get paid?'

'What?'

'Do I still get paid?' he asked again from under his grey-flecked eyebrows.

'Get paid? I was given to understand you were doing this performance as part of your two hundred hours' community service order.'

'No, madam,' he said, straightening and looking her in the eye for the first time. 'I am a professional performer and a professional performer needs to get paid.'

'Oh, I . . .' Melanie paused and then seeing no point in making a fight of it said, '. . . suppose so, though I can't for the life of me really see why. I'll put a cheque in the post.'

Julio Spuciek and Helen watched the council woman's angry, bony bottom depart. 'Could I possibly buy you a cup of coffee?'

For the first time he looked directly at her and smiled a sad rueful smile. 'Madam, that would be most kind but really I have to pack up my puppets and then there are other things that . . .'

'Oh, I can wait,' she said.

'No, really, you don't need to . . .'

'Yes, really, I can wait. It's not a problem for me.'

'Shall we go there?' Helen asked, pointing to the pub, certain that he would enjoy some nice risotto or a Barnsley chop on a bed of wilted greens, to fill him out a bit.

Before leaving the playground Julio had dumped his puppets into a big leather suitcase roughly in a tangle of strings and limbs on top of each other (Helen would really have liked to sort them out so they were lying more comfortably but kept quiet); they were with him now. His stage he'd folded with furious movements and thrown carelessly into a storeroom at the community centre.

'No, we should go there,' Julio replied, pointing instead towards the community centre café. 'The place here is where I like to go.'

Helen had to suppress a shiver of distaste as they sat down at a greasy Formica table.

'Are you sure?'

'Yes, absolutely.'

''Ello 'Oolio,' the woman behind the counter shouted. 'Coffee, is it?'

Helen ordered a KitKat bar for herself.

He said to her, 'I suppose I have to thank you for interceding for me with that ugly woman.'

'Well, she was being a bit unfair; in a way it was her fault for booking you, it's idiotic to assume a puppet show is going to be suitable for children.'

'Exactly.'

'It's like always assuming . . .' But she couldn't think of anything else so said, 'Señor Spuciek, I have always been a great admirer of yours since . . . since I was a young girl.'

She'd thought he would be pleased as she said this but he sighed, seeming to shrink a little. 'Ah yes, since you were a young girl, of course . . .' He paused. 'In the 1960s when I was a big star of the left in Argentina, an invitation came one day via the Communist Party for me to go to China to give talks and to do my puppet shows.' Again he stopped for a second, staring off into space. 'Nobody went to China then, it was easier to go to the moon than to China, what an opportunity! Also amongst my circle there was great sympathy with the ideas of the Cultural Revolution, you know. That you could turn vack the clock to a simpler life untainted by the corruption of egotism. Writers, performers, painters – individualists every single one of us – dreamt of creating a world free of egotism, I don't know why.

'Maybe because I was *simpatico* the authorities allowed me to travel around a little bit, with a minder of course but still . . . One day we were going to see a place where they made steam engines whether anybody wanted them or not and we passed a group of schoolgirls leaving their college when they all suddenly started screaming. For a second I was excited, thinking maybe it was for me, the famous revolutionary puppeteer; in that country at that time anything seemed possible. It wasn't for me though, the screaming, but vecause the young girls had seen this particularly huge poster of Chairman Mao Tse-tung travelling around on its own truck – the only behicle on the road. It was like film on the television about Elbis.'

For a second Helen was confused about who or what 'Elbis' was until she realised that like a lot of Spanish speakers he would sometimes conflate his 'V's and his 'B's.

'They were becoming hysterical over Chairman Mao – a fat old Chinaman with a vig wart on his face. I understood then that while situations may change the nature of people is fixed. Young girls they always need somevody at a particular point in their lives when they are developing . . . you know . . . in certain ways. In China during the Cultural Revolution because there was nobody else around they would get hysterical love and I guess touch themselves when they were alone to pictures in their mind of Chairman Mao, the vig fat old Chinaman who was putting their parents in prison.

'When I was picked up by the junta in '75 I got what I had always wanted: to become sort of an international political star featured in all the magazines around the free world, except of course to vecome that famous I had to be in a cell a foot deep in water veing veaten with a stick, so I didn't know about me being famous.

'Since they let me out in '83 following the war of the Malvinas, I have met a few of the ones who fell for me and they were all the same. Clever girls who thought they were a bit more intelligent than their schoolfriends. Clever pretty girls who didn't want to fall for Little Donny Osmond, so chose me instead – the poor tortured political prisoner with the soulful, brown eyes.' And here he did look at her, head lowered, with his big brown eyes and they were soulful still.

Helen felt like when she'd walked into a wall, numb at that moment but knowing that severe pain was on the way. The face of Jesus in the potato had just told the Mexican peasant girl that he didn't exist but was instead just random marks in a vegetable. To fill the space she asked, 'What was that about a community service order?'

'Ah, I have certain problems with anger,' Julio replied. 'Because of . . . you know, the things that happened to me. The prisons, the secret ones where I was taken were called Chupaderos. *Chupo* means to . . .' He made a face like a vacuum cleaner sucking up air.

'Oh yeah,' she said, 'like Chupa Chups.'

'What?'

'Chupa Chups, they're a Spanish sweet I buy for my son, a sort of round ball on a little stick, you suck them.'

'I can't have sweets I am diavetic, also have pleurisy from my time in the prison.' Julio was again silent for a while then said, 'There used to be this car that was only made in Argentina called a Ford Falcon. It looked sort of like an American car but also like a European car, voth of them from years vefore . . . old-fashioned, you understand? Just like Argentina. So when they came for you – the Triple A they were called: "Alliance, Argentina . . ." I forget the other thing – when they came for you it was always in these Ford Falcons and the cars always they had no numverplates. Everybody knew when they see this car outside your house that you are in vig trouble. I spent nine years in prison, until the junta collapsed after the war in the Malbinas. In a cell knee-deep in water. It was bery vad and worse – vy the time I got out I had gone out of fashion, yesterday's news, you know.'

He gave her a sad smile, while she suddenly remembered she'd left Timon outside playing with the Yentob twins.

'I've got to go,' Helen said, rising.

'Yes, well, goodvye,' Julio said.

'Perhaps we could meet again for coffee, at some time?' she said. 'For another chat.'

He replied with a shrug. 'Well, I am always at this place in the afternoons, this is my seat – Julio's seat, everyone knows it. If I am here I cannot stop you being here also.'

'Right, great. Afternoon coffee it is then.'

Unwrapping the silver duct tape that bound her son to the tree she heard the funny businessman saying into his phone, 'The Little One's got a funny look about her now . . .'

In bed in the early morning light Toby stared down at Helen sleeping next to him and wondered how well he really knew her. More and more he was having these feelings. Before they got together, whenever he'd seen Helen it had always been in a public place – down the pub, driving to her mother's house or at a party. When they first slept together, afterwards he had fallen asleep and on waking in the morning at first he thought that Helen had been replaced during the night by an exhausted child that had crawled into his bed for a nap. It was only when he looked down her naked body, when he saw with a start of guilt that the child had a splendid pair of breasts and a triangle of pubic hair, that he realised that it was Helen lying next to him but that their thrashing during the night or perhaps a wash had removed all her make-up.

Since then it had always disturbed him the way Helen would wake as one woman every morning then would paint on herself the face of an entirely different woman, like a police artist composing the image of a beautiful but hard-faced woman wanted for some crime of fraud or people-trafficking.

Harriet, on the other hand, had never thought it worth painting herself during her fat days and so didn't bother now and so to him there was only one Harriet and that Harriet, that true Harriet, was staggering-looking without the addition of paint. She had told Toby that for a while when going out she would apply a slash of lipstick, but her efforts had been so incompetent that she looked like she was applying for work as a clown or was somebody whose facial features for some reason needed to be seen clearly from a couple of miles away. Harriet said that men in the most ridiculous places such as the nave of Westminster Abbey or a hospital casualty department were constantly asking her how much she charged for a blowjob until finally she got the message and went out without putting on any make-up.

Toby knew that he had to change his life soon or go completely mad; he needed to make a plan right away but thinking about Harriet got him to surreptitiously stroking himself and fantasising about what it would be like having sex with his wife and her sister at the same time. At first he got really excited but pretty soon in his fantasy Helen started ordering everybody about, 'Harriet, you stick your head down there. Now, Toby, you put that in there . . .' So the whole thing dissolved as he returned to a troubled sleep.

9

Patrick had finally got an e-mail back from Martin Po but it hadn't in any way set his mind at rest. His sifu told him next to nothing about the situation over there and what little there was was written in a very confusing way, rambling and repetitious, with many outrageous claims and paranoid denunciations of those around him. Worse, at the end of the e-mail was a long list of things Martin said Patrick absolutely had to send out to him immediately. A few of them he thought he could buy in the shops: the two-way radios, canned food, medicines and the bandages, but others he had no idea what they were. Some of them like the night vision equipment and the poisons he thought might be illegal and one – a Dragunov 7.62mm sniper's rifle with infrared telescopic sights – he was certain was. Even if he knew where to get these things he was far from positive that he had enough cash to buy them. After all, he had handed over to Martin a great deal of money when he'd bought the dojo off him but he didn't seem to remember or care about that and always demanded more.

The tone of the e-mail only added to Patrick's worries. Driving around in his little red hatchback he purchased a couple of the easier items from a supermarket, a chemist and a pet superstore. He wrapped them up and took them to the post office. The cost of the postage even for these few objects was horrendous and the clerk told him that the package would probably take over two months to arrive at its destination.

*   *   *

Once Harriet had gone on a school trip to Paris; they must have visited all the museums and the cobblestone-circled palaces yet the only thing she remembered seeing was a slogan painted by anarchists on a wall near the Sorbonne to express their superior disdain for the tedious life of the wage slave: '*Métro Boulot Resto Dodo*' it read – 'Tube Work Eat Sleep'. Now it seemed to Harriet if you substituted dojo for *Métro* that was pretty much her life too. The need to keep up the exercise seemed constant: one missed training session and she immediately imagined she could sense her muscles slackening and losing definition. Since invisible mending failed to satisfy any need in her, repairs that would have previously taken a few minutes now required hours of work so that she was forced to be at her worktable on a bright Saturday afternoon. Apart from dojo and Dodo all other tasks never got done, she couldn't seem to find the time to buy herself any new clothes, for instance, but even if she did she wasn't sure Patrick would approve; it had been made pretty clear at the dojo that taking too much of an interest in your appearance was considered a distraction from the serious business of learning how to whack people more effectively. Unfortunately all Harriet had in her wardrobe that fitted her now was the stuff she'd worn when she'd last been thin, back at college in the late eighties and only just out of her teens. Catching sight of herself in a full-length mirror she thought she looked like some sort of female nonce just released from prison after a fifteen-year stretch.

From her shop window Harriet gazed gloomily at the park. The sun was shining brightly and the park bustled with people, entwined couples lay in the grass furtively feeling each other up. For the last few years the grass, trees and plants had been more or less ignored by the contractors who were supposed to come and regularly mutilate it, so while the place remained glum and sinister in winter during the spring and summer months it had grown to be almost pleasant.

This year nature having secretly gathered its forces staged a summer breakout, silver birch saplings that in the two or three years previously had lain in small cracks in the park's paths suddenly burst upwards splintering the concrete into powdery dust. Goat willow, bird cherry over a metre high and hawthorn trees hung heavy with white blossom, oak saplings sent out by the big tree in the centre suddenly stretched upwards. In the long grass native wild flowers ran unrestrained by pesticide, yellow cowslips and primrose burgeoned, while peacock butterflies flittered crazily between them.

Through the plate glass Harriet spotted Lulu and Rose rolling about on the grass, play-fighting with each other and drinking white wine.

Abandoning her work she got up and went to join them.

'You've stopped losing weight,' Lulu said to her as they lay on the grass, the sun warming their stomachs.

'Yeah, this is me now,' she replied.

'Christ, I wish it was me,' Lulu replied, running her eyes up and down her body, rather hungrily Harriet thought.

'We'd sort of hoped you'd go all stringy like Madonna,' Rose said, 'but you're hard yet still curvy where you need to be.'

'Fit, beautiful and able to fight more or less anybody in the world,' Lulu said. 'Not bad.'

'Still can't get a bloke to shag me though. I bet if I'd eaten even more and got really, really fat weighing thirty or forty stone then I'd have had my pick of all kinds of perverts.'

'I think the reason nobody'll shag you is because your clothes are an absolute bloody fright,' Rose said.

Leaving her two friends laid out on the warm grass starting on another bottle of white wine, she returned to the shop. As Harriet rose to leave, Lulu, looking around the park at the encompassing trees, the rippling grass and the nodding flowers, said, 'Funny, this place used to creep me out but now it seems sort of nice . . .'

Back at the worktable under the hot light she sat staring gloomily at a John Smedley sweater, one arm eaten by termites. The night before at the dojo for the first time she'd managed to land a couple of kicks on the side of Patrick's head. At first Harriet had felt wildly elated by this but catching a look at Patrick's wounded expression made her suddenly overcome with contrition, having to resist the urge to hug him and to kiss the livid marks that she'd just planted on his cheek.

The door of her shop opened and one of her next-door neighbours entered. He stood in front of her and gesturing over his shoulder with his thumb said, 'The old man wants to see you.'

'What, now? I'm busy,' Harriet grumbled.

'Yeah. You don't look busy.'

'I can't repair those inflammable tracksuits you lot wear,' she said, rising.

She locked the shop door behind her, then they entered the adjacent building.

The stocky young man tried to sit down on the stairlift but she placed a hand on his arm and said, 'Let's just walk up the stairs, eh?'

Grumpily he acceded and rose, and together they climbed the stairs to enter the big upstairs room. As before the older man sat at the centre of the room on his reclining chair. When she came in his face burst into a big, seemingly genuine, smile and he spread his arms. 'Ah, our beautiful neighbour! Please do sit down.'

Once Harriet had perched herself on one of the velour council-supplied couches arranged round the walls he said, 'You know I have been so longing to have a decent chat with someone intelligent such as yourself, these young men while they have their uses are not strong on conversational skills. So, Harriet, tell me what do you think of this Damien Hirst I read about in all the newspapers: a great artist or merely a dwarf for dwarfish times?'

'Well, I dunno really,' she said. 'Collectors certainly pay a lot of money for his work.'

'Yes, I see what you're saying, Harriet – that the avatars of society have given him and his ilk their imprimatur. But I still ask myself, where is the joy, the striving for magnificence? Hasn't art these days simply replaced the carnival freak shows of the 1930s? Instead of a two-headed calf, the curious go and see a pickled shark, a painting made from elephant poo or an unmade bed.'

'Yeah, I suppose, yeah . . . you might be right about that.'

'Ah, it is good to have such conversations,' Mr Iqubal Fitzherbert De Castro said. For a while he sat in silence as if mulling over the interesting things that had been said, then, adopting a less declamatory style, he asked, pointing towards her, 'Tell me, Harriet, what is that top you're wearing?'

'It's a T-shirt.'

'And who might that be who is on it?'

She had owned the shirt for so long that to her what was on it had become a collection of random abstract shapes without any meaning. She looked down at her T-shirt, pulling it out to see the figure printed in fading colours across her chest. 'Oh yeah, she said. 'It's actually a man made out of cheese kicking a football, his name's Señor Padano. I think Grana Padano is a brand of Italian cheese and it was the official hard cheese of Italia '90.'

'Ah, Italia '90. Gazza, Gary Lineker, Diego Maradona. I was in Canada then but we were all entranced. But excuse me for saying this, don't you think a beautiful woman such as yourself should be dressed in something, I don't know . . . more modern?'

'I guess . . .'

'Maybe you are wearing the T-shirt as some kind of retro fashion statement?'

'No, it was all I had that was clean.'

'Oh, that is not right, not right at all. A woman who looks as you do should have some handsome clothes. Coincidentally I might be able to help with that. I was wondering whether you might not do me the enormous favour of coming to a party with myself and my associates one evening.'

'Me?'

'Yes, in the course of our business ventures we occasionally need to throw little get-togethers or visit nightclubs and such and the women we know are either too one way or the other if you know what I mean. To be frank, if we were accompanied by someone such as yourself it would boost our status.'

'You want me to go on a night out with you. Nothing else?'

'My goodness, certainly nothing else! But we would be happy to dress you in beautiful clothes that you could keep afterwards.'

Harriet knew that if she agreed and Patrick found out that she was staying out late at parties and wearing sexy dresses and hanging out with dubious Namibians he would accuse her of diluting her Shen or some such nonsense so she said, 'Yeah, sure, why not?'

Mr Iqubal Fitzherbert De Castro made a gesture with his hands and one of the young men went into a back room. He re-emerged carrying a dress in a transparent cover. Without looking at it, Mr Iqubal Fitzherbert De Castro said, 'This is a dress by Stella McCartney which, I think, though tight, will fit you perfectly; it is made out of oyster satin apparently. The matching shoes are suede and by Gill Wing – apparently Stella McCartney being a vegetarian only makes footwear out of plastic which seems odd to me. I always thought only poor people wore shoes of plastic but there you are. We would like you to have them to keep, of course, but also to wear when you come out with us.'

'That's very kind of you.'

'It is a transaction but I hope a happy one for all concerned.'

* * *

Toby and Helen had been getting ready to go out to the launch party for the Penrith Fairground Disaster memorial crafted by a famous sculptor. It wasn't in Penrith and didn't look much like a memorial, rather it resembled a Second World War tank trap that's been dipped in breadcrumbs and it had been built in a private square in Mayfair that you could only enter with a key. Of course nobody actually involved in the Penrith Fairground Disaster was invited since they would upset everyone with their horrible injuries and their constant crying.

However, just as they were going out there'd been a hysterical phone call from Katya; apparently two days before, their builder had removed the entire back wall of the house with a JCB and then vanished without a word so now they couldn't leave their home for fear of looters. They wanted Toby and Helen to go round to their place right away for an emergency dinner party.

'I had to drive the JCB back to the hire place,' Oscar said. 'I felt awfully butch. It's surprising how fast they can go, those things, and people certainly get out of your way.'

Katya gave her husband an annoyed look and said, referring to the builder while wringing her hands, 'I'm terribly worried about him.'

'Yes,' added Oscar, 'we've been round to his house with a Thermos of soup . . .'

'Soup, swoop, loop de loop!' Toby shouted.

'. . . in case he's ill in bed but there was no reply.'

If everybody in Toby and Helen's circle was feeling calm then the talk would be all furious anger about speed cameras, parking fines and getting clamped, but if there had been a disturbance of some kind in their little pond then to calm themselves down and reassure themselves that all was well in their world, for the whole dinner they would talk about the mini breaks, weekends away, skiing holidays, diving holidays and just plain holidays that they had planned in the next year or so. Harriet once said it was as if they thought if they moved around a lot from place to place then sadness wouldn't be able to find them. That was just Harriet being her usual life-denying snippy self, Helen thought. She liked that their friends had the money to go on holiday all the time.

One secret she'd always hidden from the crowd was that she, Toby and Harriet had had to find the money to pay for their own houses, whereas their friends all had their first flats or houses bought for them by their parents or via trust funds or with a 'little legacy from Granny'. Helen had always longed to be that sort of person. Of course Harriet didn't agree, she said that they were all just big grown-up children for whom a loft-style apartment on the river is another Christmas present like a Scalextrix set or a carved rocking horse but Helen had always found it sophisticated to be free of that kind of financial worry. She liked stability and order and certainty – was there anything wrong with that? Harriet might want to go transforming herself but it would all end in tears, of that she was sure. She tried to ask Julio in her mind what he thought about her sister's change of appearance but for once she couldn't get him to say anything at all: he just sat in a plastic bucket seat sipping a cup of bad coffee. Instead she found herself thinking about the real Julio, the one that she'd met in the park. ''Ello, 'Oolio,' the woman in the café had called to him, ''Ello, 'Oolio.' Helen wondered what he was doing, where he was going, whether he was thinking about her.

One afternoon after practice at Harriet's flat Patrick asked her, 'You know sometimes in a film they have a photo that was supposed to have been taken in the past?'

'Oh yeah?'

'Well, I always feel I know when a photograph was taken, not the exact moment or anything but the period, y'know? Like I say, sometimes in a TV programme or movie you see a picture that was meant to have been taken a hundred years ago or something. The film people have got the clothes of the people perfect and the haircuts and the pose and all that, the negative might be artificially scratched and faded, and yet to me there's always something of the modern world that gets into the photo; it's sort of as if the knowledge of all the things that have happened since Victorian times – jet travel, the war in Vietnam, a sex-change woman winning *Big Brother Five* – kinda seeps into a person's skin so that they can never look like they didn't know these things. I think I can even do the same for the backgrounds in these faked pictures. To me even the trees and the bushes in the false photo look kind of up to date, like the plants know all about jet travel and the sex-change woman winning *Big Brother Five* and all that too.'

When he'd told Harriet his thing about *Film 2006* that first time up in her flat Patrick remembered how fascinated she'd been but when he finished telling her about the photos she just said, 'Oh yeah?' again.

Harriet sat on the bed naked except for a vest and white pants while Lulu and Rose applied the last of her make-up. One of Mr Iqubal Fitzherbert De Castro's young men had called into the shop that morning.

'The party's tonight,' he said.

'Where?'

'Next door,' he replied, as if she'd be an idiot to think it would be anywhere else.

'Oh, right.'

When Harriet told Lulu and Rose about her date with the people next door her two friends had got really excited and insisted on taking her appearance in hand.

'It'll be like playing with our dollies when we were kids,' Rose said.

'Yeah, you'll be our Harriet Whore Dolly,' Lulu added.

'I'm not being a whore, they bought me a nice dress and I'm going to a party with them.'

'We're not judging you, darling,' Rose said.

'But you can't go around looking so scruffy, it's like keeping a Rembrandt in a shopping trolley – your beauty needs framing.'

Immediately they'd both cancelled all their work for the day. Earlier on in the afternoon Lulu and Rose had accompanied her to the hairdresser's where they had bullied the owner into taking care of Harriet personally. Urged on by the two women, he cut her long unruly hair and straightened it into a sharp and glossy bob through which he streaked red lowlights to enhance the natural sleekness that had been there since she'd got fit. Then they had a couple of glasses of champagne in a hotel bar where some businessmen in suits tried to chat them up so they let the men pay for the drinks then went to the toilet and left by another exit.

They took a taxi back to Harriet's flat where Lulu and Rose took her into the bedroom and emptied their make-up bags on to the duvet and began to paint her face. Rose took a grubby sponge that had been lying at the bottom of her bag and used it to spread tinted moisturiser all over Harriet's face as a base, then the two of them started to describe what they were doing as if cooking an elaborate meal on television for a small child. Lulu said, 'I'm rubbing some Touche Eclat concealer by Yves Saint Laurent under your eyes to hide any bags and to make the area shine.'

Rose added, 'And I've been mixing up colours on my eye-shadow palette. I'm taking a pearlised pale pink eyeshadow which I am applying to your eyelids starting next to the edge of the lashes and blending to the outer corner of your eyes.'

Next Lulu said, 'I'm blending and smudging a brown colour with my finger underneath your eyes to give a sexy smoky effect.'

Together the two of them applied double-lash, full-volume mascara which automatically curled her lashes. Then, taking a side each, they rubbed liquid tinted cheek colour blended into the apples of her cheeks and brought up to highlight her recently revealed sharp cheekbones. With one finger Rose rubbed Clinique one hundred per cent red lipstick on to her lips, making them appear full, moist and luscious. Finally Harriet's two friends dusted her cleavage and arms with Guerlain gold powder, making her skin sparkle.

'There you go,' Lulu said, stepping back 'you don't look like a whore at all.'

'Well, the highest priced kind of whore anyway,' Rose added.

A little while later after they had dressed her, smoked a joint together and had fallen into that uneasy period when the minicab's been ordered to take you home from the dinner party but hasn't arrived yet, the entryphone buzzed. Descending the stairs with unsteady steps, feeling like she was walking on a pair of stepladders rather than high heels, Harriet opened the door to one of the young men dressed in a shiny dark grey suit, while behind her, peeking out from the bend in the stairs, Rose and Lulu sniggered and whispered like mice behind the skirting board.

'The boss sent me to come and get you,' he said, and taking her arm led her next door.

In their hallway, seeing the chairlift, she said with a giggle, 'I think it's my turn,' and with some difficulty because of the tightness of her dress sat down on the pink padded plastic seat, strapped herself in and with a beep set off for the party.

As the chair slowly turned the corner up to the first-floor landing, it momentarily jammed with a shaking and a grinding of cogs so that Harriet found herself suspended high above the entranceway facing straight back down the dirty stairs, her legs dangling helplessly in mid-air, and the young man scowling upwards impatiently waiting for her to complete her ascent.

For a second Harriet felt a distant panic but the chair began again and Mr Iqubal Fitzherbert De Castro was waiting for her in the doorway of the big room.

'Harriet, welcome.' Taking her hand and helping her out of the chair he asked, 'I hope you didn't have any difficulty getting here?'

'No,' she replied, 'it's not too far to come.'

Leading Harriet by the fingertips into the big room, he said wistfully, 'Ah well . . . you know, it would have been nice for me to take you to some smart place on the river perhaps or a fashionable restaurant in the West End but it is unfortunately not possible at the moment for us to travel very far. This city we live in, it is all overlapping territories. Areas we mark out, over which we try to exert influence. A male cat, an unneutered one of course, has a territory sometimes miles across that he must patrol every night before he can rest. For me there are certain streets in our neighbourhood where I am welcomed with gifts, while there are others especially in areas of Tooting and Streatham where I could not walk without serious risk of being killed. You, on the other hand, would be free to parade up and down those same streets all day and nobody would bother you. So for the moment we have to hold our parties in this house.'

In the room, the lights were turned down low; seated on the low couches were various stocky men in tight suits. Harriet felt with a shiver their eyes run up and down her body like an MRI scan. She didn't know what food she expected these people to eat but on a couple of side tables were the same cheap supermarket quiches and wrinkled cocktail sausages that the poor serve at funerals. The drink was those stubby bottles of beer smuggled in from France and the litre bottles of whisky, vodka and gin from the same Pas de Calais drinks warehouse.

On the council-supplied couches the older men in suits sat nursing drinks, while in the centre of the room younger men, some in suits, others in expensive round-necked jumpers and cotton combat pants, danced with young women who were naked except that they wore gold shorts or black thongs and on their feet cheap high-heeled shoes. Though she kept her face blank, inside Harriet was feeling the same dark excitement as she'd experienced in the days after Patrick first made her jump from the tree. She'd heard that crack addicts were always chasing that first irretrievable high but here she was and she'd managed to get the exact same feeling back, except this time it was better because now she was the one in control. Harriet wondered whether she was right to be so thrilled by this decadence; maybe identical parties were going on all around the neighbourhood where young women detached themselves from those they danced with to be fondled by men old enough to be their accountants then led off to the bedrooms in ones and twos.

Though they all wolfishly looked her over, nobody tried anything with Harriet. She assumed they thought that she belonged to Mr Iqubal Fitzherbert De Castro. Yet after a little while it was clear to her why her presence would bring him status. Sure, she thought, looking them over, some of the girls, especially the younger ones, were extremely pretty, springy unmarked bodies, lush hair and so on but when you looked closely there was some corruption that spoilt all of them: partly it was a hardness, she guessed – the imprint of the dreadful things they had done in their short lives – partly it was their brittle insincerity and partly it was simple fear. The girls covered up their fear with spiky bravado or a brittle sexiness but there was still the whisper of the knowledge of what these frightening men might do to them on every one of their pretty faces. All these things, Harriet told herself, were missing from her own features, making her easily the most beautiful woman there.

She knew at last why she had learnt to fight and why she had put up with the rigours of training though it went against so much of her nature. Sure, it had made her cool to look at but if she ever tried to use the blows and strikes of Li Kuan Yu outside the dojo she'd most likely end up in prison. That wasn't it, here she was amongst these terrifying men unafraid – that was what her fighting skills were for: to give her the confidence to do exactly as she wanted. She'd tell Lulu and Rose tomorrow that she'd been accepted as an equal by a group of men who didn't care what anybody thought about them, who lived a life of danger and debauchery. She was free and she loved it. As the voice of Dr King often shouted at her over the hidden speakers in the lavatories of the Admiral Codrington, 'In the words of the old negro spiritual, "Free at last, God awmighty, free at last!"'

Mind you, there were other people to whom Harriet would not mention this night at all: Helen for one, Toby as well and, though she would be seeing him for practice in about six hours' time, Patrick.

Toby and Helen had been watching the television, a gardening show which they were both keen on: over the years they'd got a lot of interesting ideas for features in their own garden from it. About halfway through the show, though, Toby suddenly began shouting at the television, 'Tree surgeons! Tree surgeons! Tree surgeons! They're not fucking surgeons! How can they call themselves surgeons? They're just gardeners! Not even proper overall gardeners, they're just tree gardeners! A pack of jumped-up pretentious twats. I mean a mechanic's not a car consultant, is he? A plumber's not a drainage doctor! A window cleaner's not a . . . a . . . a window surgeon!'

Then suddenly he began crying.

'Toby, what's the matter?' Helen asked, touching his hand.

'Can't you see?' he said, glaring at her furiously. 'It's the tree surgeons, they make me so angry . . .'

'But I couldn't help feeling that it had to be more than that,' she told Julio, 'though God knows what.'

'It's another woman,' Julio stated bluntly.

She felt herself blushing bright red. 'Another woman! Toby?

You don't know my husband if you think it's another woman.'

'Well,' he said, 'I don't know of any other thing that would make a man so crazy.'

'No! No! No! Maybe in Argentina, with all that tango dancing and machismo and the cars with no numverplates,' she told him, 'but not here in north London. He has a very stressful job – it's probably something to do with that.'

Then it suddenly struck her that the Julio she was talking to inside her head was the old grumpy fellow she'd just met rather than the optimistic younger version. With an effort she conjured the younger man out of the shadows at the back of her brain.

'Of course it's not another woman,' young Julio told her, 'after all he is your husband as you say and you are such a beautiful woman, how could anybody ever tire of you?'

'Exactly,' Helen replied, finally satisfied with the conversation.

Yet the picture of the Argentinian that she held in her mind, an image of a handsome, long-haired, athletic youth, was constantly being overlaid like a faulty, juddering, antique videotape with the likeness of a mournful, bad-tempered, crippled old man.

The back of the mournful, bad-tempered, crippled old man was towards her as she sidled between the tables in the park café. It wasn't true, despite what he'd told her, that he was in there all the time. She knew this because she'd called in on several occasions at different times of the day and there'd always been somebody else sitting in the seat he'd said was Julio's seat. She knew in her heart that she should leave him be but there was a terrible compulsion within her to get him to conform more closely to the image of Julio she held in her mind.

She nearly missed him this time as he was at a completely different table by a window staring out into the busy, sunlit park.

'Oh. Hello, the lady from the puppet show,' he said, rising

formally from his seat to greet her, at least remembering who she was but not smiling fondly as she'd imagined he might. 'Please sit down,' Julio said, gesturing to a red plastic bucket seat opposite. 'You seem tired, it makes you look old.'

'Oh well, you know,' Helen replied, sinking down into the unyielding sweaty chair, 'it's my work. I work for a charity that looks after talking birds and there's been sudden tribal uprisings in Papua New Guinea. The mudmen, after like fifty years of being peaceable, have suddenly taken to raiding Western targets. They attacked the British Consul's summer residence in the Southern Highlands two weeks ago and they've taken his daughter's parrot, Polly Williams, hostage. They've already released a video of Polly pleading for his life and saying he'll be killed if the British government doesn't meet a number of insane conditions. We're trying to put together a team of negotiators to go out there but it's hard finding the right people, it's wearing me out . . . worrying about that poor bird, poor Polly. I guess that's me, I worry too much.'

'It occurs to me you all worry too much, all you women,' Julio said. 'You know when I am in the newsagent's I look at the men's magazines and there's hundreds of them about their many hobbies – trains, guns, cars, sailing, Asian women with enormous breasts. But then I look at the women's magazines and I see every one of them is to do with self-improvement, a constant stribing to make yourselbes one hundred per cent perfect. Lose weight, get fitter, speak Chinese, knit this, weave that. The men they are completely happy with themselves the way they are, the women all hate themselbes.'

'Yes, you're right,' Helen said, smiling – she loved it when he said wise things – 'we make it such hard work being a woman.'

Julio said, 'When I was a child we were quite rich, so my mother didn't need to work but still she couldn't enjoy herself. Instead she was always going to night school, taking classes and half learning languages but then becoming dispirited and giving them up because she hadn't become fluent in two weeks.' Here he paused. 'Then one day without warning she disappeared.'

'Oh, Christ!' Helen gasped. 'The Triple A!'

'No, nothing like that,' he replied, annoyingly smiling a tiny bit in a pitying way at her melodramatic interruption. 'It was long before the Triple A; even so the family were out of our minds with worry because she was gone for a month vefore we found out where she was. When we discovered her do you know what my mother was doing?'

'No.'

'Working as a chamvermaid in a hotel.'

'A chambermaid?'

'Yes, this woman who had servants to do any little thing she wanted was cleaning toilets and was happier than she had been for a long time. My mother told me afterwards when we got her home that it is many women's plan if things become too much for them, they think they'll run away and work in a hotel.'

'Why a hotel?'

'She said you are part of a community but have no responsibility. You get told what to do, a vit of a wage and somewhere to sleep. Working in a hotel lets you off all the endless effort of being a woman, all this responsibility to improve yourself.

'Yes, you are still caring for other people but at a distance, not too involved. Because that is the women's other thing: that they think secretly that they all are in charge of everything and have to work every hour of the day to make everyvody happy.'

IO

The pond in the park, once dead and stagnant, now fumed with life, starlings, sparrows and blackbirds came to drink from its soupy waters, house martins and swifts looped low over the black surface to scoop up the dragonflies and water boatmen that skimmed across the surface. Wood pigeons cooed in the trees, dandelions, daisies and native poppies spotted the emerald grass. Harriet said to her sister, 'The hardware store's closed down, I hear it's going to be a fucking Starbucks or one of those places that sells sandwiches made in India the day before and then packed into triangular little packs by people suffering from cholera.'

'Well, you know times change, if people can't pay the going rate for a property . . .'

'It doesn't seem fair.'

'I'd have thought you'd be all for change,' Helen said.

'You're confusing my personal growth with a guy being thrown out of his shop after thirty years: they're not the same thing.'

'What about Starbucks' personal growth?'

'What the hell are you talking about?'

When Harriet and her sister argued they never argued about what the argument was about. Like the superpowers in the last century fighting their surrogate wars over the territories of smaller nations, so Harriet and Helen would conduct furious rows over Vatican foreign policy or the correct way to make couscous with roasted Mediterranean vegetables, each of them adopting more and more extreme positions they didn't believe in, while the real disagreement was over Harriet being expected to babysit at a moment's notice or her dropping out of night school yet again. Sometimes it was unclear to both of them what the buried subject of the argument was: Harriet could remember one furious row over the ecological effects of tourism on the Great Barrier Reef where they both forgot what rabid views they'd started out with and had to end it with weak and confused agreement.

She supposed really it was always ultimately about the same thing – the upper hand.

'Anyway,' Helen said, 'I've always found when a shop closes, a few weeks later I can't remember what it used to sell. It's only sometimes when you need some nails or a copy of the Koran you recall there used to be a shop that sold what you wanted round the corner but then you go and get it somewhere else. And restaurants . . . think of the number of restaurants that have come and gone, you always know they're in trouble when there's a waiter standing in the doorway staring miserably up and down the street. That's not going to encourage you to eat there, is it? Like that old-fashioned Italian place up the hill, do you remember it? That closed down last week because it was useless.'

Toby spent most of that sunny Saturday buying a light bulb. In their house there seemed to be an almost infinite number of different light fittings: there were lamps that required small continental screw fittings, lamps that required large continental screw fittings, some that took small bayonet bulbs and some that took large bayonet bulbs, not to mention all the halogen lights that were almost impossible to fit with their fiddly little prongy things.

In the past he could have got what he wanted from Mr Sargassian's hardware store which apparently now was going to be a fucking Starbucks or one of those places that sells sandwiches made in India the day before and then packed into triangular little packs by people suffering from cholera. Now he had to drive into Wood Green, find a parking place, find a lighting shop, then had to phone Helen. 'What am I looking for again?'

'Large continental screw-fitting energy-saving pearl candle.'

'Right.'

'That's a small continental screw-fitting clear candle non-energy saving,' Helen said when he got it home.

'Oh.'

When Toby returned to Wood Green the lighting store was closed so he had to drive to a DIY warehouse off the North Circular Road. 'What was it again?' he asked his wife on the phone.

'Large continental screw-fitting energy-saving pearl candle.'

'Right,' Toby said but the DIY warehouse didn't have any of those so he had to drive back into Muswell Hill where he finally got the bulb in a shop identical to Mr Sargassian's hardware store. The store was two shops down from the boarded-up Italian restaurant; a temporary sign on the hardboard window said it was soon to be a fitness place called Pontius Pilates.

'Are you still looking for people to go to Papua New Guinea?' Toby asked Helen as she wobbled on their dangerous stepladder trying to fit the bulb.

'Yeah, why?'

'I'd like to go.'

'You?'

'Yes.'

'You?'

'Yes, why not me?'

'What is wrong with you, Toby?' she asked, descending the stepladder and facing him.

'My life's too comfortable.'

'Well, you could buy some shoes that don't fit, then, instead of going to Papua New Guinea. You'll have to camp, you know, in the jungle. I mean you don't like staying in any hotel that doesn't have at least three AA stars.'

'That's the point, I want to rough it, while doing something worthwhile, for talking birds in danger of course.'

'I know they're not up to strength yet,' Helen said doubtfully. 'I suppose I can have a word with the PNG group coordinator,' but Toby knew from her tone of voice that she wasn't convinced and almost certainly nothing would happen. On the other hand, he told himself, at least he'd tried.

Unlike 'her Julio' – the one inside her head who was nearly always courteous, polite and kind – the 'real' Julio could sometimes be rather too crude for Helen's taste. He said to her as she waited for them to leave his flat, 'You know what my theory of human evolution is?'

'No, natural selection maybe or the intervention of some all-knowing, all-seeing, essentially kindly spiritual entity like in the books of Paulho Puoncho?'

'That *pinche cabron*! No. My theory of human evolution is shit.'

'Shit.'

'Yes, shit. You look at other animals – their arseholes are right on the outside of their vodies so their waste comes out nice and easy but we have these vig fat vuttocks that trap our shit. I think maybe we evolved so we could wipe our asses and get away from the stink of our own vacksides.'

Not very nice and terribly negative; she knew he'd been tortured and everything, but still. This conversation took place in Julio's 'apartment', as he called it, actually a one-bedroomed flat on the Watney Estate. There were Spanish-style wrought-iron grilles over the windows and an ornate black security gate covering the front door which looked both vaguely exotic and sad at the same time and also looked stout enough to keep the emergency services out if there was a fire. Inside, the walls were painted in ochre reds and yellows, there were colourful posters with words in Spanish on them and on his desk piled with papers and magazines sat the corpses of his inexpertly mended marionettes Margarita, Tio Pajero, Abuela, El Gordo and Señor Chuckles.

As Julio moved about the flat preparing to go out, forgetting where he'd left his keys, patting each one of the many pockets of his trousers to ensure he'd got his reading glasses and his heart pills, the slow, jerky movements of his body reminded Helen of those badly repaired puppets. Surreptitiously she looked at his body but was disappointed that there were no apparent signs of torture on his stick-like arms projecting from the flappy short sleeves of his faded white shirt. Certainly he didn't seem to be quite able to stand up straight, his body etching a slender, shallow 'S' in the overheated air of the room; this she took as evidence of abuse at the hands of Fascists. Of course you saw lots of elderly people just like that down the post office and nearly all of them hadn't been tortured by a right-wing military junta so perhaps she was wrong.

A familiar but distant sensation had been dogging Helen since entering his flat and it was only now that she realised what it was: the feeling of being on a date. Trying to recall, Helen wasn't sure she'd been alone in a room with a man for more than a few minutes since marrying Toby. All the people they saw socially were couples like themselves so the men came with the women, the women with the men. Before that the only males she'd been alone with she'd been having sex with. It seemed odd to be by herself with a man who had shown no interest in her. Helen wasn't completely sure how to behave; in the end she thought she'd try for flirtatious indifference.

The experience of being in some guy's flat, of looking for clues to his personality like a detective, of simple objects taking on the qualities of heroism or cuteness or repulsion, flooded back to her, almost like a memory of childhood. Helen cruised his books and his walls for revealing insights. Coming upon a group photo in black and white she picked it up to study more closely. The photograph showed a group of youngish men and women dressed in the style of the 1960s under a banner that read 'Congreso des Marionetas. Buenos Aires 1970.' With a jolt Helen recognised the young Julio Spuciek, the one who had lived in her mind for the last twenty years, standing in the centre of a group amongst whom to her kind of person were a selection of living gods. There was Borges, Mario Vargas Llosa, Marquez and even the elusive Paulho Puoncho.

'Quite a photo,' she said to Julio, indicating the picture.

'Oh yes,' he agreed, shortsightedly peering at it. 'At that time there was a great deal of Norwegian money abailable for those interested in writing for puppets, so many came. Though from what I remember we spent most of our time in and out of the brothels.'

'The brothels?' Helen repeated, though there isn't really another word that 'brothel' can be confused with.

'Yes, brothels, whorehouses, vordellos. Everyone in that group thought women were only truly beautiful when they were very young girls. There was a particular house in Vuenos Aires off the Abenida Florida, I think it was, Paulho Puoncho used to go there all the time. The girls were perhaps fourteen, fifteen, sixteen, at least that's what the madam said and we chose to velieve her.'

Then Julio said, 'At least I am no longer interested in any of that, thank God! At my age I will never fall for another woman. Now, shall we go and eat Chinese food?'

A few days before, Helen had gone to the café at the time of day when she thought he might be there. At first she couldn't see him but sat at a slimy table anyway and ate a stale Mars Bar with a sell-by date in the last century. Through the dirty windows looking out over the playground it seemed to her that all the middle-class mums looked so terribly worried, while the few working-class mothers happily chatted and smoked as their kids fell off the swings and cracked their heads on the concrete.

''Ello, 'Oolio!' she heard behind her and he was there.

'Listen,' Helen said after he was seated opposite her and she'd paid for his coffee, 'I'd really like to take you out to dinner one night this week. I can get us a table at the Ivy with a couple of days' notice if you'd like to go somewhere like that.'

'No, I don't think so . . .'

'Please, maybe not necessarily anywhere fancy.'

'Well,' Julio said, a distant look coming into his eyes, 'I have heard that there is a place in Wood Green Shopping City. I read about it in the local paper, they say it is called Wow Tse Tung and you can eat all the Chinese food you wish to for nine pounds and ninety-five pence. Their advert in the local paper declares that a person can choose from over one hundred and twenty dishes – there's sushi and roast Peking duck with pancakes on the weekends. Can you imagine that? So much food for so little money.'

This must be what they mean by 'the Fat of the Land', Helen thought to herself, surveying the customers of Wow Tse Tung. Or rather, she amended, 'the Fat of the British Commonwealth'.

On this Friday night the place was full of the overweight of the United Kingdom's former empire. There were fat Cypriots, fat Sikhs, fat Bangladeshis, fat Nigerians, fat Maltese, fat Chinese, fat Australians, fat Papuan Pygmies. Morbidly obese Guyanese overflowed their groaning plywood and chrome chairs, while enormous-bottomed Jamaican women creaked over the protesting blond laminate floor and corpulent Malays queued impatiently beside clinically overweight South Africans for their turn at the chicken wings. All of them made her feel sick. Helen was certain she had never revealed her revulsion –

her extreme dislike of fatness – to Harriet but secretly she had always thought that to be overweight was simply a failure of personality, an inability to exert sufficient control over your body. She admitted to herself at that instant why she'd married Toby: it was because he had been so in love with her that she would always hold the power and he would never be able to hurt her, she would always be the one in control.

She and Julio had taken a minicab the mile and a half to Wood Green Shopping City, a red-brick ziggurat of shops, restaurants and walkways that had furious winds blowing down them on even the calmest of summer days.

Wow Tse Tung was on the second level and an elephantine pair of Hindus were just about to snag the last good table opposite the large plate-glass window overlooking the treacly traffic outside, but the Argentinian who up till then had been shuffling like an old man developed a sudden turn of speed and grabbed it for him and Helen. Outside, the buses, the dented vans and the Asian kids in their tricked-out Hondas and Subarus ground up and down the High Street as once their table was secured they ordered two Singapore Tiger beers and were free to start on the hunt for food.

'There are six different kinds of soup!' Julio said in wonder, staring at the stainless-steel tureens.

Soup, swoop, loop de loop, she was surprised to think but at least didn't say out loud.

Helen helped herself to a small bowl of hot and sour and sat down; she took a couple of sips but found herself oddly unable to enjoy the food in front of her. In turn she tried to listen to what Julio was saying but instead all she could think about was what item of food she was going to have next. She said to herself, As soon as I get through this hot and sour, I'll have a bowl of chicken and sweetcorn. Yet once an overflowing white bowl of wallpaper paste was in front of her her mind was already churning over which starters she was going to choose. First time round I'll stick to dumplings and the smaller spring rolls, she thought. Then on the second run I'll go for chicken wings, grilled prawns in chilli sauce and the Peking duck with hoi sin wrapped in pancakes. After her fourth trip to the servery for satay sticks, seaweed and char sui buns Helen thought if she forced herself to pause for a while her mania might subside, but as she sat at the table, her fingers fidgeting on the polished wood trying to listen to what her companion was saying, she could only count down the seconds until she would be able to return to the buffet.

Through the disturbing thoughts of Chinese food dancing across her mind Julio seemed to be going on about the time when he had first come to Britain as a refugee from Fascism. From what information managed to fight its way past the dumplings and spare ribs singing their siren songs, she was able to gather that he had in those days been a much more significant figure, almost at the centre of trendy London life. He babbled about the takeover of the magazine *Puppetry Today* by a group of Marxists, of the early days of *The Muppet Show* at Elstree studios and he made a violent denunciation of the man who'd had his hand up Roland Rat.

Halfway through one particular tale of a drunken wrestling match with a ventriloquist's dummy who Julio had mistakenly thought was a dwarf that had been shouting insults at him, Helen could sit still no longer. She jumped up and ran back to the counter, this time for main course food, and returned to the table carrying a plate piled high with a massive mess of curries, sweet and sour pork in a strange orange sauce, chicken legs and wrinkled beef and black beans. Abandoning her chopsticks she also brought back with her a big spoon from the servery so that she could shovel food into her mouth more effectively until there was a sharp pain across her chest and a sheet of sweat was running down her face, but still she was unable to stop.

Used to having her rapt attention, after a while Julio lapsed into silence. He ate in a different way to Helen, laying out his choices in a pattern on the plate then raising it to his lips slowly, taking tiny little bites of each morsel like a rodent. From time to time he would surreptitiously slip a chicken wing wrapped in a napkin or a peanut-sauce-coated satay stick into her handbag with a stagey wink.

In the humid night air they came out of the back of Shopping City and headed towards home accompanied by the bass beat of the air-conditioning units. The mismatched couple slipped past the wheely bins piled high with rubbish, their feet sliding on the greasy service road, the future behind them and solid Edwardian suburbia in front. Soon Helen and Julio passed the old-fashioned Italian restaurant now shuttered and boarded up. Helen had only stopped eating when Julio decided he wanted to leave. 'I haven't had any puddings,' she moaned like a petulant child.

'Chinese desserts are always a disappointment, just sponge cakes with soya veans in them,' he said, unbending, then taking her under the arm led her to the cash desk to pay for them both and afterwards out of the shopping centre.

'So did you enjoy that?' Helen asked as she waddled down the tree-lined hill and over the railway bridge, the pain in her chest slowly transferring itself to her stomach.

'No,' he said, sighing, 'I feel soiled . . .'

'Well,' she replied, relieved to understand why he'd wanted to leave so abruptly, 'that can happen if you eat too much Chinese food but it's nothing to be ashamed of, we can go back to your place to change your trousers then you'll be—'

'No! I mean I feel dirty, I tried to enjoy going to that place but there is something terribly wrong with such avundance, for people to dine every night as if they were at the wedding of the King of China for nine pounds and ninety-fibe pence.'

Helen found herself thinking, Oh, for fuck's sake, it's only dinner! then gasped, she was arguing with Julio Spuciek! The man who had always agreed with her, whose opinion always concurred with hers, was talking miserable crap. Confusion filled her mind.

Not noticing any change in Helen's manner, the old man grumbled on. 'I went to B&Q only last week. I went in there only to get a right-angle square and a hammer but for the price of these two things I could buy a complete set in its own box, comprising over one hundred and fifty different tools, ratchet heads, socket sets, screwdrivers, craft knife, so many things for so little money. It made me weep right there in the hardware section to see it.'

They came to a stop outside the Watney Flats.

He said, 'May I ask you something, Helen?'

'Of course.'

'Does your husband have a toolbox?'

'A what?'

'A toolbox. Well, not necessarily a toolbox but does he have some tools, a selection of screwdrivers and what do they call them, *llaves Ingles* – Allen keys – does he have a few of those with a rusty saw perhaps and a hammer in a carrier bag?'

'Why do you ask?' she said. 'Do you want Toby to do some repairs for you?'

'Oh no, it's just that there is a certain type of man who has a toolbox, perhaps nothing fancy, with different compartments for screws and nails but at least he has some tools in a drawer or on a shelf and he is a man who can do things, change a plug, put up a picture, fix a leaky hose on the dishwasher perhaps, a man who thinks a little about the world outside himself, a man who can help others. Then there is another type, a certain type who doesn't have these things, who cannot do these things, often a weak creature suffering from allergies and intolerances, who only thinks about the world inside themselves, who works in an office perhaps or a limp creature reading the news on the radio. I'm not sure this is truly a man.'

'Do you have a toolkit, Julio?'

'Of course I do, I told you, a complete set in its own box, over one hundred and fifty different tools, ratchet heads, socket sets, screwdrivers, craft knife, so many things for so little money. So does he, your husband?'

Helen tried to think whether Toby had a toolkit or not; certainly she couldn't recall him ever doing any repairs. 'Yes, I'm certain he does,' she said, then changed her mind to speak the truth, 'No, he doesn't, I'm pretty certain he doesn't, no, but he does play football every Thursday.'

'That is something but not enough,' the Argentinian replied like a High Court judge summing up in a murder case. 'You are married to a weak man and a woman who marries a weak man is . . . a woman who likes weak men. Goodnight, Helen.'

Then he turned into the flats, leaving her alone on the pavement.

'Why does your handbag smell of meat?' Toby asked groggily as Helen came to bed.

She said, 'I do love you, you know, Toby.'

Coming slightly more awake he said, 'I've booked on to the Papua New Guinea trip. I spoke to your boss today and he said it'd be fine. I know you don't want me to do it but it's something I have to do to test myself.'

'Well, I was against it but I don't know now,' Helen said. She didn't add that she didn't know about anything any more.

Every year there was held in and around the wooden hut and the playground in the park what Toby referred to as 'The Pointless Park County Show' and what the council called a Community Sharing Experience. On a hot summer Saturday under the spreading sycamore and horse chestnut trees small, dark, silent men and women from the local Colombian population manned a pasting-table stall serving maize buns and stews of chicken simmered with plantain; the Turks and Kurds sold grilled meat and fluffy bread studded with caraway seeds cooked on smoking charcoal grills; Punjabi women produced polystyrene tubs of dhal and thick vegetable curries; and the elderly, shrivelled, little white men and women of the local Communist Party Branch stood behind a stall that offered spindly, unwell-looking house plants and the works of Joseph Stalin.

Mr Iqubal Fitzherbert De Castro and his group of young associates had mounted a splendid stall supposedly representing something called the Namibian Disaster Relief Fund Steering Committee, which everybody steered well clear of.

'Which particular disaster would that be?' Harriet asked Mr Iqubal Fitzherbert De Castro.

'Well, there's always some bloody disaster happening somewhere over there,' he replied, then added in immigrant-speak 'innit?' making her laugh.

On a small stage with a howling sound system, between the compulsory Caribbean steel band and a samba school of overweight social workers led by Oscar and Katya's builder (who had turned up for work at their house one day offering no explanation for his abrupt disappearance and who was dressed today in a sparkling yellow bra/thong combination, glistening yellow gossamer wings rippling behind him topped off with a towering green and black feathered headdress), the regulars at the dojo were scheduled to give a demonstration of the deadly martial art of Li Kuan Yu.

'The pale creepy one's looking sick with worry!' Harriet heard the Tin Can Man, hidden in the undergrowth, shout into his phone.

Patrick told himself he should be reasonably confident over how their Li Kuan Yu demonstration would go. He knew you wouldn't have seen such a thing in Martin's time but then

Martin hadn't faced the problems he had to face. Patrick had asked the community centre people if they could perform at the community fair knowing, since he'd been attending it from childhood himself, that they'd be grateful for anything to break the usual tedious parade of well-meaning multi-ethnic crap. The reason he'd decided they should perform was to instil a greater sense of solidarity at the dojo. Recently there had come a number of threats from outside: a bloke purporting to be a genuine Shaolin monk had opened a dojo in Wood Green teaching Southern Crane kung fu and since then three members of his dojo had stopped coming. Patrick didn't think it was a coincidence. Jack reported that this man – the monk in Wood Green – had stated in an internet chat room that as a fighting style Li Kuan Yu was 'monkey poo'. 'That's very nice language for a man of the cloth to use,' was all that Patrick said to Jack.

He went round to the houses of the people who'd dropped out, trying to persuade them to come back, but they either said point-blank that they wouldn't return or hid behind their curtains and refused to answer the doorbell. Patrick made disparaging comments about them to the other students but inside he felt like his authority was being undermined. Perhaps Jack sensed this too – the old man being the only one who had also been taught by Martin Po, Patrick had often suspected he'd always been resentful that the sifu had appointed Patrick his successor rather than Jack. Of course maybe, Patrick thought, if he told him about the huge amount of money that he'd handed over for the privilege of being made new sifu he might shut up about it. Perhaps he'd stop contradicting Patrick at practice, constantly suggesting that the Founder would not have done certain things as Patrick said they should be done.

If he was honest Patrick had to admit that he didn't like Jack, he was one of those people who could instantly sense the weaknesses and insecurities of others. He'd sidled up to the younger man one evening after practice at the dojo.

"Arriet's doin well, ain't she?' he said, which was odd for a start, since he didn't usually praise anyone. 'Surprisin' considerin'.'

'Considerin' what?' Patrick asked.

'Well, I was walkin' Rufus,' (that was his dog) 'round the park, about four in the mornin' it was. Me insomnia's been playin' me up lately and I saw your 'Arriet comin' out of 'er neighbour's flat all dressed up like a tart. You know, *those* neighbours.'

He wasn't entirely surprised to hear that Harriet hadn't been telling him the truth about what she got up to when she wasn't training, knowing already that she was disobeying his orders on whom she socialised with. OK, you could understand why she kept on seeing her sister and her brother-in-law, people said family bonds were strong. What was unacceptable was her not dropping those two awful women she hung around with, who smoked and drank and whose internal chi must be all over the place, even though he'd more or less ordered her to stop seeing them. Now to discover that she was staying up all night with a gang of . . . well, whatever they were. He found that hard to bear.

He supposed she would have to be disciplined but he had no idea how to go about it. A wave of bitterness swept over him at the unfairness of it all: he practised all the time and had dedicated his life to living as the sifu said he had to, he had given up everything, practised and trained and thought about Li Kuan Yu every single minute, did not spill his fluids, didn't mix with anyone outside the dojo and yet Harriet's behaviour didn't seem to be affecting her development as a fighter in any way. Even if she was leading a dissolute life, went to places like the pub and all-night parties where she did God knows what with those people, her fitness, speed, flexibility and determination just seemed to keep on getting better – in some ways he was forced to admit she was becoming his equal. There were times when they fought that she moved faster and punched and kicked with more ferocity and accuracy than him and managed to land some quite hard blows to the side of his head. One day he'd have to sort it all out but not right now, there was another matter he wanted to talk to her about first.

The usual routine was for Harriet to put on her martial arts pyjamas at home as there were no changing rooms in the community centre but for the big demonstration she instead chose to cross to the park in jeans and a T-shirt. Once there, undressing in the small office set aside on this one day for women to change in, she recalled all the times when she'd been fat, how at all times she'd hidden her body away from other women. Now she slipped out of her pants and, naked, put them into her sports bag, then sorted through it to bring out her fighting gear. All the time as she was bent over the desk she was aware of other women looking at her body, admiring and envying it and wishing it was theirs.

One night back when she'd been fat, Harriet remembered watching the evening show on ITN when they did one of those features they have on most weeks when there's not much news, about the rising tide of obesity that threatens to kill us all. As usual there was a clip of enormous fat people waddling about the street but shot only from the neck down so they wouldn't feel humiliated and sue. Suddenly she got a horrible sick feeling on seeing a gigantic blobby gut that she was almost certain was hers slithering past the camera in slow motion. Even that didn't stop her eating. Harriet felt so bad about her weight being shown on television that she ate a whole bag of chocolate-covered mini muffins.

All around her while she was changing she could hear women moaning about different parts of their bodies that appeared absolutely fine to her: tits, arse, leg, neck, ankles, parts that she didn't even think of as separate like the back of the forearm. Harriet congratulated herself that this body dysmorphic disorder was one female characteristic she didn't possess. She thought, perhaps because her body had once been so absolutely out of control, that these days every single bit of it was a pure delight, a pure delight that she was happy to share with others of her sex.

Once dressed, Harriet made her way to the backstage area of the open-air platform where they were due to give their display. The others were already there, fidgeting and stretching nervously while she just stood still, calm and composed. That little shit Jack came up to her and said, 'With all your gadding about you're not too tired for this then, Harriet?'

'Not too short and bald for this then, Jack?' was her reply.

The steel band clanked to a ragged halt and took so long trooping off stage that by the time the dojo got into the light and lined up behind Patrick whatever atmosphere that might have existed had long dissipated into the warm air. Patrick tried ineffectually to corral the attention of the crowd over the howling, railway station-standard PA. As he haltingly and confusingly attempted to explain the basics of Li Kuan Yu, a gang of twelve-year-old boys began to laugh and jeer at him until Harriet saw Toby stalk across the grass and tell them to shut up. She tensed, seeing the boys considering whether to make something of it, but his bulk and demented expression caused them to think better of it. Harriet wasn't certain but to her Toby seemed drunk.

Patrick had told them the night before at the dojo that he'd sent out invitations printed on his home computer to leading journalists on all the major newspapers, important magazines, radio and TV stations, but staring out from the stage at the few people scattered on the grass Harriet guessed that about a fifth of the audience were her friends and family and none of the rest looked like columnists on the *Daily Telegraph* or reporters from Sky News. From the stage she made a surreptitious little 'calm down' gesture to Rose and Lulu who were openly sniggering at poor Patrick as he stumbled through his opening remarks. Her sister and Toby sat way on the other side of the compound from her two friends and her eyes were drawn to a thin, shabby-looking man of sixty or so standing behind them who stared at the stage almost as intently as Toby.

Finally, once Patrick had ensured that almost nobody was watching, the demonstration began. The whole dojo did the opening form, then, with Patrick giving a commentary over the screaming microphone, they stepped forward to perform in pairs: when Harriet's turn came she faultlessly exchanged elbow strikes and blocks with Jack. Holding her fists in front of her face, elbows akimbo, she blocked while he attempted to hit her cheekbones with his elbows, then they reversed and she struck out at the little man, rocking him back on his heels with the speed and violence of her blows. As Harriet did this Toby, Lulu and Rose whooped and hollered encouragement and the noise began to bring others towards the stage.

They all did Roll Eyes Fall on Enemy, with the whole dojo staggering around pretending to be drunk before falling on top of their imaginary enemies; Patrick couldn't understand why the crowd all laughed at this but at least they were watching now. They only stopped when a little while later Harriet again came forward to demonstrate Passing Swoop Knee Grab, her speciality Broom Staff Pike Stance and Split Fingers Cobra Eyeball Strike. As she twisted and turned, even though it was on this stupid little stage doing this silly dance, she suddenly knew she was experiencing what great dancers feel when every move they make is exactly the right move and people stand and stare open-mouthed to see your body do these things.

Once Harriet had gone to an air show with a guy who was

disturbingly keen on these things and had seen a fighter jet take off. Once the plane was airborne the pilot had gone to 're-heat', injecting raw aviation fuel into the flaming red-hot exhaust stream so that the fighter had shot straight up into the air with an unimaginable scream of power and was gone from sight in seconds. That was Harriet right then – a woman on re-heat.

The show ended with a mass demonstration of Anaconda Tree Jump Vine Strike, half the class pouncing from their wobbling stepladders on to the shoulders of the other half. The watching crowd had grown to over a hundred people by this time and the climax of the demonstration was greeted with enthusiastic clapping and whistling, though Harriet thought it was clear to all of them that this applause was mostly for her.

Lulu and Rose were sitting at a bench table: they had bought paper plates of food from every nationality and bottles of beer illegally sold by a stall of Kurdish separatists. 'At these prices we can't afford *not* to be sick and drunk,' said Lulu.

Now changed back into her street clothes, Harriet skipped over the grass to them, glowing and happy.

'Hey, look at you,' Rose said, stroking her arm as she sat down.

'Christ! You were incredible up there,' Lulu added.

'Oh well . . .'

'No, you got that quality, girl, people can't take their eyes off you.'

'That is my feeling exactly.' This last statement came from Mr Iqubal Fitzherbert De Castro who had silently appeared behind them.

'Why thank you,' Harriet said, smiling up at her new friend. 'Mr Iqubal Fitzherbert De Castro, let me introduce you, these are my dear friends Lulu and Rose.'

'Delighted to meet you.' He took their hands in both of his and pressed down as if making hamburger but still he spoke of

Harriet. 'Isn't she lovely? And now I know she can fight too, what a marvellous modern woman.'

'Blimey, he's even scarier than you let on,' Rose said after Mr Iqubal Fitzherbert De Castro and his following pack of young men had left.

'I never said he was scary.'

'Ah, must have been a warning voice whispering in my ear.'

'Don't be like that, he's . . . they're exciting.'

'Hello, Patrick,' said Lulu, looking up from her plate of black beans.

'Hello, Patrick,' said Rose.

The two women knew they discomfited her teacher and liked to play on it.

'Erm . . . yes, hello, erm . . .' He gave up trying to remember their names and instead asked, 'Harriet, can I have a word with you?'

'Sure.'

He led her away from the music and the press of people. They walked together in silence across the rolling grass until they stood hidden by clumps of pampas grass planted by the council when small but now grown tall and wild; the jangling noise of the fair seemed distant and muted. Harriet stiffened herself for praise concerning her performance on the stage, a small smile on her face, but Patrick never referred to it. Instead he said, 'Why have you never asked me what happened to Martin Po?'

Even at the height of her belief in Li Kuan Yu she'd always had the most trouble with Martin Po, choosing in the end to see him as some sort of distant, possibly safely dead, saint-like figure who without being susceptible to human failings embodied all good things people should aspire to – sort of like Gandhi, Che Guevara or Freddy Mercury.

'I kind of assumed you'd tell me when the time was right, when I was ready for the knowledge.'

'Well, I can't tell you where he is.'

'Er . . . right, you can't tell me where he is but . . .'

'I can only say this. A few years ago we had many discussions. Martin had come to feel that he'd reached the end of what he could do in Britain. He had developed all these fighting skills but couldn't use them outside the dojo unless he debased himself doing security work or something equally demeaning; he couldn't kill anybody without risking getting locked up, no matter how much they deserved it. So he finally decided to go abroad, to find a wild place where he could teach fighting skills, the code of Bushido – the way of the warrior – to people who could put them into practice. Where people could use Li Kuan Yu in a real conflict situation.

'Now I can't say where he's gone but we're still in touch. There is a problem though: the problem is there's things he needs that he can't get where he is. Some of these things I know you can get here, others I'm pretty sure they're illegal but if you know the right people . . .'

'Right, so . . . ?'

'You're more wordly than me, Harriet, you know more about life outside the dojo. Can I show you the list of things and ask what you think?'

'Sure, I guess.'

He handed over a long list of items which he'd printed off from his computer. Studying it, she thought Martin Po might as well have been asking for winged unicorns and a magical goose. If she hadn't been angry at him for ignoring how brilliant her performance had been she might not have said, 'Well, I know some people might be able to fix you up with some of this stuff, at a price.'

'Good, perhaps you can contact them for a meeting?' he said. 'I'll see you on Monday for practice then.' And pushing through the pampas grass he disappeared.

As she was sitting back down at the wooden bench table with

her friends, Lulu said, 'Here comes Toby and your sister. Christ! He looks pissed and she looks . . . I dunno, sort of weird.'

Julio Spuciek was at the fair! Helen had caught sight of him amongst a bumbling little group of junkies and petty thieves, all of them she supposed under community service orders, who shuffled narcoleptically around picking up litter and emptying the bins like a Southern chain gang but without the gospel singing. It was a shock to see him; since their dinner at the Chinese all-you-can eat place she'd had to force herself not to go down to the café daily, she'd fought the urge to stand for an hour or so outside the Watney Flats hoping to see him leave or to take food or hot soup, swoop, loop de loop round to his apartment.

Though she knew she shouldn't she still couldn't prevent herself from going looking for him and finally tracked him down beside the football pitch where he was idly poking at a discarded crisp packet with a pointed stick.

'Hi, Julio,' she said. 'Have you been all right?' She noticed he seemed to have a silly smile on his face.

He looked up with a start. 'My goodness your sister, what a woman! So beautiful,' was the first thing Julio said to her. 'I started looking at her on the stage because I see this woman and there was a strong resemblance to you. How can this be? I thought. Then when she started to move I fell in love with her beauty just like that! I thought I was finished with such things but there you are, it's happened.'

'But,' Helen stammered '. . . I thought you said only young girls of fourteen were beautiful?'

'When? When did I say that?'

'You said you and all your lecherous South American mates agreed that women are only truly beautiful when they are young – fifteen, sixteen, seventeen, eighteen. You and Paulho Puoncho went to a brothel off the Avenida Florida where the girls were maybe fourteen, fifteen.'

'Oh, that was some nonsense that we used to say when we were young. I went along with it but never really believed. No, your sister up there on the stage, a body of such grace, such power and, I think the most attractive of all, capable of great cruelty.'

'My sister capable of great cruelty! Hat? You must be joking.'

'No, she is magnificent.'

She couldn't stop herself asking, 'What about me?'

'What about you?'

'Don't I have grace, power, cruelty?'

'You?' He looked at Helen and laughed. 'You are a girl. A pretty girl, sure, but one whose looks mean too much to her. Everyone must love you or you feel you are nothing. Perhaps you will introduce me to your sister Harriet?'

She was saved from figuring out what her response to this would be by a young community worker rounding the corner. 'Oi, 'Oolio!' he shouted. 'You've been warned about chatting to the girls. Do you want another two hundred hours?'

So he scuttled off, leaving her feeling even more uncomfortable and confused.

Martin and Patrick had once discussed the idea of whether it might be possible to form a squad of trained killers, of ninjas, from those who are suffering or who had suffered from panic attacks and related acute anxiety disorders – phobias, obsessive compulsive behaviour, intrusive fearful thoughts and so on. Sifu Po had a notion that if getting out of the house in the morning was the most frightening thing in the world then a midnight parachute drop into the Yemen would be no more frightening. He reasoned that if you are frightened of everything you are therefore frightened of nothing. If you are phobic, he said, it takes as much courage to touch a frozen chicken as it does to murder a Russian gangster in his sleep, if you are scared nearly to death of the voices in your head telling you to take your pants down in public then going up against the Colombian drug cartels might be a cakewalk by comparison. As he said to his young disciple, 'Let's face it, Patrick you can run away or kill the Colombian drug cartel but the voices in your head, you're stuck with them.' For a while the two of them had hung around outside the Nightingale Clinic which Martin said was a famous mental place and eventually they found a number of people who were suffering from anxiety disorders, but when the two men tried to take these people somewhere to explain their ideas they kept crying, fainting on the pavement and begging the martial arts adepts to let them go. Still, it had been a happy time for Martin and Patrick travelling around together, stalking the mentally ill.

Patrick had thought that maybe with Harriet he would become Martin – the wise sifu – and she would become him, sort of – the disciple, the one who learnt and admired. But she seemed more interested in the gangsters next door.

Harriet sat in front of her computer, accessed Google and started looking for information on Li Kuan Yu. She didn't know why she hadn't done it before; perhaps it was because when she had been in love with it, she'd wanted to think that Li Kuan Yu was unique, a private magical thing that existed in a world outside the tawdry goings-on that you found on the internet.

The first few searches produced bewildering references to impossible Chinese classical books, myths and legends, but no martial arts, apart from a reference to Kuan Yu, apparently the god of choice of the Triads, the police and kung fu masters. Changing the spelling to Lee Kuan Yew brought reams of entries referring to the semi-retired dictator of Singapore but this wasn't what she was after.

Altering the spelling several times, 'LKY: Kettering: Martial Arts' finally produced a number of entries. In a Forum on the site 'www.Obscurexternalmartialarts.com' she read: 'Web-forum: The Master of Northampton. Does anyone know what happened to Martin Po?' Somebody calling themselves 'Tim from Vancouver' asked this question.

There were a number of replies.

ENTRY: From William Tang, PhD, Dept of Sino Tibetan Studies, University of Durham. Posted 16/10/99.

Martin Po was reputedly master of the Legend of Li Xian Ieou (Silver Fin Fish Fist), an allegedly deadly martial arts form. There are no published photographs either of the art or its founder.

Origin: Some trace the roots of Silver Fin Fish Fist to Tönpa Shenrab, the founder of Bön, a shamanistic folk religion which pre-dated Buddhism. He is said to have been born in the mythical land of Olmo Lung Ring, whose location remains something of a mystery. The land is traditionally described as dominated by Mount Yung-drung Gu-tzeg (Edifice of Nine Swastikas), which many identify as Mount Kailash in western Tibet. Due to the sacredness of Olmo Lung Ring and the mountain, both the counter-clockwise swastika and the number nine are of great significance. (See Snellgrove: *The Nine Ways of Bon*, 1957.)

Certainly the swastika featured large in the sect which surrounded the cult of Li Xian Yeow. The Happy Garden, headquarters and temple, was situated at number 9 Boncastle Road, Kettering. See *Leicester Mercury*, Jan. 1982, pp. 2–3, 'Chinese Nazis in Northampton?'.

Though never numerous there have been no known references to Martin Po since 1997.

There were several other entries, one from somebody calling themselves 'Iron Fist Tony Roberts' which read: 'Sure. I studied his so-called LKY some time back. He's a fraud. It doesn't work.

I hurt my back quite severely from falling off a ladder practising one of the forms. Don't go there.'

This had led to two responses:

From Anna Conda, Leipzig, Germany: 'Fraud yourself. Liar! LKY is best world martial art. I will defend my master to the death against all detractors, you crippled pimp. Martin Po is in the Far East, by the way, learning at the feet of his Master. He will return and crush his enemies, probably soon.'

And lastly from somebody called 'John in Daventry', who wrote: 'I went to school with a Chinese kid called Martin Po. I seem to remember he got done by the police for jumping out of trees and wrapping his legs round schoolgirls, after that he went away. I don't know anything about LKY but students should try Drunken Monkey Fist. Much more effective and no trees.'

Not a unique, private, magical thing that exists in a world outside the tawdry goings-on found on the internet then.

It was a particularly busy time at work for Helen since the following week would be National Talking Bird Awareness Week. However, since the same seven days were also European Leprosy Awareness Week and had within it UK Banana Day and National Ride to Work Day not to mention the entire year being United Nations International Year of the Environmentally Aware they struggled to get media attention. Sometimes she thought that perhaps the authorities could extend the year, say, to six hundred days then every cause could have its day. Yet she knew that inevitably even this unlikely solution would lead to problems; the football season would be too long for a start and the worthwhile days, weeks and months would simply expand to fill the extra time. Maybe, Helen thought, some of these special days could be combined so that you'd get something like National Ride to Work on a Leper Day. It might be nice for people to chat to a leper while they were carried into work, they might learn something about the disease that they wouldn't get from reading an article in the paper.

It occurred to her that she might be able to conserve two birds with one stone. The rescue of the British Consul's daughter's parrot from rebel mudmen in Papua New Guinea was just the kind of heartwarming story Warbird needed to put it in front of other charities. Secondly, if the rescue mission was led by the husband of one of the charity's senior administrators that would certainly help her standing within the organisation; after all it had been a while now since the Rwanda triumph. Or it might all be a complete disaster.

II

The summer was hot with periods of humidity ('humadidity' as Toby called it) mixed with warm rain that in previous years would have sent plant diseases racing round the park. However, because of their wild mongrel nature the plants were strong this year and fought off illness with ease. The store that had once belonged to Mr Sargassian finally reopened but not as predicted as a corporate coffee shop or a place that sold sandwiches packed in India, rather as a charity shop supposedly for the Namibian Disaster Relief Fund.

'They've opened a shop now,' Harriet heard the Can Man say, 'yes, *them*.'

As she browsed the store, it seemed to her that many of the products on show appeared to be at remarkably low prices and were suspiciously new compared with the cast-offs in other charity shops she'd visited. Stacked up were the latest DVD recorders, top-of-the-line computers and iPods that she thought were only on sale in the United States alongside huge piles of round tins of mackerel from Turkey and big fat rolls of shiny black rubbish bags for a pound.

Since the party at the flat next door there had been several excursions and on each occasion there had been a new outfit for Harriet. Often these were waiting for her in the next-door flat but at other times Mr Iqubal Fitzherbert De Castro took Harriet to smart clothes and jewellery places in Crouch End and Muswell Hill where the women serving in the shops would give her funny looks. Sometimes they went to nightclubs, once to the dog racing at Walthamstow and once to a party in a flat on the Greenwich Peninsula over-looking the Dome.

Sometimes when they went out they'd travel around in one of those stretch limousines; with its dimly lit interior yawning off into the distance it felt to Harriet like they were travelling around outer London in a carpeted coal mine. The gang of young men dressed in smart suits would perch sideways on fold-out chairs and drink whisky from a line of cut-glass decanters arrayed on a drinks cabinet to the side of the limousine, their contents described on a little brass dog tag worn round the neck.

One night as she came out of her shop towards the limousine the Tin Can Man was on the opposite pavement standing just inside the park, knee-deep in the long grass; unusually she could see the silver glint of his phone as it hung silent in his hand.

Clambering into the back seat of the limousine, Harriet cast another quick look at the silent watcher. Following the direction of her gaze Mr Iqubal Fitzherbert De Castro asked, indicating the Tin Can Man, 'Friend of yours?'

'No, not really, I just see him around, you know, and he says things about me or he used to . . .'

'I see. Well, actually, we used to be quite close to him.'

'Him?'

'Yes, before his troubles he was something of a wealthy man.'

'Really? He doesn't seem like it now.'

'Nevertheless it is true; you know, he owned that building where the gym that is only for women is now. Used to manufacture women's clothes there. When he had his troubles we were luckily able to help him out a little by buying the building off him. Unfortunately he was not grateful because by then his mind had turned; still we tried to be his friend and that is the main thing.'

When Harriet had first become involved with Mr Iqubal Fitzherbert De Castro and the Namibians and had gone to that first party she'd wondered whether she'd finally found her gang of travellers, her posse, her tribe, her crew. Certainly being in their company gave her a delirious sense of being unrestrained. To Harriet Mr Iqubal Fitzherbert De Castro and all the others whom he mixed with were not bound by parking tickets, planning regulations and refraining from putting your rubbish out until after 8.30 on bin night. They did not submit to the petty rules of society. Of course there was a price to pay for this freedom – the price they paid was that they didn't have the protection of society and other people sometimes tried to kill them but they seemed OK with that.

Yet as she spent more time with them it slowly became clear to her that they weren't free at all, that their lives actually required much, much more effort than the average law-abiding civilian's whom they so despised. The Namibians had no friends who hadn't been bribed not to rat on them and they had to act, to keep up a front of hardness at all times like they were in some sort of a twenty-four-hour British gangster film. Worse than that they weren't nice and nobody they knew was nice, the normal give and take of human contact didn't apply, every second everybody they came into contact with was looking to achieve some advantage over them and they were trying to do the same. The revelation to Harriet was that knowing all this didn't affect her attitude towards them – they were fun, a welcome contrast to Patrick's gloomy asceticism, Toby's mooning devotion or the constant struggle with her sister for the upper hand. Which didn't mean she could relax; there was no doubt it was her physical beauty that bought her a place at the party. Each time they asked her to go somewhere with them it meant that she was still beautiful.

But going out all night meant she needed to train extra hard during the day; if she let her workout regime slip for even an afternoon she instantly thought she could feel her muscles softening. Sometimes when her bones were burning from exercise and her knuckles bleeding from punching practice she wondered what it was about Old Fat Harriet that was so bad that she'd had to be starved to death. She'd certainly required a lot less upkeep than the new Harriet and she'd certainly been a lot better off financially. The thing that suffered most in all her constant exercise and late-night partying was the shop, her credit card bills lay unpaid and she had to fight really hard not to remember that she was way behind on the mortgage.

'Is Mr Iqubal Fitzherbert De Castro around?' Harriet asked one of the young men manning the counter in the Namibian Disaster Relief Fund shop. Sulkily he turned to a doorway which led to a back storeroom and called out; after a few seconds she heard the older man emerging.

'Ah, Harriet,' he said with a big smile when he saw her, 'just the person I was wishing to see. I was wanting to see you to ask whether you thought that the invention of the camera had destroyed painting and sculpture or had liberated it?'

'Liberated it?'

'Really? But don't you feel that photography reproducing this perfect representation of the external world meant painting and sculpture went from attempting faithfully to express the universal world of everybody to instead representing the interior world of only the artist? Maybe as you say that was liberating but surely it made things much more difficult for the viewer since we can never know precisely what's going on in anybody else's mind, crikey! It's hard enough to know what's going on in your own.'

'Yeah, you might be right.'

'Also this abstractionism that you so champion so forcefully, Harriet, means that the average person can no longer know whether a work of art speaks to them or not. Nowadays a cabal of high priests, critics and gallery owners tells the public what is worthy and what is not and they follow like a herd of concrete cows.'

'Yes, you've convinced me. Now look,' she said, 'there's a friend of mine who wants to acquire a number of items that aren't, shall we say . . . available on the open market.'

'I see,' replied Mr Iqubal Fitzherbert De Castro, his manner changing completely, stiffening a little like a gun dog at the scent of a business opportunity. 'Do you have a list of these things?'

'I do,' Harriet replied and handed over the sheet of paper Patrick had printed out on his computer with Martin Po's requests on it.

She'd been fairly certain that he would laugh at it, this long catalogue of ludicrous items, yet Mr Iqubal Fitzherbert De Castro, after studying it for a few seconds, simply said, calmly folding the list and putting in his top pocket, 'Hmm . . . These things are not easy to come by and I do know they will be expensive but I think at least half of them are possible.'

That morning Toby had sent a text message to Harriet's mobile phone; he never used any of the abbreviations commonly employed so she reckoned it must have taken him over half an hour with his big hands to type in: 'Dear Harriet, today I am having numerous injections in preparation for my Papua New Guinea trip in a privately owned travel clinic situated just off Regent Street and was wondering whether you would you like to join me for a relatively late lunch. Kind regards, your friend Toby.'

'OK Gr8.2?' she'd sent back. To which an hour later Toby replied with the full name of the place including what floor of the building it was on, its complete postcode and complex directions for how to get there.

As Harriet walked towards the train station she passed the woman from the gift shop standing in her doorway staring up and down the road. Seeing her she said, 'Oh, hello, Harriet, how are you? I was beginning to think you'd moved. You used to be in here all the time buying presents but you haven't paid us a visit in ages.'

'No, well,' she replied facetiously, 'I don't have any friends any more.'

'Oh, I know, did they get pissed off when you got too pretty?'

Recently she'd stopped carrying any kind of handbag; when Harriet had been obese her bag had been almost as overweight as its owner. Looking back she didn't know why she thought she needed to carry a spanner around with her – Harriet imagined the feeling of liberation achieved in getting rid of it was similar to what a man might experience the first time he got his head shaved. Now all she took with her was some money, her phone and a comb.

She sat on the clammy blue-chequered moquette of the train feeling light and free. Harriet hadn't been out with Toby since they'd gone to the Italian restaurant and she told herself she was looking forward to chatting and laughing with him just like they had in the old days.

Since the railway companies had in recent years managed to stop vandals daubing their tags in spray paint on the outside of the rolling stock they'd instead taken to scratching their names on the carriage windows. Though the train in which the passengers swayed towards King's Cross was relatively clean, the window through which she attempted to see out was as deeply etched as that of a Victorian gin palace. To Harriet it was as if they were travelling along with a smoke cloud of names that blew down the track with them.

As Harriet walked down Regent Street, slipping in and out of the bovine crowds of tourists, she caught sight of Toby standing outside the building where they were due to meet, staring across the road, looking for her in the wrong direction. The injections he'd been given had frozen his mouth so she could see his face was lopsided, and dribble oozed from his lips to drip over his chin. She stopped and after a few seconds went to stand in the doorway of a tartan shop. Harriet took her phone out of her jacket pocket and texted Toby: 'Soree Tobes, got urgnt repair at shop, cnt cum. Hat xxx.' She saw him start jumpily, then after searching through all his pockets take out his own mobile and stare down at the screen, read the message and then after half a minute's thought begin to thumb in a reply.

She slid away down a narrow side street and walked east. Harriet had not been into the centre of London for months; the parties she went to with Mr Iqubal Fitzherbert De Castro were always in places like Tooting and Walthamstow, places that, like them, weren't at the centre of things. The thundering, relentless traffic and the foetid diesel-soaked air made her feel like a character in a Thomas Hardy novel who'd taken three days to walk into the big intimidating town to buy a wife at the Michaelmas Fair. Though lunchtime was over all the cafés still seemed to be crammed full of office workers and tourists. Along the main streets there was a continuous dreary succession of chain sandwich bars followed by chain coffee shops, mobile phone shops and ugly building society branches, yet once she got out of the centre, on the side streets there was a more varied and attractive life. The cafés and sandwich bars with tasteful tables and chairs outside were family-run places, the delicatessens and grocery stores managed to be both modern and old-fashioned at the same time and it was the owners of the isolated, empty American franchises who stood on the step and stared up and down in a despairing way.

About twenty-five minutes later she got the message: 'Dear Harriet, I am so sorry that we couldn't meet for luncheon, nevertheless I will see you on Saturday at the Admiral Codrington for my leaving party. I sincerely hope your emergency repair went well. Regretfully yours, Toby.'

It had been hard to tell from the facial paralysis but to her the expression on his face when Toby got her message had been one of relief.

* * *

Of late when attending all the film premieres, restaurant openings, charity events, Helen tried hard to make sure she didn't get her picture taken. At all these parties there was always the same photographer from the London newspaper, a swarthy little Armenian man whose pictures were featured in the Friday magazine that came free with the paper. A little while ago when she scanned one of his spreads of a Warbird-sponsored polo match to see if she'd been featured it suddenly seemed to her that there was a quality in these pictures that made everybody in them appear to be dead. Actually dead wasn't the right word, maybe doomed was a better one. Somehow she felt there was a melancholy property that infused these images, a feeling that she was looking at people who died fifty years ago, passengers having a last drink prior to boarding an ill-fated airship, grinning cadavers partying while all the while under their table an anarchist's bomb ticked away the seconds, stiff and starchy regimental dinners captured on the eve of First World War slaughter.

As Lulu rampaged around the Admiral Cod, her digital camera flashing like lightning, Helen recalled seeing in the London paper a grabbed photo of the author Martin Amis 'dancing' at a party. She had always really liked Amis's books, even the ones nobody else did, but this photo did for all that. First of all there were the clothes: some sort of wrinkled linen jacket worn over a pair of jeans with a neat crease pressed in them. Then there was the pose: Martin was facing a corner obviously dancing away by himself and appearing to be totally absorbed in the track; for some reason she was certain it was 'You Spin Me Right Round Baby Right Round' by Dead or Alive. Then there was the dancing itself: though it was a still photo you could tell Martin Amis was one of those middle-class white guys who form shapes with their bodies so disharmonious that dogs start howling on the Isle of Man every time they take to the dance floor yet who still believe deep in their hearts that they are really, really great dancers. After seeing this photo Helen was unable to read any of his books or even look at their covers without feeling queasy.

She didn't know why Toby thought he needed a leaving party: he was only going to be away for three weeks and if he did need one why not a nice dinner at home with their good friends, Oscar and Katya and Martin and Swei Chiang, or perhaps a drunken do at the community centre with those guys from football or a few drinks at the office. But he had been insistent that he only wanted to go to the Admiral Codrington on a Friday night with Harriet, Lulu and Rose. Helen had said to Harriet, 'Would you like to bring your friend Patrick along?'

She replied in quite a nasty voice, 'Why would I want to invite him?'

'I don't know – he seemed good enough to bring to Christmas dinner.'

'Oh, that was ages ago.'

'Yes,' Helen said. 'It feels like it was ages and ages ago.'

''Ello, Dollface!' Toby heard Cosmo the waiter shouting, and turning saw Harriet sashaying between the chairs as she crossed the heaving floor towards them. Somehow his sister-in-law seemed able to slide through the tiny slivers of space left by the shouting, waving drinkers without touching any of them.

Sometimes like, say, the other day in Regent Street, if he'd seen her then, he thought catching sight of her wouldn't have affected him that much because he was prepared, whereas now the vision of her caught him unawares and he felt like he'd just donated two litres of blood: light-headed, silly and afraid. She was wearing combat pants low on her hips, a tight white vest (worn with no bra so that her nipples were outlined against the material) that didn't quite reach the top of her pants and dull black chunky walking boots. Harriet slumped down at the table where Helen, Lulu, Rose and Toby had been drinking white wine for about three-quarters of an hour already, the muscles of her tanned arms shifting under the skin as they rested lightly on the candle-wax-coated pine surface.

'Hey, Cos,' she shouted back over her shoulder, then looking around said, 'Christ, it's busy in here.'

'It was quieter earlier, when we got here,' Helen replied.

'Yeah, well . . . I'm here now so gimme a drink.'

'There you go, Dollface,' said Rose, passing her the bottle.

'Is there somewhere else you'd rather be?' Helen asked her sister.

'Well, no, there was a thing in Dagenham I was invited to but I'm happy to be here instead. With my beloved friends and family.'

'So how long will you be away?' Lulu enquired, turning to Toby.

'Well, the trip there will take nearly a week. We fly to Perth in Australia, then on to Darwin in the Northern Territories, take a smaller plane to Port Moresby, then a Land-Rover and finally we walk up into the Southern Highlands. After that it depends on how negotiations go, but I expect to be back within three weeks.'

'Isn't it dangerous? Aren't there cannibals and stuff?' Rose enquired.

'Oh no, there used to be years ago but that's all died out. The towns can be a bit rough actually but once you're in the jungle it's fine.'

After that there were more drinks, toasts to Toby. Harriet gave him a tropical hat with corks dangling from it. He thought there might have been dancing at some point.

He did recall he said to Harriet, 'Hat, you know when something bad happens to a couple? Say one of them is arrested for some terrible crime, like those women who were convicted of killing their kids on the say-so of that mad old paediatrician and all the husbands said, "I'll stand by you forever, darling. I believe totally that you're innocent, I know absolutely you didn't do it."'

'Yeah?'

'I really admire those men but I don't think I'd ever do that. Personally, I think I'd pretty much believe anything bad about anyone that anyone told me. If somebody came up to me and said you were a murderer or Helen was a robot or was having an affair with a horse I'd more or less believe them right away, even if they weren't somebody I knew particularly well.'

Harriet laughed, which made her look more lovely than ever to Toby, then said, 'You're giving yourself away there, Toby. Because what you're saying about other people is what you believe about yourself. You would never believe somebody else no matter how close they were to you would be incapable of doing some terrible thing because you believe that you're capable of doing something truly awful yourself.'

.'Oh, Christ, does it?' he exclaimed. 'I just thought it was a funny quirky thing I was telling you so you'd find me amusing. I didn't think I was accidentally giving stuff away, shit! But, Hat, I just sort of assumed that those men, say, who stuck by their wives they were doing it for other reasons. That they didn't really believe their partners were innocent.'

'No, they really believed their partners were innocent.'

'Blimey, do they?'

'Yes.'

'Do you feel you'd behave like that?'

'Yes, I do. See, you've just told me you think that you're a potential killer or something worse. But I won't believe it of you, even if there's documentary evidence backed up with CCTV footage and sworn statements from members of the clergy and the House of Lords.'

'I don't know whether to be pleased or not, you're saying that you don't think I'm capable of anything above the banal.'

'Yes, but in a good way, Toby.'

'Night, night, Angel,' the Tin Can Man was saying as they came out of the pub long after midnight, 'give the kids a kiss for me and tell them I'll see them soon.'

From across the pub seeing Toby and Harriet talking with their heads so close together like they shared some sort of secret made Helen feel somehow horribly alone; the irresistible urge rose in her to talk about Julio so since there was nobody else around she was forced to speak to Lulu and Rose, even though they were both rubbery with drunkenness.

'This erm . . . friend of mine,' she said, 'guy I know, he says that women when they have a crisis in their lives they want to run away and work in a hotel. How weird is that?'

'Oh yeah, sure . . .' said Rose, trying to focus on her, 'it's in Eastbourne.'

'No, it's not,' Lulu contested hotly, 'it's in the Lake District about five and a half miles outside Keswick on the A66. Big half-timbered place, I'm going to be looking after the plumbing once I go nuts.'

'Well, my place is definitely in Eastbourne,' Rose persisted, 'on the seafront, painted a sort of rusty blue. I'll work on reception after I go mad.' Then, putting on the sort of fluting voice she thought a receptionist might use, said, 'Do you have any baggage, madam? Can I order you a newspaper in the morning? Could I take the imprint of a credit card for room service items?' She smiled triumphantly at the two other women. 'See, I could do that.'

12

Soft grey cloud the colour of gravel hung low over the rain-forest. The platoon of Australian SAS soldiers, their sweat-rimmed tropical hats, baggy shorts, knee-length socks, unshaven chins and black M16 rifles cradled in their arms making them look like a troupe of dissolute boy scouts on a high school killing spree, had walked with Helen across the mountains from where the road from Port Moresby had run out, hacking their way through the malodorous, leech-dripping foliage for three long days. As they pushed through the clinging jungle Helen was pleased to discover that although admittedly not carrying a heavy pack she was more or less able to keep up with the Aussie soldiers; she guessed that natural fitness must run in her family.

When she had seen Toby off in the minicab to Heathrow Airport Helen had felt no concerns for his safety. The plan had been for Toby and the rest of the negotiating team, protected by a detachment of the Papuan New Guinean army, to trek to a village in the Highlands where they would meet representatives of the rebels who'd taken Polly Williams. Warbird had been through negotiations of this kind a number of times before and they'd always been able to buy the natives off with the equiva-lent of a bag of balloons and a pencil. Helen had spoken to Toby once from Australia and again on a landline from Port Moresby, but since then nothing. She wasn't disturbed by this – communications were bound to be difficult.

So when the director of Warbird had come into her office looking all serious she had suspected nothing. 'Helen,' he said, 'we've just had a message from the UK Consulate in Port

Moresby that Toby's party may have been taken hostage by rebels and the troops who were supposed to be protecting them have fled.'

She sat silent for a second. The thing was that since her last meeting with Julio at the Pointless Park County Show it had become much, much harder for her to know what to think about anything; she was adrift now without Julio's guiding voice telling her she was right all the time. She felt like the population of one of those little Baltic countries that had gone overnight from communism to unrestrained capitalism, and the one clear message of the government radio station had been replaced with a thousand different exhortations.

To Helen's shame the first thing she could think to ask was, 'Any news of Polly Williams?'

'For God's sake, Helen,' he said, 'aren't you worried about your husband?'

The days and nights were at their hottest now, the pub folded back its doors and drinkers often carried bottles and glasses across the road to sit sprawled in groups on the edges of the park where the uncut grass was as glossy as the brushed coat of a racehorse and in places grew waist-high. Rose bay willow herb and foxglove hung heavy with swollen red flowers, there was ragwort, wild parsnip and yellow buttercup in profusion. In the middle of the night, as a recently arrived owl hunted for rodents, Harriet saw from her living room window the Tin Can Man creep from his hiding place somewhere in the centre of the park to feed himself on the wild strawberries that grew in abundance. In the night-time silence she heard him tell Lynn, 'They're tinier but many times more delicious than the commercial variety.' To her mind the two of them seemed to be getting on much better these days, maybe there'd be a reconciliation; how would that work?

One of Mr Iqubal Fitzherbert De Castro's underlings came

into her overheated shop, where she was staring hopelessly at a dinner jacket as if it was the corpse of a beloved pet that she needed to bury in the back yard, and said, 'The boss says he's having another party tomorrow night and why don't you bring your friend who wants the things so we can talk about it.'

'Oh, OK, great,' Harriet said, putting the jacket aside. 'I'll phone him and tell him it's on.'

Nobody was particularly happy for Helen to be attached to the rescue party as liaison but she had insisted and since Warbird was paying for a Hercules transport aircraft, which should have been delivering famine relief to the Sudan, to be kept on permanent standby at Port Moresby and for the soldiers' ammunition no one felt able to stop her, especially given her determined but demented demeanour. In the churning washing machine of her mind a tiny degree of certainty was beginning to return. Now she had a project to concentrate on, a project that was to restore the world completely to the way it had been. If she could just get Toby back safe then everything would follow; maybe at a later date she might even be able to seek out Julio and heal his unhinged mind. She castigated herself that she should have realised the devastating effect torture can have on a person. It was clear to her now that the old man's experiences in the Chupaderos had given him an unpleasantly negative view of the world; it was hardly surprising given the terrible things that had been done to him and she should have understood this.

Despite the seriousness of their mission Helen was pleased to find she was able to take a good deal of pleasure in the mindless physicality of walking. It struck her as odd how so much of the vegetation that blocked their path was a vigorous, feral version of the pot plants you found tamed back in everybody's home: from time to time she had the odd sensation that she was chopping her way through the gardening department of a large B&Q. On the second day, climbing upwards along the muddy path, they had picked up three of the original party sent by Warbird to negotiate the release of Polly Williams the parrot. Confused and dehydrated, the trio had no up-to-date news of what had happened to Toby and the rest of the party; instead they babbled about the treachery of their Papuan army guards and of being held in terrible conditions by the rebel tribesmen before managing to escape through a hole eaten by termites in the longhouse in which they'd been held. Fed and watered as best they could, the survivors had been sent back down the track with a couple of soldiers to wait for the Land-Rovers at the rendezvous site.

Helen had spoken to Timon the day before on the satellite phone; he'd been sent to stay at Martin and Swei Chiang's place in Andalusia. 'Why can't I go and stay with Auntie Hat?' he'd asked for the hundredth time. She told him he should be grateful to be able to enjoy the splendours of Seville and Granada.

'Any news of Toby?' Rose asked Harriet in the pub that night.

'No, but I'm sure he'll be all right.'

'Why?' asked Rose.

'Dunno,' Harriet replied glumly. 'Just trying to stay positive. You know, I dislike everything about them but I'm beginning to think life would be a lot easier if you could be one of those religious people that thinks God's watching over them and everything's going to turn out fine in the end and that life isn't really dangerous and a big random nothing.'

Lulu said, 'Oh that only works as long as things are going well.'

'How do you mean? I'm always reading in the paper or hearing on the radio that religious believers have better lives. They always tell everyone they do.'

'Well, you say that, kitten,' her friend replied, 'but some of them are lying and as for the rest, well, when they have a crisis the religious people suffer post traumatic stress disorder much,

much more severely than those like us who don't believe in anything.'

'Really? Wow . . .' Harriet's awed tone wasn't solely for the information she'd just been given but was also because it always came as a shock to her when Lulu showed any signs of having special knowledge and expertise and wasn't just a crazy woman who drank and acted mad for a living. Helen, on the other hand, had always refused to accept Lulu's eminence.

'But, Hel,' Harriet would always say to her sister. 'She studied for five years.'

And her sister would inevitably reply, 'It doesn't matter how long you study something if the thing you're studying is idiotic and wrong in the first place and the person studying it is a drunken whore.'

Harriet asked Lulu, 'But don't the religious people live longer, suffer less stress, have better hair then?'

'Yeah, up to a point, except that's only as long as nothing bad ever happens to them ever. But if they do have some sort of a disaster, couple of family members killed in a car crash, severe illness or losing their house keys then wallop! They fold like a map, go around tearing at their clothes, weeping, stamping on their bishop's mitre and wailing about God having forsaken them and how could it happen to them and what kind of a world is this we're living in? Where are their personal angels now they need them? And yadda yadda yadda, blackness, despair, the horror, the horror, all that. The big crybabies!'

'Do you think you should call your patients big crybabies?'

'What, you don't think we hate you all? And the religious ones *are* big crybabies. See, deep down I don't know what they really, truly believe. I do know that if you're a fervent believer you have this desperate air of needing to be right all the time and if you're religious you can be because you've got the word of God in your head to tell you you're right all the time and these idiots feel all safe and snug on the surface seeing as the

Lord is looking out for their family and pets and their career in the civil service. Until he stops of course. Then the world falls to bits and it's terribly hard for them to get it back.'

'So in some ways what you're saying is,' Harriet mused, 'you'd actually be doing somebody a favour by proving to them that their religion, what they believed in, was nonsense. You'd be saving them pain in the future?'

But she didn't get an answer from her friend as Lulu was staring at a harmless-looking man at the bar. 'I'm sure that's the bloke who's been putting poison in my rubbish bags,' she said.

On the third day of walking when they were a little way from the village there was a sudden crashing up ahead of them on the trail; the Australian soldiers immediately raised their rifles and slipped the safeties off but it was only one of the doctors from Medicos Sin Sombreros, accompanied by a native guide, red-faced and sweating. Ignoring the captain he located Helen halfway up the file and reaching her breathlessly said, 'Madam, we have found your husband, he is injured but alive and God willing will make a full recovery.'

All the emotions Helen had been holding back, like a hundred unwatched TV programmes held on a digital hard-drive recorder, poured out of her now. Images of herself as she had been before flashed into her vision, the endless pointless parties, the conversations about nothing, her anger and intractability, her obsession with Julio, all these could be recorded over now and they could start again.

In a rush the party tumbled into the village square. On the rectangle made of tightly packed earth an impatient group of natives stood waiting, short, ageless and deep brown. These too joined the press of people heading for the air-conditioned Portakabin that by day served as the clinic of Medicos Sin Sombreros.

The doctor, Helen and the SAS captain squeezed through the door first and then the soldiers barred the way of the tribespeople who were forced to peer over each other's shoulders into the frigid air.

On simple hospital beds, gauzy white mosquito nets giving the place the air of a Tennessee Williams play, lay the rest of the Warbird party.

Toby was in the centre bed. Helen frantically scrabbled under the net and crouching by his side took her husband's hand.

He was in a bad way, bandaged and bruised, his skin purple and verdigris, a drip disappeared into his arm, yet at her touch he woke. Prising his gluey eyes apart he managed to croak, 'Hi, babe.'

'Oh Toby,' she sobbed, 'I'm so glad you're all right, I've been such a cow to you, I've been so distracted lately I feel like I haven't been there for you . . .'

'No, no, it's OK,' he replied feebly, patting her arm, 'this was a thing . . . a thing I had to do.'

'I drove you to it . . .'

'No, no.'

'Well, everything's going to be better from now on.'

'I'm sure it will be . . . and I did it, you know, I did it.'

'Did what, darling?'

'Tested myself, like I came here to. They kept us all tied up in the one longhouse; things weren't too rough until those others escaped then the bloke who was leading the rebels, the one who was urging the tribespeople to turn their backs on modern things, to drive out the white men, revive cannibalism, all that, Chinese guy, very fit but well over sixty, dyed black hair, he went completely mental, yelling at the natives and beating them with a stick.

'All us hostages got pretty sick with hunger and dehydration and malaria, so sick we could hardly move. One night I had a dream, we were in the Admiral Codrington, me, you, Harriet,

Oscar and Katya and Oscar and Katya's builder wearing quite a restrained black and gold bikini and Polly Williams was there too. So Polly Williams says to me, "You remember we were watching that documentary the other week about social conditions in London in the 1950s?" Do you remember, babe, it was on BBC 4?'

'I think so, Toby, yes.'

'Anyway Polly Williams says, "And do you remember that the landladies who rented flats used to have signs in their windows that read 'No Blacks, No Irish, No Dogs' but what I want to know, Toby, is why were the dogs trying to rent flats? They didn't need their own flats, did they, the dogs? Not like the Blacks and the Irish." Then Polly Williams pointed to Oscar and Katya's builder with his wing and he said, "But he built them the flats, he was their friend and he built them all the flats, the Blacks and the Irish and the Dogs . . .'"

'Right . . .' Helen said.

'Do you see what Polly Williams was trying to tell me? Oscar and Katya's builder, I used to laugh at him because he was friendly with simple foreigners but I was wrong. I was being a fool, a supercilious fool. So I got sort of talking to a couple of them, the natives who were guarding us, in sign language and pidgin English. Turns out they'd been enthusiastic at first but were going off the whole idea of being rebels. Didn't like being cruel to us or being nasty to Polly Williams the parrot; they were worried that if he was killed his spirit would come back and haunt them.

'Apparently the Chinese guy, his whole plan was he wanted to lure the Australians into a trap, to jump on them out of the trees, seize their weapons. He had been expecting to receive a big shipment of things that would help him march on Port Moresby and declare himself King of Papua New Guinea or something but they hadn't come through. So anyway one night these friendly natives freed me and the other hostages and together with stones and sticks we jumped the Chinese guy and his lieutenants while they slept. Christ, Helen it was nasty . . . I didn't know, babe, I could, I didn't know they could . . .' During the last few minutes Toby had become increasingly agitated, a fuddled look rising in his eyes.

The Spanish doctor lifted the mosquito net, a syringe in his hand. 'Tovi,' he said, 'Tovi, you need to calm down,' as he injected clear liquid into the prone man's arm.

'Now one thing, Helen,' Toby said, grabbing her arm, 'I need to tell you, one thing, at the banquet tonight . . . at the banquet don't, whatever you do don't . . .' then he slumped abruptly into unconsciousness.

As Toby had said there was a banquet that night. The doctor told them, 'Yes, I'm sorry about this but the headman wants you to come and eat with the tribe tonight, it's a big honour so you can't really refuse without giving offence.'

She asked, 'Are any of the hostages well enough to attend?'

'No, they are all sedated, they've had a tough time, but on the good side several of the tribespeople have told me that Polly Williams was able to fly away in the confusion and that they have seen him since sitting in a tree telling them wise things.'

The houses in the village were divided into those for the men and those for the women, all were built on stilts with open sides and intricately thatched roofs. In the centre of the community to one side of the square there was a longer house which was kept for ceremonial occasions such as the dinner tonight.

The doctor, the captain and Helen arrived just as night abruptly fell. When they trooped up the stairs, women led them to the middle of the hut and they sat cross-legged in a circle on a woven mat alongside all the elders of the tribe, several of whose ceremonial dress included red and yellow face paint and large human-hair wigs trimmed with yellow everlasting daisies.

Helen asked the SAS captain, 'If they'd jumped on you out of the trees what do you think would have happened?'

'We'd have shot them, I'd guess.'

'Yes, that'd be my guess too.'

Young girls dressed only in long cloth skirts with garlands of flowers round their necks entered bearing large roughly carved wooden bowls containing a thick, gluey broth in which were suspended masses of strange tuber-like vegetables and lumps of grey stringy meat. As the bowls of soup were placed in front of them, there was a significant pause during which the headman climbed slowly to his feet, made an expansive gesture extending both his arms out wide and, smiling at his honoured guests, declared in a sonorous voice: 'Soup, swoop, loop de loop.'

Because she wanted something from this party Harriet didn't ask for a dress to wear but instead took out from the very back of her wardrobe a Mary Quant minidress in black velvet shot through with silver thread, already vintage when she bought it in her last year of college from a shop called the Frock Exchange in Muswell Hill and already too small for her to fit into. She chose to wear black suede high-heeled shoes by Patrick Cox with it; these had been given to her by Mr Iqubal Fitzherbert De Castro.

She phoned Patrick and told him that the Namibians would like to meet him but he'd need to come to a party next door. Harriet detected a note of girlish panic in his voice when he said, 'Party, but I don't have anything to wear to a party, they wear sharp suits at those parties, I don't have anything to wear, not a sharp suit.'

Sighing, she replied, 'I'll find you something.' Rootling in the back amongst the thinned-out ranks of hanging garments in her shop, Harriet finally located a dark blue Hugo Boss suit in Patrick's size that had had a couple of tiny holes in it, brought into the shop by a City trader and never picked up.

'I don't have any shoes apart from trainers,' he then moaned.

'You'll get away with that,' Harriet said, 'a suit and trainers is quite fashionable, and I'll bring you round a white shirt from Gap or somewhere.'

That evening, in the coppery sunlight, Harriet strode round to Patrick's flat in her high heels, carrying the suit in a bag over her shoulder. When she'd been fat, men on the street had often shouted insults at her about her weight, now instead they came close and whispered entreaties and compliments, offers of dinner or electrical goods; at first she'd liked it but after a while it seemed the same as when she'd been obese.

Again she thought about Old Fat Harriet. Wasn't her new thin self a sort of collaborator, keeping herself thin for a pack of gangsters? The old her had been kind, considerate, had lots of friends, a good business and didn't feel sour and exhausted all the time.

Up in Patrick's bare flat the stiffness between them made her want to say something nice to him so she said, 'I must say it's very clean in here.'

'Well, you know,' he replied, 'I never really had any hobbies as such. If any of the women in the gym ask I always say "cleaning". What I really like is to use a cotton bud soaked in lemon oil to get at the space behind the taps in my bathroom, an area a lot of people ignore, then later give the taps an extra sparkle with a little glycerine. I find it's easy to get the bloodstains out of a white T-shirt with little dabs of detergent, followed by hydrogen peroxide and then I rub on my secret weapon – unseasoned meat tenderiser. Of course I use cold rather than warm water for this, only fools use warm water which would just set the stains. To clean my floors I wipe the lino with one part fresh milk mixed with one part turpentine.'

Then he experienced a feeling of panic. Patrick had never got on with any of the teachers at school but the ones he hated most were those who tried to be your mate, who said, 'Call me

Steve,' who offered you a fag or amphetamine tablets and asked what kind of rap music you were into. Had he become that kind of teacher? Should he have been more distant with Harriet, not got her into this? Well, no, who was he kidding? In this situation it was Harriet his pupil who was protecting him; he felt so out of his depth and suddenly wished he wasn't going to this party but could instead stay in his flat repeatedly punching a bucket of gravel to toughen up his knuckles.

Still, he had to admit to feeling immensely proud entering the party with Harriet on his arm. Of course he had been much closer to her, had touched her all over when they fought, but there was something about the sweetness of her perfume, something about her dress – what it revealed and what it hid, something about the material of her dress and her body moving beneath it that prompted faint and unfamiliar stirrings within him, feelings long suppressed but moving closer like a two-stroke motorbike heard far off on a country road.

In the big room the lights were low and the music loud, yet the darkness was alive with a squirming of bodies that reminded Patrick of worms in a Tupperware box when as a kid he used to go fishing.

Mr Iqubal Fitzherbert De Castro came towards the two of them; he took Harriet by the hand, kissed her cheek, then shook hands with the younger man. 'Ah, I believe you are the fellow who would like to get his hands on the various . . . shall we say hard-to-procure items.'

'That's right,' Patrick replied, trying to keep his voice neutral.

'Well, let us sit down and discuss it.' He led the couple to a low table in the corner where the noise was slightly less.

'Would you like a drink?'

'Of course. A white wine, the good stuff not the crap you'd give to anyone else,' Harriet said, smiling fondly.

Patrick tried to ask for a tomato juice but Mr Iqubal

Fitzherbert De Castro said, 'No, you must have a drink with us.'

'I couldn't . . .'

'Tell him, Harriet, tell him he must have a drink with us, we will be offended if he does not.'

'C'mon, Patrick,' she said, 'one drink that's all, don't be a stiff.'

A bottle of white wine was soon brought to their table. Harriet took a glass and handed it to him.

'Well, I suppose so.'

Patrick took a sip of the wine; it was cold and oily and sharp at the same time. He wondered how they'd managed to get so many more sensations into a drink since he'd last had one.

Seeing the direction Patrick was looking in, Mr Iqubal Fitzherbert De Castro smiled and asked, 'You like that, do you?' He hadn't known he'd been staring but when the Namibian spoke Patrick realised he'd been gazing at a redheaded woman who'd been dancing almost naked in front of an elderly, moustachioed, white-haired gent with a silver-topped walking stick.

Patrick thought he'd emptied his wine glass but it seemed to be full again. Taking another long pull he replied, 'She seems like a nice girl.'

'Would you like me to get her to dance for you?'

'Oh, c'mon, Akbar!' he heard Harriet say.

'What?' he asked, turning to her. 'Patrick's a grown-up, if he'd like a dance he should have a dance.'

'I would like a dance,' he said.

'See, he would like a dance.'

He smiled at Harriet, his pupil, his friend; she seemed to be scowling back at him but he was the sifu. Like Akbar said, he could do what he wanted. Mr Iqubal Fitzherbert De Castro summoned one of his young men who went and brought the girl over; she couldn't have been more than twenty and she still wasn't as pretty as his Harriet but on the upside she was more or less naked.

'You 'ave to keep your hands by your side,' she explained to Patrick.

'Right,' he said.

Then she began to dance in front of him; it was a bit like when they went to museums and art galleries with the school – you couldn't touch anything there either and this was confusing too but in a different way. Her bottom was so close to him that he could see the tiny bumps on her skin, at other times a breast came so near it went all blurred in his vision. To Patrick it seemed impossible that somebody could do this in front of you without being yours to do with as you wished.

When she had finished Mr Iqubal Fitzherbert De Castro tucked a twenty pound note into her thong; the younger man wanted him to buy him another one and at the same time for it never to happen again.

'Would you like another one?'

'Yes,' he said, feeling like some sort of sultan in a film, 'but a different girl.'

This one was older with black hair but a much better dancer.

As he called another girl over to dance Mr Iqubal Fitzherbert De Castro caught Harriet looking at him. She didn't know quite what he read in her face but while the new dancer wriggled for the mesmerised, unhearing Patrick, the older man said to her, 'That man who shouts into the sardine tin he loved us at first, he would come around all the time and I must admit it was good to have him there, to talk to him like I talk to you.

'Then after a time he became disenchanted with us and quite abusive; one thing he said, he said people like me and my associates are shown on the TV and in movies as being as diverse as ordinary people, some are nice, some are nasty, but he said it wasn't the truth, he said you cannot do what we do and be nice, because of what we do every one of us is horrible, horrible people.'

*   *   *

Hours later Patrick and Harriet came out of the flat into the hot, lethargic night air scented with the musky odour of the climbing roses that grew in the gardens of the nearby houses. Harriet's observation was that Mr Iqubal Fitzherbert De Castro had looked Patrick over and found him not worthy of exploiting with his silly list of impossible things. She calculated that he had drunk nearly a whole bottle of wine which must have been quite a shock to his system after whatever it was, nine years? Harriet couldn't remember if he'd he stopped drinking at the same time as he'd stopped spilling his seed; was not drinking supposed to help make him immortal as well or was there no connection?

In the end who cares? she thought to herself, it was all crap anyway; it might be good if he appreciated that then he might be a bit less of a freak.

Harriet said, 'Let's take a walk in the park.' When they reached the edge of the grass she paused and resting one hand on his shoulder took off her high-heeled shoes. The earth was warm under her feet as they crossed the springy turf, coloured grey under the sodium lights but turning silvery as they pressed deeper towards the trees where the only illumination was starlight.

The wine had given Patrick a kind of loose feeling inside and this made him want to try and let Harriet know a little more of what kind of man he was and how much she meant to him. He knew he had somehow lost her over the last few months, lost her admiration and respect and it might be a way to get her back. Patrick said, his eyes a little unfocused and his brow dusted with sweat, 'You know, Harriet, I hear the women talk at the gym and from what they say it seems there's this thing between friends where if one of them does something – juggling, cooking, accountancy – then everybody has to pretend to them that they're brilliant at it. If you go to watch a performance or eat dinner at their house everybody has to act like it's brilliant even if it isn't. Thing is though' – his voice rough with sentiment – 'the special thing, Harriet, is you're beautiful and a friend and I can say honestly that you are really good at Li Kuan Yu, you know that, don't you? Almost as good as me in fact.'

Better than you, she thought to herself but just said, 'Thank you very much.'

He said, 'Did you ever see any of those early Clint Eastwood movies?'

'The cowboy ones?'

'Yeah, those. The guy he plays in them movies, he's got this blank face, hasn't he? And everybody takes that to mean that he's really brave and cool but really a guy who has to keep his face that straight all the time, he must be terrified of showing his feelings, scared that if he lets anybody see who he really is they'll hate him.'

They'd reached the oak tree; she reached out for him and said, 'Kiss me,' and he said, 'No,' once as Harriet pressed him back against the rough bark but soon her lips were on his and his hands were reaching under her dress. Quickly Harriet took her pants off, slipped her dress over her head, then she dragged the jacket and T-shirt from his body, undid his belt and slipped her hands down the front of his trousers beneath his underpants. It had been such a long time since Harriet had had sex with a man that she'd forgotten how hot cocks could get when they were really hard and filled with blood; she felt as if she was holding the wooden handle of an expensive French frying pan or one of those things you put in your gloves on freezing cold days to keep your hands warm.

Their bodies were familiar to each other through fighting and the way they touched now was sort of the same but very different; they pawed and pulled at one another, Harriet caressing his whole torso, feeling the muscles shift against one another under the translucent skin before they both began to concentrate their questing hands and mouths exclusively on each other's secret places.

'It's gone, you took it!' he screamed.

'What?'

'My immortality! You've stolen it!'

They had fallen asleep underneath the branches of the oak tree. After perhaps an hour, slowly surfacing, Harriet had got up and found her dress in one of the lower branches and pulled it on before going back to lie next to him, her cheek against his chest.

She was wondering how long it would be before she could wake Patrick or maybe simply leave him there to creep back to her own warm, welcoming bed when he had come to with a sudden jolt, knocked her aside and scrabbled to his feet still naked. Harriet slowly got up so that she was facing him.

She couldn't say it made her feel good that the recollection of what they'd done a little while ago, the first sex she'd had in years, produced that sort of reaction.

'Nine years!' he shouted. 'Nine years of not spilling my fucking seed. Not touching a woman or even myself; can you imagine what that's like when you're a young man only in your twenties? Do you understand what you've done?'

'As far as I can see all I've done is to give you a really good night out and a fuck.'

'You've stolen my immortality! You got down on your knees and with your dirty little lips sucked my immortality out of me! You straddled me and pulled out my power!'

'And I enjoyed doing it too.'

His voice rising hysterically Patrick yelled, 'Now I'll have to save up my fluids for another nine years before I'm safe and who knows what'll happen in that time. I could be killed at any moment!' And he actually looked around for lurking predators as he said this.

'Oh, don't be such an idiot, can't you see all that stuff was mystical crap? I've done you a favour by taking your stupid fluids. Maybe now you can start to live a proper life in the real world and have some fun.'

As she finished speaking he took a step back and gave her two hard rapid punches to the face, the first almost certainly breaking her nose. She staggered back, bumping into the tree, blood and snot rolling down over her lips and chin.

'Oh Christ,' he said, looking horrified and holding his cupped hands to his face. She took advantage of him leaving his body wide open to punch him between the legs with her right fist. For a follow-up Harriet tried to kick him with her left leg, but Patrick countered by hooking under her ankle with his foot, unbalancing her and sending her slamming backwards to the ground, banging the back of her head hard on the solid soil as she landed, leaving her stunned for a second. Keeping to Harriet's side Patrick lifted his leg and tried to stamp down on his adversary's face. Rolling sideways, just missing his plummeting foot as it hit the ground raising a cloud of dust, she snapped back and grabbed his stamping leg; finding the nerve point four inches above the ankle on the inside with her thumb, she pressed hard. As the paralysing pain shot through Patrick he buckled slightly; taking advantage of his temporary weakness she grabbed the lower leg up to the knee and jerked. They both fell backwards, Harriet on top, Patrick legs apart, disoriented. She went for his eyes with a split two-finger strike; it failed because Patrick raised his hand edge outward along the nose.

As she raked and gouged, he flipped her over, drew back his fist and punched again, hitting Harriet full in the face breaking her cheekbone. She struck back, snapping upwards with an open palm blow which landed perfectly under his jaw and jolted his head back.

It wasn't enough. Patrick straddled her and pushing the

shoulders down crossed his wrists over her collarbone. Grabbing Harriet's top for leverage, he dug his knuckles into the carotid arteries and pressed down. The light was going out in her head, fading into a warm, welcoming silence when she heard a distant screaming that sounded confusingly as if it was approaching from beneath the ground. Groggily she wondered whether demons were coming to get her and after all there was a heaven and a hell, wouldn't she be embarrassed if that was the case? As the screaming reached a pitch the earth beside the flailing couple exploded, clods of turf, soil, branches and leaves flew upward from the ground to rain down on to her face, gritty soil filling her open gasping mouth as the upper part of the Tin Can Man's torso appeared abruptly beside her.

'I'm here now, Lynn,' he said quietly, staring into the woman's eyes. Then, face smeared with dirt, the older man climbed from his muddy hole in the ground.

Patrick, relaxing his grip on Harriet, rose to face him. 'Look, mate,' he said, 'this don't have nothing to do with you.'

The Tin Can Man opened his mouth and laughed, revealing two neat rows of little yellow teeth, then without any change of attitude struck. When Harriet had seen people fight at the dojo it was always a choreographed dance, while the way the Tin Can Man came at Patrick reminded her more than anything else of an enraged baboon. There was no precision, no elegance, no move you could put a nice name to: simply there was the flailing fury of a man who's lost his family and lived in a hole in the ground for three years, who's had his belongings pissed on, who didn't care about, indeed welcomed, pain.

Patrick successfully countered the Tin Can Man's first assaults with a series of blocks and punches then tried to get him on the floor with a move that was called Passing Swoop Knee Grab. Harriet remembered he'd told them at the dojo that this was based on the tango and had come to Martin Po from his days in the ballrooms of Hong Kong. Now in a real fight it looked ludicrous. The homeless man shook Patrick off easily and instead threw his opponent to the ground then crouched over him. She'd heard people speak about somebody 'having lumps torn off them' but nobody could imagine they'd ever see it, yet with his grimy, dirt-encrusted, claw-like nails and his little teeth the Tin Can Man ripped at Patrick's flesh, spittle and blood flying from his mouth.

'Harriet . . .' Patrick called, reaching out his arm, 'Harriet, help me . . .'

The Tin Can Man hunkering above Patrick also turned to her. 'You don't want to see this, Lynn,' he said.

'I'm not . . . I'm not Lynn,' she replied after a second's pause.

'I know you're not, darling,' he said. 'Now leave us alone, the men have things to do.'

And he turned and began again tearing at Patrick. Harriet knew that she should try to intervene: she was supposed to have all these fighting skills, all this strength and agility but she knew, deep in her bones, an animal knowledge, that no matter what she did it would be of no use at all. She would be unable to make any impression on the ferocious attack. There was an implacable quality to the Tin Can Man's violence as if something metal or glass, a bus shelter or a railway engine, had come to life and was ripping at Patrick. She had not imagined such a level of violence could possibly exist in the world and in that moment a terror rose inside her so strong that it sent Harriet running out the park, her dress streaming in rags around her.

When she awoke in her flat it was mid-morning. Harriet was amazed that she'd fallen asleep but it turned out that staying up all night for months then rising at six to jump out of a tree, getting badly beaten and witnessing . . . no, she wasn't thinking about that yet . . . that could really exhaust a person. She took herself alone to the Casualty department of the North Middlesex Hospital, where they strapped up the broken ribs and patched her broken nose and cheekbone. She supposed she could have got Lulu or Rose to come with her if they weren't tied up with work but Harriet didn't want to explain anything, and more than that she wanted to be alone. On the way back to the flat she forced herself to limp across the park. A couple of young mothers, their buggies parked side by side, sat with their backs against the oak tree chatting happily. There seemed no sign of last night's disturbance, perhaps somebody had cleaned it up, she thought, it was impossible to tell.

For the rest of the day Harriet wandered up and down her house, from the shop at the bottom which today she kept closed, up to the living room and the bedrooms. She sat in a corner of her big room for a time while the sun carved its way across the floorboards. At dusk Harriet rose from the couch, put a couple of changes of clothes in a carrier bag and descended the stairs. All day there had been an insistent thought in her head that she needed to get away to some place where she could rest; there was a crushing tiredness that threatened to squash her like a flatfish. Scotland seemed like it might be a good idea, mountains, castles, heather, all that.

Euston Station late in the evening, empty and echoing, reminded her of one of those badly designed cathedrals of the 1960s built after people had forgotten what religion was for. Staring at the big black departure board she saw that there was a night train leaving for Glasgow in twenty minutes; the ticket for a one-way first-class sleeper compartment almost cleaned out her current account and what remained she took from a money machine on the concourse. The attendant brought a cup of tea and a biscuit before they departed.

Through the early hours the train crept gently north, lingering on remote platforms of Midlands stations for half an hour at a time while freight wagons clattered past on parallel tracks.

The night train came to a halt once more at some dark stop, though she couldn't tell where since a long, unrelenting brick wall blocked the view out of the window. Since she had been lying fully clothed at least there was no delay in getting dressed. Nobody saw her open the train's door and step down from the carriage, no one saw her walk along the dark, sticky platform, no member of staff stopped Harriet passing through the barriers and walking out on to the Nantwich Road where the traffic lights changed unheeded from red to green and back again as a motorbike with a faulty silencer raced from miles away to racket past her down the dead straight road.